THE FRIEND

JENNA JORDAN

BLACK SWAN
DIGITAL

1

The headset tone cuts through the room. Leah Hunter sits upright, lifts the receiver to her ear, and speaks before the second note fades.

"911. What is your emergency?"

A boy answers. His voice is thin, breathless. "My dad fell. He is on the floor. He is not breathing."

Leah finds the address. Her fingers move without sound. The map locks to a square of Phoenix where cul-de-sacs curl like broken shells. She confirms the street and number and sends the call to paramedics with a keystroke.

"Tell me your name."

"Ty."

"Ty, I am here with you. We are going to help your dad. I need you to do something important. Put your hand on his chest. Tell me if it is rising."

A dog barks in the background, frantic and high, and the television clicks through a daytime ad. Ty's breath hitches on the line. "It is not moving."

"Okay. We will begin compressions together. Put the heel of

your hand in the middle of his chest. Put your other hand on top. Lock your elbows. Keep your arms straight. Push down hard and fast. I will count."

She counts. He follows. In the dispatch hall, other voices fold into hers. Operators speak in low, even tones. Behind her, a printer hums. Leah holds the rhythm and listens for Ty's breath as if it were the only sound that matters.

"You are doing well," she says. "Help is close."

The boy sobs once and keeps pushing. Sirens rise somewhere beyond the line. Leah hears a door open, boots on tile, clipped words. A medic's voice reaches the phone. "We have him."

Leah speaks to Ty, softer now. "You can let them take over."

He begins to cry in a way that sounds like relief and fear at the same time. Leah waits. When the medic confirms control, she thanks Ty for what he did, tells him he was brave, and ends the call.

The room does not go quiet. It never does. Monitors still glow and keyboards still chatter, and the wall clock ticks forward repeatedly. Leah takes off the headset and sets it down with care. Her hand shakes once, then steadies.

Miguel Ortega stops at her station. He is tall, shoulders square inside a navy polo. He chews mint gum to stay awake, always mint. "Good job, Leah. Textbook," he says. "You kept him alive until they got there."

"Ty kept him alive," Leah says.

Miguel taps the back of her chair with two fingers. It's a habit he does not know he has. "Take five."

"I am fine."

"Take five anyway." He moves down the row, already reading another screen.

Beside her, Bree Lowe swivels toward Leah. The junior

dispatcher's desk is a small storm of sticky notes, energy chews, and a plastic cup with a cracked lid. "Legend," she says, grinning. "If I flatline, I want you on my speaker."

"Do not do that," Leah says.

"Deal." Bree pops a grape in her mouth and turns back to her board. "You want coffee?"

Leah looks at her paper cup. The ring around the rim is the color of old pennies. "I already have coffee."

She does not drink it. She logs the call instead, putting data into boxes and seconds into fields. The interface is pale blue and neat, a calm face for the worst days people ever have. When she clicks submit the record slides into the archive as if it were only a receipt.

The next call blinks red. Bree snags it with a quick tap. "911. What is your emergency?" Leah listens to the younger woman's tone, bright and firm, and returns to her own screen.

Five minutes in the break room. That is what Miguel asked. Leah obeys the request like an order. She steps under the hum of fluorescent bars and stares at a vending machine lined with candy and instant noodles. The glass reflects the colorless light across her face. She presses her palms to the counter and breathes in for four, hold for two, out for six. The air smells like reheated soup and bleach.

Her phone vibrates with a message from her boyfriend, Sam. *On the late shift again. Be safe.*

She types back a quick reply, *Another one saved. Heading home soon.* She locks the phone and slips it in her pocket and returns to the floor.

The morning moves through her like sand through a timer. Calls stack and clear, covering a welfare check, false alarm, crash without injury, and an elderly caller who cannot find her dog, crying so softly Leah has to lean into the headset to hear. Leah keeps the voice level and the words simple. She holds each caller steady for as long as they need and then releases them when the line belongs to someone else. The work is a tide. You learn to read its ebbs and flows.

By the end of the shift, Leah's head aches from pressure and her throat feels scraped. She removes the headset and coils the cord. She checks the time. Three fifty-nine. The hands move together to four.

Miguel appears. "Good work," he says. "Twenty-three calls. No outstanding callbacks."

"Thanks."

"Go home."

"I am gone."

She logs out, slides the chair in with a soft knock against the desk, and walks the short hall to the exit. The double doors release a rectangle of white heat.

Outside, the parking lot bakes. The dispatch building sits low and brown under a sky without a cloud. A line of vents along the roof sheds a steady whine. Leah shades her eyes with the side of her hand and crosses the bright concrete to her car.

Inside, the air is a furnace until the vents begin to push cool through the cab. She lets the engine idle, waiting for the temperature to come down and feels the silence hit her chest. It feels so clean. And after eight hours of panicked voices, clean can feel violent.

In these moments after a shift, she can always hear them echoing in her mind. Not the words, or even the full phrases, but the tone or the breath of them. The count that she used with Ty, the pace of hands on a chest. The mind tends to keep the shape of what it does most. She rests her forehead against the steering wheel until the echoes soften. Her phone lights with another message from Sam. *Proud of you, always.*

Sam means it. He means it every time. She types *Thank you*

and sends it, before fixing her seat belt and pulling onto the road.

The city is a wash of heat and low buildings, with palm fronds shaking in the dry air. Traffic is thin, and Leah drives without the radio on, enjoying the silence. At a light she checks her face in the mirror. The skin beneath her eyes is gray, her mouth is a straight line. She looks like someone who sleeps in short pieces, or at least like someone whose body forgot how to switch off.

Her apartment complex sits behind a row of palms that lean toward the street. The stucco is the color of toast. She parks under a sun-bleached cover and takes the stairs. The metal rail is hot enough to sting the palm of her hand, but inside, the air holds at a cool, even number. She drops her bag by the door and stands in the living room enjoying the cool, the quiet, and the sense of being home and at peace.

She makes coffee because the motion fills the space. She leaves it on the counter and moves to the window where the blinds are half closed, and light falls in thin bars across the floor and across her hands. She can see the edge of the city from this angle, where the low buildings dissolve into open land. She thinks about the boy named Ty, probably now sitting beside a bed in a hospital room that smells like antiseptic.

A work alert pops up on her phone asking for general cover for the evening shift. She ignores it without responding, she's done with calls for the day. The next tone belongs to Sam. *Heading to the clinic. It's been a long day. Miss you.*

She types *See you on the weekend* with a heart and sends it, before putting the phone face down on the table and grabbing her coffee. She places it on the small table in the lounge and lies on the couch, closing her eyes. She tells herself she will sleep for an hour, but she does not set an alarm. The room is golden and still, but the stillness is not empty. She hears the calls she took and thinks about the ones she did not. She hears the woman who hid in a closet and whispered "he is still here" and the teenager who said "it just happened" and then said it again as if saying it twice could make it true. She hears her own voice, even and calm, inside the voices of strangers.

When she wakes she is not sure how long she slept, or if she even did. Her body feels heavy. The clock on the stove reads five seventeen. Her chest tightens when she thinks about going back, then loosens because going back is the only plan she has.

She showers and dresses, tying her hair into a tight ponytail and smoothing the stray pieces with water from her fingers. She checks her face. She looks ready enough. That is all there is. In the kitchen, she pours out some cereal into a bowl and adds milk, washes it down with coffee and sends Sam a quick message. *Morning. Hope your shift was okay. Just about to go in. x*

Outside, the light is shifting to a pale yellow. The heat has lingered through the night and shows no sign of shifting at all. She crosses the lot, opens her car and turns the ignition. The radio comes on low and she shuts it off, wanting the silence to carry her in. When she reaches the road, her phone buzzes. *Be safe.*

She replies with one word, *Always*, and places the phone in the holder on the dash, fixing her eyes on the road. The dispatch center waits on the edge of a commercial strip, a squat block with tinted glass that reflects the color of the sky. The parking lot is relatively empty, and she finds a spot in the half shade of a tall tree and goes in. The air inside has the same measured chill as every morning, the air conditioning cranked up to the max. Time bends in buildings like this, with its filtered air and artificial light. You leave the building and when you return it's as though the room has not learned you were gone long enough to miss you.

Someone calls her name and waves a greeting. Leah nods

back, not slowing, letting the familiar motion carry her toward her station. Once she sits and logs in, the headset comes down over her ears, the pads settling with a pressure she can feel in her teeth. Her fingers hover over the keys for a moment before the tone lands.

"911. What is your emergency?"

A woman whispers that someone is in the house. Leah's voice finds its line, steadying the space between them. She asks which room the caller is in, whether the door is locked, what the windows look like, whether there are footsteps. She guides the woman into breathing with her, matching pace and sound. She keeps the quiet from growing large enough to swallow them both.

When patrol takes the line, Leah lets it go and sits back. Water replaces the coffee she's been avoiding. From the next desk, Bree laughs at something on her screen, and a small, simple affection for the younger woman warms the brief gap between calls. It is the closest thing to ease Leah allows herself while she is in the chair.

Hours make a slow loop. The room's scent shifts from fresh coffee to reheated food and eventually to something dry, like paper and fatigue settling in the vents. Through it all, Leah's voice never lifts or dips in ways that might unsettle anyone on the other end. She keeps to simple words, repeats instructions, and promises that help is coming—promises she tries to make true as often as possible.

Toward the end of the shift, the headset band feels like a ring tightening on her skull. She presses her thumbs into the hinge of her jaw until the ache eases. A quick message goes to Miguel about a flagged address. Then she clears her board, watches the screen return to neutral, and logs out.

Outside again, the day is fierce and bright. The air has changed, feeling thicker now with the weight of the day, but the temperature is as hot and sticky as it has been for days, made more cloying by the cool of the building she's just stepped out of. She walks to the car with the sound of the room still running under her skin like current, each step carrying a faint ghost of the calls she took. When she sits behind the wheel, she doesn't turn the engine on. Instead she watches her reflection dull and brighten in the glass as thin clouds drift across the sun. For a moment she imagines she can still hear the click of the wall clock, the soft hiss of the vents, and the steady count of hands on a chest that might or might not rise. All of it lingers like an afterimage she can't blink away.

She tells herself to go home. Eventually, the keys turn, the engine picks up its quiet hum, and she pulls into the slow river of afternoon traffic.

At the next light, she reads Sam's message from last night again. *Proud of you, always.* The words hold both distance and devotion, as if affection can reach her but cannot fully land. She thinks about the kindness in them, the effort. When the light turns green, she rolls forward and lets the thought settle somewhere she doesn't have to touch.

Back in her apartment, she sets her keys in the dish by the door and toes off her shoes. She doesn't bother with a light. The kitchen holds its shape around her, a stillness she steps into rather than breaks. The hum of the refrigerator is the steady voice that never asks for anything. She pours water from the tap and drinks it in three slow swallows that feel like a small reclaiming of herself.

The couch remembers the shape of her body. She lies down with a folded towel under her head, the fabric warm from her hands. Her notebook opens to a blank page. She writes the date, then the name *Ty*, then the words *father collapse* and the phrase *units on scene within minutes.* She leaves out the dog. She leaves out the television left running. She leaves out the boy's thin, shuddering relief, and the way it sounded like someone surfacing after a long dive. Some details don't belong anywhere except her memory, and even there they scrape.

She closes the notebook and tucks it under the table. Sleep is the plan. Sleep does not come. Her mind cycles through addresses, names, and tiny bright details that refuse to stay still. After a while she rises, crosses to the window, and parts the blinds with two fingers. The parking lot below glows under sodium lamps, flat and unreal. A single moth taps at the glass, unable to find the gap that would free it.

She lets the blinds fall. Darkness folds back in. The apartment is cool, clean, and obedient to her silence. It does not argue, does not answer, does not echo anything she does not give it. For a few breaths she allows herself to feel the steadiness of it—this one unmoved part of her life.

Her phone vibrates on the table. She looks at it without picking it up. Not an emergency. Not tonight. Just someone who loves her asking for a piece of her she has nothing left to give. Guilt rises and recedes, and she lets it pass through her without making a home.

When she finally sleeps, the sleep is thin. In the dream she is back in the chair and the tone lands again and again without end. In the dream she speaks, but no one hears her. She wakes with a small sound in her throat and a film of sweat cooling on her skin. For a moment she is certain the headset is still clamped to her skull. Her hand lifts to remove it and meets nothing but air.

She rises. She drinks more water. She sits on the edge of the bed and waits for the sense of a voice in her ear to fade. It doesn't. It settles instead, returning to the place it always waits when she is not at work. A low echo. A line that hums.

Morning comes with no ceremony. She pulls the blinds, showers, dresses. She ties her shoes with care, as if steadiness can be built stitch by stitch. She picks up her bag and texts Sam. *Can't wait to see you later. I'll call you after my shift.* She hits send.

And as she steps toward the door, the day feels ready to begin. Another turn in the loop, another voice waiting somewhere she has not yet heard.

2

The training room smells faintly of coffee and toner, the kind of scent that belongs to long days and recycled air. Light hums from the ceiling panels, flat and white, giving everything a slight overexposed sheen. Leah sits near the back, her chair angled just enough toward the exit to make leaving easy, though she tells herself she isn't thinking about leaving. On the front screen, a slideshow loops, showing the Phoenix Emergency Communications logo spinning slowly through shades of blue, as if even the software is tired. HR has laid out name cards for the newcomers, but the edges have already begun to curl from the warmth of too many bodies in a small room.

Tom Watkins from Human Resources stands beside the projector, clipboard in hand. A soft man with a voice built for reassurance, he clears his throat before beginning.

"We're happy to welcome a few transfers this quarter," he says. "Please make them feel at home."

The room nods as one. Leah joins in, the motion automatic. She has been through so many orientations that the edges of them have blurred together in a vague memory of new faces, tight smiles, nerves telegraphed through jittery knees and overcaffeinated chatter. She's polite to them all, but names dissolve after a week, sometimes sooner. Her shift pattern keeps her swimming in and out of sync with everyone else, and familiarity fades fast in a place where survival depends on conserving just enough of yourself.

Tom consults his list. "From Albuquerque Dispatch, Amber Klein."

A woman near the door raises her hand. The gesture is small, almost tentative, but the smile that accompanies it has an unmistakable steadiness. When Tom beckons her forward, she steps into the aisle. The others clap once, a ripple of sound born more from habit than enthusiasm.

Leah looks up and stills. She knows that face.

Amber's hair is pale gold, pulled into a low, efficient ponytail. Her uniform polo is a shade lighter than regulation navy, the collar crisp as if she ironed it that morning. Her eyes are a bright, almost cold blue, and hold a practiced steadiness that looks rehearsed. When she meets Leah's gaze, her smile widens with recognition.

During the coffee break, Tom busies himself arranging name tags and handing out pens that will, inevitably, go missing. Amber doesn't hesitate. She walks straight to Leah's table.

"You remember me," she says. It isn't remotely a question.

Leah hesitates, caught between the safety of detachment and the tug of truth.

"Yes. From the national seminar," she says at last. "Two years ago. You were in my practice group."

Amber's smile deepens, becoming something warmer, almost grateful.

"You helped me with the cardiac arrest simulation. I was panicking, and you stayed after the session to run it again until I got it right. You even showed me how to control my breathing between sentences."

Leah blinks, surprised by the detail. "You have a good memory."

"I remember how calm you were," Amber says softly. "It was the calmest voice I had ever heard."

The words land with too much intent. Leah looks toward the front of the room where Tom is calling another name, as if the motion might dilute the moment. She can feel Amber's attention on her, steady, warm, and expectant.

"It's all part of the job," she murmurs.

Amber takes the seat beside her. "Not everyone can do it," she says. "Most people's voices crack when someone screams at them. Yours doesn't."

Leah doesn't know how to respond. Compliments about professionalism are fine, but this feels too focused, too precise. She offers a polite nod.

"Thanks."

Amber folds her hands neatly on the desk, posture perfectly composed. She keeps darting small glances at Leah's notebook, the way someone might wait for a cue or an opening.

When Tom starts the safety briefing, Leah faces forward. She listens without absorbing, aware instead of the quiet rhythm beside her, and the slow, measured breathing that almost matches her own. It feels intentional, as though Amber is syncing herself to Leah's cadence.

And that, more than any compliment, makes something inside Leah tense up.

By the afternoon, everyone has migrated to the call floor. The room hums with overlapping voices of dispatchers in mid-sentence, callers in panic or confusion, and beneath it all, the muted, ceaseless click of keyboards. Screens glow in long rows.

Headsets flash their small green LEDs like a constellation of steady signals. Miguel moves through the aisles, introducing the newcomers to their consoles, pausing here and there to adjust a monitor or offer a quick word of reassurance. When he reaches Leah's desk, she slips her headset off and lets it rest around her neck.

"This is where you'll be," he tells Amber. "Sit with Leah for the next few days. She'll show you the ropes."

Amber's smile brightens as though she's been waiting for that exact instruction. "Perfect."

Miguel turns to Leah. "You good with that?"

"Sure," she shrugs. "Why not?"

Amber pulls up a chair. The wheels squeak softly on the polished floor before settling into place beside her. Leah shifts slightly so their screens form a shared horizon. She walks Amber through the essentials of the mapping software, incident codes, dispatch hierarchy, the flow from call to console to patrol. Amber listens with the focused attention of someone who has rehearsed being attentive, her eyes tracing each movement Leah makes. Every so often she flicks a glance toward Leah's face, as though checking whether she's performing the right kind of understanding.

The first call comes through before Leah finishes her explanation. She fits the headset over her ears and answers, her voice dropping into its familiar cadence. "911. What is your emergency?"

A sobbing woman reports that her husband has locked himself in the bathroom with a gun. Leah's fingers move at once, fielding the storm with practiced calm, quickly flagging a patrol response, looping in the sergeant through the chat window, pulling details from the woman piece by piece while keeping her anchored. She stays steady through the entire six-minute call, never letting the silence slip into fear, never letting her voice waver. When she disconnects, Amber exhales as though she has been holding her breath the whole time.

"You didn't sound nervous once."

"Training," Leah says. "Years of it."

Amber shakes her head, her expression almost puzzled. "No. That's something else. It's like you turn a switch and your voice becomes... safe."

A faint smile tugs at Leah's mouth. "That is the idea."

Miguel strolls past again, scanning the room the way he always does near the start of a shift. "Everything okay here?"

Amber nods quickly. "Great. Leah's incredible."

Miguel chuckles. "Told you she'd show you the ropes." He keeps moving.

The next hour unfolds in a steady, reliable rhythm of call, log, dispatch, breathe, repeat. Amber mirrors Leah with uncanny precision, her hands hovering above her keyboard in the same poised readiness. When Leah types, Amber's fingers twitch as though preparing to echo the same motions. When Leah says a phrase, *Stay calm, Help is on the way*, Amber mouths the words a second later, shaping them like incantations she plans to master.

A few consoles down, Bree notices and leans over with a grin. "You two sound like clones already."

Leah glances up. Amber laughs, cheeks warming to a soft pink. "I guess I have a good teacher."

Leah forces a small smile, though the back of her neck prickles. "Guess so."

Amber's eyes linger a moment longer, bright with an eagerness Leah isn't sure she wants aimed in her direction.

At lunch, the cafeteria smells of other people's reheated food, the usual midday mix that settles low in the air. Leah normally eats alone, tucked into a corner or by a wall, but today she gestures for Amber to join her. It feels rude not to, and avoiding it would draw more attention. They choose a table by the window, where the blinds slice the sunlight into narrow, slanting bars across the linoleum.

Amber unwraps a turkey sandwich, the crinkle of plastic loud in the lull between conversations. She watches Leah stir sugar into her coffee, her gaze steady. "How long have you been here?"

"Almost ten years."

"That's a long time to hear everyone else's worst moments."

Leah shrugs lightly. "Someone has to do it."

Amber tilts her head, studying the shape of that answer. "Doesn't it stay with you?"

"Sometimes." Leah pauses, searching for a version of truth that won't open too much up for this relative stranger. "You learn to make space for it."

Amber keeps watching her. "You say that like it's easy."

"It isn't," Leah says. "But you can't take it home."

Amber's eyes linger on her mouth when she speaks, a detail Leah notices in the edge of her awareness. The focus unsettles her. She drops her attention to her salad, grounding herself in the motion of shifting greens with her fork.

"Your voice doesn't even shake when you're talking to them," Amber says softly.

A breath of laughter escapes Leah. "You'll learn. It's muscle memory."

Amber shakes her head. "I don't think so. I think it's who you are. You sound like you could talk anyone through anything."

Leah pushes her fork through the lettuce, feeling the weight of the compliment settle in a place she doesn't want it. "Maybe that's why I'm tired all the time."

They eat in silence for a few minutes, the cafeteria noise rising and falling around them. Bree passes their table with a tray piled high with chips. She waves. "Orientation buddies," she says, nodding at Amber. "You surviving?"

Amber smiles quickly. "More than surviving."

When Bree moves on, Amber lowers her voice as though confiding something. "She seems nice."

"She is."

"She talks a lot."

A faint smile crosses Leah's face, smaller than before. "That's part of her charm."

Amber looks down at her hands, tracing a thumb across her knuckles. "I talk too much sometimes."

"Can't say I've noticed that so far."

Amber seems genuinely pleased by that. She finishes her sandwich and folds the wrapper into a perfectly neat square, aligning each crease.

Leah checks her phone. No new messages from Sam. She had texted him hours ago when she first got in to work. *First day of training new team. Wish me luck.* His reply had been a single thumbs-up. That was six hours ago. She tells herself he is busy at the clinic, that this is normal, that relationships can run quiet without it meaning anything.

Amber follows her gaze. "Boyfriend?"

Leah hesitates, just a beat. "Yes. His name is Sam."

Something shifts in Amber's expression. Just a tiny twitch around her mouth, gone almost before it forms. "He's lucky," she says. "Not everyone can handle someone who hears other people's pain all night."

Leah studies her. "He tries."

"I can imagine." Amber's tone softens. "Do you ever tell him about your calls?"

"Never."

"Because you don't want to bring it home?"

"Because I don't want him to see how much it affects me."

Amber nods slowly, the gesture thoughtful, almost intimate in its understanding. "That makes sense."

Leah glances at the clock above the serving line. "We should get back."

Amber stands, smoothing her cardigan down her sides as though preparing for something more formal than the call floor. "I'll follow your lead."

Leah feels the weight of those words in a way she can't quite name.

The afternoon drifts by. The room glows with its wall of screens, each square of light holding another emergency unfolding somewhere in the city. Leah's voice remains steady through the chaos, a kind of metronome that settles the edges of each call. Beside her, Amber listens closely, absorbing every inflection.

During a break, Miguel stops at their station. "How's it going?"

Amber beams. "Leah's amazing. She explains everything."

Leah closes a file, keeping her tone even. "She's picking it up fast."

Miguel nods. "Good. We need steady hands."

When he moves on, Amber leans a little closer. "He trusts you."

"He trusts anyone who does their job."

"Still. You can tell he listens when you speak."

Leah types a note, choosing silence over encouragement.

As the shift nears its end, she walks Amber through the end-of-call protocol step by step. Amber repeats each part exactly, matching even Leah's phrasing. Leah corrects her once, only to realize the adjustment makes the imitation even closer. She decides not to push it further.

At four, Miguel gives the signal to wrap up. Leah removes her headset and stretches her neck, rolling out the stiffness. Amber watches her, then mirrors the same movement a beat later.

"You should rest your voice," Leah says.

"I like the sound of the room," Amber replies. "All those voices at once. It's like listening to the inside of a storm and knowing exactly where the calm part is."

Leah studies her for a moment. "That's one way to describe it."

Amber smiles. "You're the calm part."

Leah turns back to her console, busying herself with shutting everything down, before heading out.

Outside the sun is sinking, red across the horizon. Bree calls goodbye as she heads to the parking lot. Leah waits by the door for a moment, letting her eyes adjust to the light. Amber joins her.

"Want to grab dinner? Show me around the place?" Amber asks.

"Thanks, but I have plans."

"Sam?"

"Yes."

Amber's lips form a polite smile that doesn't reach her eyes. "Another time, then."

"Sure."

Amber walks to her car, waving as she goes. Leah watches her drive away before heading to her own. The encounter leaves a faint pressure in her chest that she can't name.

Amber's admiration feels like sunlight that stays too long on the skin.

~

At home Leah cooks a small dinner of pasta, nothing special. She hasn't got anything much in, since she and Sam were supposed to be meeting for dinner, but he messaged earlier to cancel. *I have to work late again. Rain check on dinner?* Now, as she eats alone, she wonders if this is just a heavy workload or if he's starting to cool on her. Chewing slowly, she suddenly finds the apartment too quiet. There's no sound except for the hum of the refrigerator.

She turns on the television for noise but lowers the volume until it is only a murmur. Her eyes keep drifting to the notebook on the counter where she records all of her most difficult calls. She considers writing about Amber instead, and the way the woman's voice carried that strange echo of her own, but she dismisses the idea.

Meanwhile, across town Amber sits cross-legged on the floor of her apartment, a headset plugged into her phone. The room is small but clean, the walls bare except for one pinned note that reads: Calm keeps the chaos away.

She scrolls through the training recordings that Leah sent to help her practice tone modulation. Leah's voice fills the headset's earpieces. It is gentle, precise, and unhurried. Amber breathes in time with it, counting silently as she exhales. She replays the same clip three times, mouthing the words along with Leah.

"I'm right here with you. Stay calm. Help is coming."

She closes her eyes and says it again in a whisper until her own tone matches perfectly. The mimicry feels natural, like learning a song she already knew the tune to.

She reaches for a sticky note and writes a note to herself. Practice breathing to match hers. She sticks it beside the first one. Her desk is a small shrine to routine, with its color-coded pens, the headset cradle polished to a dull shine, and a single mug identical to the one she saw Leah using that afternoon.

Amber presses play once more. Leah's voice fills her ears, calm and sure. Amber repeats each line in perfect rhythm. When she stops, the silence feels wrong. She leaves the headset on, listening to the faint hiss of the connection even after the recording ends. Her breathing stays slow, matched to Leah's remembered pace. Somewhere in her chest, a rhythm begins to settle that isn't entirely her own.

3

The storm breaks without warning. By mid-morning the city has become a patchwork of blue light and moving sirens, the sky strobing as if under interrogation. Wind presses hard against the windows of the Phoenix Dispatch Center, rain dragging itself down the glass in erratic silver lines. Inside, the air hums with electricity and voices. Every console blinks red.

Leah Hunter adjusts her headset, straightens her posture, and answers another call.

"911. What's your emergency?"

A woman screams about a downed power line sparking in her yard. Leah dispatches a unit in the time it takes for the woman to finish the address. Her fingers move quickly, each command a precise strike. The room pulses around her with overlapping noise as reports of crashes, power outages, and floods blend with the usual dispatch codes, and clipped sentences snapping into place. The rhythm is familiar, almost comforting. This is where she lives best, inside the chaos, but holding it steady.

Beside her, Amber Klein works with her headset already in place. She has learned the system fast. The soft glow from her monitor lights the planes of her face, her eyes focused and still. The two of them move in an easy, uncanny sync, hands hovering and clicking in near unison. They hardly need to look at each other to stay in rhythm.

Miguel walks the rows, tie loosened, shirt sleeves rolled.

"Stay sharp, people. There's a power outage across the south side, so comms might drop out. Keep manual notes if you have to."

Leah nods without looking up. "Copy."

Amber mirrors her. "Copy."

From three stations down, Bree's voice rises, bright with nerves. "Feels like the end of the world out there."

"It isn't," Leah says quietly. "It just sounds like it."

Another line lights. Another call. A man trapped in his car beneath a fallen tree, shouting that water is rising around his door. Leah sends a rescue unit, coordinates with the Fire Service, and keeps her voice calm and clipped and even. Beside her, Amber takes a call about a transformer explosion and repeats Leah's phrasing almost word for word.

"Stay calm. Help is on the way. Keep your distance from the fire."

Her tone is identical, using the same cadence, the same quiet authority. Leah glances across. Amber meets her eyes, and for a breath they fall into the same rhythm, inhaling and exhaling as one.

It feels, for that small, suspended moment, like standing in the eye of the storm with both of them anchored to the same still point while the city roars around them.

Miguel pauses behind them, watching their movements line up without effort.

"Look at you two," he says, voice half joking. "A two-person symphony."

Amber smiles. "She sets the tempo."

Leah pretends not to hear, keeping her eyes on the screen. She types another report and moves straight into the next call.

Hours pass in fragments of voices, sirens, and thunder cracking overhead. The power flickers once, plunging the room into instant darkness before the backup lights flare on. A low murmur of tension rolls across the floor. Leah feels it but doesn't react. Her body knows this rhythm and it moves before she has time to think. This is far from the first storm she's weathered on a shift. Her voice is the metronome that holds strangers steady until help arrives.

When there's a lull in the call traffic, the brief moment of silence lands like a physical weight. The whole room exhales. Leah removes her headset and rubs her temples. Her throat burns. Rain still drums hard on the roof above, a relentless, steady percussion.

Amber appears beside her with two paper cups. "Black coffee," she says. "One sugar, no cream."

Leah looks up, startled. "How did you...?"

"I watched you make it yesterday." Amber hands her the cup, smiling. "You're predictable in the best way."

Leah takes a sip. It's exactly right. She can't tell whether that makes her feel seen or exposed. "Thanks."

Amber settles onto the edge of the neighboring console, one hand curled around her own cup. "You ever get tired of saving people you'll never meet?"

Leah stares into the dark liquid. "Sometimes."

"But you keep doing it."

"It's what I'm good at."

Amber nods slowly, a contemplative tilt of the head. "Do you ever still hear them after your shift?"

The question lands softly but with weight. Most people don't ask that. Leah hesitates.

"Sometimes," she admits. "The ones who don't make it, mostly. Or the ones who sound like they might be children."

Amber's voice lowers, almost reverent. "Me too. It's like their voices stay in the wires."

Leah studies her face. The glow of the monitor gives Amber's eyes a faint glassy shine. For a moment Leah sees herself reflected there as another exhausted dispatcher, another pair of hands holding chaos at bay. The recognition sits too close, almost invasive, like someone stepping a little further into her space than she expected.

They sit like that, two silhouettes in the dim light, with the rain hammering above, until Bree bursts in with a paper bag and a grin that cuts through the tension.

"You two still okay? I brought donuts before the world ends."

Amber doesn't move. She stares at Bree, with a smile frozen on her lips. The sudden brightness of Bree's voice grates like static. Leah watches Amber's smile curl before she turns away.

"Take one," Bree says, waving the bag.

"I'm fine," Leah answers.

"Suit yourself." Bree leaves, humming a tune that clashes with the steady pulse of rain.

When she's gone, Amber exhales through her nose. "She's loud."

"She's just young."

Amber's tone softens. "You like her."

"She's easy to like."

Amber's mouth twists slightly. "Easy isn't always good."

Leah lets it pass. She drinks the last of her coffee, the bitterness grounding her. "Come on. Let's clear the backlog before shift change."

Amber stands, her expression resetting to calm. They return to their consoles and for the next hour, the room settles into a weary rhythm. The worst of the storm has passed. Now come the follow-ups, as the power company runs checks, the stranded motorists get towed, and the quiet voices of people afraid of the dark, or the stranger there with them, return.

In another quiet moment, Leah leans back. "Well, that was a tough one, but we survived."

Amber smiles faintly. "Together."

Leah logs her last call. "You should take a break. Get some air."

"I don't want to miss anything."

"You won't."

Amber lingers anyway. "If you go, I'll go."

Leah stands. "Fine. Five minutes."

The breakroom is half lit, one flickering bulb above the sink. A half-empty pot of coffee sits stewing on the machine, thick as syrup. The vending machine hums a low mechanical sigh. Leah makes fresh coffee for both of them, rinsing out the sludge already in her cup. Amber watches her every movement, as if studying choreography.

Rain hits the windows in bursts. The city beyond is a blur of light and water. Leah sits at the small table, stirring her drink while Amber takes the seat opposite.

"You ever think about quitting?" Amber asks.

"Every night around three."

"What stops you?"

Leah shrugs. "Habit, I guess. I'm not built for quiet."

Amber nods. "Me neither. It sets me on edge."

They sit for a while without speaking, watching the storm fade and the skies clear. Leah lets her shoulders relax for the first time all night. The quiet between them feels almost intimate, a small bubble carved out of the chaos.

"I used to count breaths," Amber says suddenly. "Back in Albuquerque. When I couldn't sleep. I'd match them to the sound of the phone tones. It helped."

Leah tilts her head. "You mean the call alerts?"

"Yes. The short ones between transfers." Amber smiles faintly. "You can hear a pattern if you listen close enough. Like a heartbeat."

Leah looks at her. "That's strange."

"Maybe. But it works."

Bree's laughter echoes faintly down the corridor. The sound pulls Leah back to the world. She finishes her coffee and stands. "Time to get back."

Amber stands too, moving in sync. "I'll walk with you."

By the end of the shift, the storm has thinned to a tired drizzle. The emergency board shows only a handful of pending calls and most of the screens dim to standby blue. Chairs creak as people lean back for the first time in hours. Miguel walks the line one last time, checking logs, and even his steps are slower now.

"Hell of a night," he says. "Good work, all of you."

Bree yawns so hard her headset slips. "I might sleep for a week."

"Not before the debrief," Miguel replies, though his tone is soft enough that no one believes he'll hold them to it.

Leah gathers her things, sliding her notebook into her bag, the weight of the shift settling in her shoulders. Amber mirrors her movements a station over, quiet and composed, as though she's been working here for years, not days.

At the exit, Leah pats her pocket automatically, left, then right, and freezes. Her keycard is gone. She checks again, slower this time. But the pockets are empty.

Before she can retrace her steps, Amber steps forward, the card pinched between her fingers.

"Looking for this?"

Leah blinks. "That's my...How did I...?"

Amber offers the card out, her expression perfectly neutral.

"You must have dropped it ," she says. "I found it by your chair."

Leah reaches for it, and their fingers brush. Skin against skin, warm and brief. The contact jolts through her before she can stop it. Amber doesn't pull away quickly; her smile holds steady, gentle and a little too intent.

"Thank you," Leah says, voice catching on the edge of relief.

Amber's gaze lingers. "Anytime."

"Right, well, see you in a few days," Leah says.

Leah steps into the corridor. The heavy door swings shut behind her with a muted thud. She breathes in the cool air and feels the relief rush over her like a wave, washing away the static of the room. For a moment she stands still, head tipped back, the metallic scent of rain drifting through the vents. She'll be grateful of the three day break in shifts now, and the chance to get away from the phones.

Outside, the sky is a pale, washed-out gray. The parking lot gleams with shallow puddles, reflecting the early light in trembling shapes. Leah unlocks her car and the soft click echoes in the damp quiet. Her reflection in the window looks ghostly, almost translucent. She lowers herself into the seat and rests her hands on the wheel, grounding herself with the familiarity of the gesture. Across the lot, another engine starts. Leah looks up. Amber's car idles three rows away. Headlights on but not moving. Amber's silhouette sits perfectly still behind the glass.

Leah hesitates. She tells herself Amber is probably waiting for the windows to defog, for the heater to warm. Something normal. Something ordinary. She starts her own car, reverses slowly, and pulls out. In her rearview mirror, Amber's car remains where it is, unmoving, as though she's watching. The image of it grows smaller and smaller until it becomes only two faint circles of light swallowed by drizzle.

Amber doesn't move until Leah's taillights fade completely

into the gray. The windshield wipers sweep back and forth in slow, steady arcs. She sits with both hands on the wheel, breathing in time with the rhythm. The radio glows faintly, tuned to a static-filled frequency that hums like distant rain.

She whispers the words she has heard Leah speak a hundred times. "Stay calm. Help is on the way."

A small, secret smile unfolds. Then she turns the key, shifts into gear, and glides out of the lot just as the first thin thread of sunlight stretches across the wet asphalt.

4

Leah arrives for her next shift just after sunrise, the sky a pale lid over the city as the light gathers at the edges. The lobby doors breathe cold air when she badges in. The corridor is warm, quiet, faintly stale. She turns the corner toward her station and stops without meaning to.

Her desk is perfect. The headset is coiled on the right, looped in the tidy spiral she uses only when she is the one who closes the row. Her mug rests beside the keyboard with the handle turned outward at its familiar angle. The monitor tilt is set precisely to the height she leaves it at when she plans to return the next morning. But she has not worked in three days. And others would have used the station in her absence.

Leah looks around to see who might have prepared her desk. The room is still asleep. Screens are dimmed, chairs tucked in, nothing disturbed. No one sits at the neighboring consoles. She reaches out and brushes the headset cord with the back of her knuckle. Strange, she thinks, how perfectly it's been arranged.

She sits down and logs in. The system blooms to life in soft blues. She straightens the stapler out of reflex, not choice, and tells herself someone from maintenance must have tidied the row. But the thought doesn't fit. Maintenance never notices mug handles and screen tilts.

A voice calls out behind her. "Morning."

She turns. Amber is at the end of the aisle with two paper cups. She's wearing a gray cardigan the exact shade Leah owns. At her lanyard hangs a small brass compass charm that catches the weak light. Leah bought the same charm online two weeks ago, after she'd lost her old key ring in the parking lot.

Amber lifts one cup. "Twin fuel."

Leah forces a small smile. "You're in early."

"Couldn't sleep," Amber says, stepping closer and setting a cup beside Leah's mug. She gestures lightly toward the desk. "Someone knows you well."

Leah keeps her tone mild. "Maybe the cleaning crew got observant."

Amber laughs. "Sure. Or someone wanted to be kind." She nods toward the charm at her lanyard, then at Leah. "Twins, huh?"

"Twins," Leah echoes, though the word lands wrong in her mouth.

By the time the floor wakes, the small scene has already folded under the routine of the day. Miguel passes with a stack of printouts. Bree slides into her chair with a whispered complaint about the broken vending machine. Calls begin to land, light as drips on water. Leah takes one about a chirping smoke alarm, then another about a stalled car in a resurfacing lane. The city settles into its usual morning pulse.

At ten, her phone buzzes against her thigh. Sam's name flashes up. She declines the call, sends a quick text: *In the chair. Break soon.*

He replies before she sets the phone down. *Dinner tonight still on?*

A small warmth flickers at the thought. She'd seen him once

during her days off, a hurried lunch that felt like sunlight. She texts: *Yes. Looking forward to it.*

He sends back: *Good. I miss you.*

It's simple, earnest. It sounds more like him than the brittleness he carried last week. She places the phone face-down. Amber is suddenly at her shoulder with a file Leah doesn't need. "He sounds protective."

Leah looks up, slightly annoyed to have Amber reading over her shoulder.

"It's fine. We just don't get much time together."

"People hate competing with this job," Amber says softly, as if she knows. "They want a version of us that doesn't get pulled away."

Leah presses the phone under a notepad. "It's fine between us."

Amber nods, as though the comment included her. "Of course. Just... if you ever need to talk..."

"Thank you." Leah returns to her screen.

The next call hits fast. It's a teenage girl finding her grandfather unresponsive. Leah slips into the familiar rhythm. Calm voice, clear step, watch the breath, keep her anchored. She sends a unit. The girl apologizes for crying. Leah keeps her steady.

At the next console Amber answers a call in a gentle, firm, unwavering tone that sounds almost exactly like Leah's.

Bree swivels around. "You two are scary similar."

Leah glances over. Amber's posture mirrors hers perfectly, too. Her left hand hovering above the function keys, right hand typing. Their voices fall into the same cadence on separate lines, echoing each other until Leah briefly wonders which voice belongs to her.

The call resolves. The girl sobs with relief as paramedics take over. Leah ends the line, logs the event, and presses her palm flat to the desk to still the tremor that comes only after crisis passes.

"Break?" Bree calls.

"In five," Leah answers.

"I can go now," Amber says brightly.

Leah ignores the small tug beneath the words. "I'll catch up."

By the time she reaches the lounge, Bree is gone. A tired coffee pot sputters on the warmer. A jar of powdered creamer sits open, a soft drift forming around the rim. Leah chooses tea for a clean taste and leans against the counter while it steeps. Amber enters without a sound. She holds out her phone.

"Look at her."

A photo of a gray cat appears on the screen, perched on the arm of a couch. The eyes glow from the flash. The picture is casual, almost sweet. Leah smiles despite herself.

"She's beautiful."

"Juniper," Amber says, pleased. "She runs the place."

Leah's gaze shifts behind the cat to the table. A ceramic mug sits beside a stack of mail. White with a pale blue ring. A hairline crack near the handle.

Leah has the same mug at home. Not just the design. The same mug. With the same crack. Amber pockets her phone.

"She likes my voice," she says lightly. "Calm keeps the chaos away."

Leah wants to ask about the mug. She doesn't. Her tea suddenly tastes metallic, so she pours the rest out.

Back on the floor, a commercial kitchen alarm triggers on the south side. Calls stack. Leah lets the nothing of the break room fall away and reabsorbs the something of the work.

The afternoon passes in shards of traffic calls, small crises, one whispered voice behind a locked bathroom door. Leah stays with the caller, pacing her words to the woman's breath until the police knock and take over.

By the time the shift ends, Leah's voice feels frayed at the edges. She shuts down her console and coils the headset exactly as she found it that morning. The repetition prickles beneath her skin.

Amber appears at her shoulder. "Fancy grabbing some dinner?"

Leah startles. "Oh. Not tonight. I already have plans."

Amber's expression doesn't fall. If anything, something in it settles. "He isn't going to keep you from me forever," she says lightly, a joke that isn't a joke.

Before Leah can respond, Amber steps back and gives a small wave. "See you tomorrow, twinny."

The word follows Leah into the corridor feeling too bright, and too sharp. Outside, the light has collapsed into early evening. Heat presses low over the lot. She drives home with the radio off, the city sliding past in thin, paper-like layers.

By the time Leah reaches her apartment, she feels scraped thin, like someone has turned the day inside out and left the seams exposed. At her door, a parcel waits against the mat. Small, brown and neatly taped. There's no sender listed, only her name and unit number in clean printed type.

She carries it into the kitchen and sets it beside her cracked blue-rimmed mug. The sight of the two objects together makes something at the base of her skull tighten, but she pushes the thought aside and reaches for a butter knife. She slides it under the tape, careful not to split the cardboard clean through. Inside is a compact case in matte black plastic.

Even before she lifts it, she knows the weight, the hinge, the exact click of the latch. They're noise-cancelling headphones. Her usual brand. The model she buys every couple of years when the old pair finally quits. But she hasn't ordered any, and there's no note, no receipt, and no packing slip tucked under the molded insert to give her a clue who sent them.

Her thoughts go first to Sam. This afternoon's messages sit like grit under her ribs. They had made dinner plans for tonight, but she'd been too worn down to decide what she wanted, too fogged by the shift to persuade herself she was up for much of anything. He'd texted, *Any ideas where you want to go?* She'd replied that her head was pounding, that the day had hit harder than expected.

He'd been the one to suggest postponing. *Another night is fine. I'm wiped too.* Then: *Love you. Proud of you.* It had softened her, the way it always did.

She looks at the headphones. He sends small peace offerings sometimes, like books she's mentioned, a new kettle after hers cracked. So she tells herself he probably sent these too. She sets the case on the counter and looks again for a gift message she already knows isn't there.

The kitchen hums around her waiting for her to decide which version of the truth she wants. She takes a picture of the open box, the case, the lid. *Thank you. You didn't have to.* She types the words but doesn't send them. Instead, she deletes them and slides the phone into her back pocket. She'll talk to him later.

She showers, letting the hot water run in steady sheets. In the mirror afterward, her eyes look pale, the skin beneath them paper-thin. She dresses in soft clothes and carries the case to the couch. The apartment holds a quiet she once found soothing. Tonight, it feels like a pause she didn't ask for.

She opens the case and lifts the headphones. The moment they settle over her ears, the world folds inward. The outside traffic noise disappears, the clock disappears, even her breath becomes distant, as if heard through walls. The pressure around her head feels like hands cupping her skull, steady and enclosing. She closes her eyes and waits to see whether the quiet will soothe or scare her. Strangely, it does both.

Memories flicker in fragments of the perfect coil of the cord on her desk, the small compass charm flashing on Amber's lanyard, the gray cardigan in the same shade she owns, and the cat perched beside a mug with a crack that ran the same impossible line. Coincidence sounds reasonable until it gathers enough weight to stop sounding like coincidence at all.

When she removes the headphones, the apartment returns in a soft roar of gently sounds. She sets the case on the table and stands up, walking to the kitchen to pick up her own mug. The crack beneath her thumb is familiar, intimate in the way injuries can be. She places it down and turns off the light.

Her phone buzzes with a message from Sam. *Made it home. Let's make sure we do dinner tomorrow? And... I love you.*

Relief opens something warm in her chest. She types, *I love you too.* Before she can talk herself out of it, she sends another message *Did you send headphones?*

The dots appear. Pause. Reappear. *No. Should I have? Why?*

No reason, she types. *Ignore me. Rough shift.*

You okay?

I will be. Call you in the morning?

Of course. Sleep. Proud of you.

She powers the phone off and carries it to the bedroom. She leaves the headphones on the table and the open box on the counter, as though keeping them in plain sight might help prove, to herself more than anyone else, that they are only objects, and not warnings. Not messages and not anything else.

∼

Across town, Amber lies on her back on a narrow bed. The room is dark except for the blue of a phone screen propped against a stack of books. A headset is plugged into the device. The training clip Leah recorded for the new recruits plays in a loop, the volume set low. Leah's voice fills the space, steady and precise.

"I am here with you. We will do this together. Breathe in for four. Hold for two. Out for six."

Amber repeats the words under her breath. Her own breathing falls into the rhythm Leah describes. The room seems to expand and contract with the count. On the bedside table, a small compass charm rests in a shallow dish with keys. The same gray cardigan hangs over the back of a chair. A white mug with a pale blue ring sits by the sink, drying on a folded towel.

Amber speaks into the dim. "Stay calm. Help is coming." She says it again and again until the phrase no longer feels like words. It becomes a shape in the air. It becomes the sound the apartment makes when the phone stops talking, and the silence begins to breathe.

She picks up the headset and presses the ear cushions tight until the outside world thins to almost nothing. She closes her eyes and listens to Leah's voice. She does not think of the word boundary. She just sees a line and thinks only of how easy it is to cross when the ground is already even.

5

Leah feels happier on the night shift again. The city feels different at this hour, with its thick air, heavy sky. Leah arrives early for her shift, hoping a few quiet minutes will settle her before the noise begins. Behind the glass frontage the Phoenix Dispatch Center hums like a machine idling low, waiting to be pushed hard. Corridor lights buzz overhead, tired and warm.

Inside, the room looks unchanged, with its rows of consoles, screens glowing blue, a calm that feels temporary. Amber is already there. Two takeout coffees wait on Leah's desk, steam drifting upward in the fluorescent light. Amber sits cross-legged in the neighboring chair, hair braided tight, lanyard charm glinting each time she shifts. She turns when Leah enters, smiling as though she has been waiting for her arrival.

"Hazelnut, right?" She nudges a cup toward Leah. "One pump, no sugar."

Leah pauses mid-reach. "How do you know that?"

Amber lifts a shoulder. "You mentioned it the other day."

Leah is almost certain she didn't. But the coffee smells right, and the first sip is perfect, barely sweet, exactly how she takes it.

She tells herself it's harmless. Just good listening. The kind of attentiveness she drills into every new hire.

Miguel strolls past with a clipboard, nodding at them on his way to the supervisors' desk. "Storm building in the north. Expect volume."

Leah tucks her bag under the console and logs in. "Copy."

Amber watches her over the rim of her cup. "You get headaches when the pressure shifts in the weather, don't you?"

The question catches Leah mid-keystroke. "Sometimes."

Amber smiles, pleased with herself. "Me too. It's like the whole city presses down on you."

Leah returns a polite smile, unsure how to answer. The headset settles over her ears and the tones begin as the shift opens like a door.

Two hours in, as predicted, the night turns violent. The storm sweeps across the city faster than anyone thought it would, dragging a snarl of rain and blown transformers behind it. Calls flood the board of collisions, alarms, trees down, wires live. Leah slips into the narrow focus she's honed over a decade, listening to one voice, one crisis, one map square at a time. The world shrinks to what she can steady.

Amber sits one console away. The calm in her expression echoes Leah's so precisely it almost unnerves her. Her eyes flick from screen to screen, matching Leah's phrasing, holding the same clipped certainty. A man shouts through static. "We've been hit, it's multiple car. People are hurt."

Leah maps the location as she speaks. "Sir, stay on the line. Tell me where you are."

Across the console, Amber mirrors the tone for her own caller. "Stay calm. Tell me where you are."

Bree passes behind them and mutters, "You two could share a brain."

Leah almost laughs but keeps her gaze forward. Amber is

coaxing details from a frightened woman, syncing her breaths to Leah's without looking. Their screens populate with paired coordinates, mirrored notes, two halves of the same rhythm.

When the last unit clears and the storm noise falls back to routine chatter, Leah leans away from the console. Her shoulders ache. Amber exhales loudly, slipping off her headset and twisting her braid into a new knot.

"That was intense," she says. "Just knowing you were there grounded me."

Leah glances over. "You handled it well."

A slow curve lifts Amber's mouth. "Only because you were there."

The warmth in the words is real, but its wrapped around something sharper. Leah can feel the edge of it. Miguel appears again, clipboard in hand.

"Good work, both of you. Seamless."

Amber beams. Leah nods, grateful for the interruption. By the end of the shift, the board has quieted, the storm broken apart. Leah finishes her report and signs out. Amber stands at the same moment, as if their movements were tethered.

"I'll walk out with you," she says.

Leah shakes her head. "You don't have to."

"It's late," Amber says lightly, though the look in her eyes is too steady to be casual. "And you always park in the corner lot, right?"

A small hesitation opens in Leah's chest. "Yes."

"Then I'm walking with you."

Leah doesn't argue. The corridor feels longer after a storm, the lights humming louder, the whole building exhaling spent air. Outside, puddles shimmer under the lamps. The wet asphalt breathes heat.

Amber keeps half a step behind her, close enough to watch, far enough to seem polite. At Leah's car, Amber stops just short of the driver's side. "Text me when you get home, okay?"

"I'll be fine."

"Please. We both know what it can be like out there."

The insistence is soft but firm. Leah nods. "All right. Thank you."

Amber's smile settles into place, satisfied. "Goodnight."

Leah unlocks her car and slides inside. Through the windshield she sees Amber linger, unmoving, watching her. Only when Leah's headlights wash across her face does Amber turn back toward her own car. Leah's pulse runs faster than it should.

Home is dark except for the small lamp she leaves by the couch when she's on night shift. She kicks off her shoes, grabs some food from the fridge and when she sits at the table, she checks her phone. There's one new message from Sam.

Why did you text me "I'm done"?

Leah stares at the screen.

"What?" she whispers aloud. She scrolls through her sent messages but finds nothing there. No message, no draft, and nothing sent and deleted. She checks her call log, her chat history, her email. Nothing. Her stomach tightens. She types quickly.

I didn't send that. I've checked my phone. There's no sign. Must be a glitch. I'm sorry.

He replies a minute later. *Then who did?*

I don't know.

A long pause. *It came from your number.*

Leah sits on the edge of the couch, gripping the phone. She rechecks her folders, her backups, anything that might explain it. The silence of the apartment presses close. The shadows feel thicker, like soundproof foam.

She types, *Maybe my phone's acting up. I'll have IT look at it.*

No reply. Just the read receipt, glowing small and final. Leah locks the phone and sits for a while, her heart still tripping over itself. She thinks about how Amber always plugs her phone into the same charger during breaks. How she always asks, "Want me to grab yours too?" It's probably nothing. Probably.

She showers and tries to let the water strip the noise away. It doesn't.

The next day, Leah drags herself into work, eyes burning from lack of sleep. Bree greets her with a bag of pretzels and a smile.

"Tough sleep?"

"Something like that."

Amber appears behind her. "You look pale." She sets a coffee down. "I got you a latter. Hazelnut, one pump."

Leah blinks. "You didn't have to."

Amber shrugs. "You'd do the same."

Bree raises an eyebrow, glancing between them. "You two need name tags that say 'same brain.'"

Amber laughs softly. "Maybe we share one."

Leah forces a smile and sits. She checks her phone and types a message to Sam. *We okay?* It stays on unread.

The first few calls come in routine. Faint echoes of last night's chaos—follow-ups, insurance queries, cleanup reports. Amber handles most of them, her tone clipped and professional. She never misses a cue. When the board clears, she turns toward Leah, face full of concern.

"What's up?" she asks.

"Just tired."

"Did you and Sam fight?" The question feels too quick, too close.

Leah looks up, caught. "What?"

"You look worried. Like you've had a bust up."

Leah nods slowly. "No, not a bust up. Just distance I guess. He's upset with me over a message I didn't send."

Amber's voice softens. "He should be more supportive."

"It's not that simple."

Amber tilts her head. "He sounds like he doesn't really understand what you do."

Leah doesn't answer. The observation is sharp and smooth, like a blade drawn under silk. Amber reaches for Leah's wrist but stops just before touching her.

"You carry everyone else's pain. You shouldn't have to carry his too."

Leah withdraws her hand to the keyboard. "I'm fine."

Amber leans back, eyes still on her. "It's probably just stress."

Leah exhales. "Yeah. Probably."

When she reaches for her charger that afternoon, it's gone. She checks under her papers, behind the monitor. Nothing. The cable she's used for months, always in the same locker compartment, isn't there. She asks Bree, who shrugs.

"Check the lounge. People are always moving stuff."

Leah does but with no luck. When she returns to her station, Amber is waiting, holding up the white cord.

"Looking for this?"

Leah freezes. "Where was it?"

"In the breakroom. I thought it looked familiar."

Leah takes it slowly. "Thank you."

Amber smiles, lips pressed tight. "You're welcome."

That evening the sky turns purple behind the apartment blocks. Leah drives home without music, the steady hum of the engine filling her ears. At her door, a delivery driver waits for a reply to his knock, a paper bag steaming in his hands. He turns as she approaches.

"Leah Hunter?"

"Yes."

"Pad Thai, spring rolls, extra lime. Paid already." He offers the receipt.

Leah signs automatically. She carries the food inside, setting it on the counter. The smell is comforting, and familiar. She hasn't ordered Thai in weeks. She assumes Sam did it as his version of peace, maybe. She texts him. *Thank you for dinner. It was sweet of you.*

He replies within seconds. *What dinner?*

She reads it twice. The receipt still sits on the counter., and when she picks it up, she sees a customer note which says: From: A. Maybe it was a coincidence. Maybe it was someone else's order misdelivered. But it's her exact usual from the same restaurant, same combination of dishes. And the only A she can think of is Amber. But how would she know what to order and which restaurant, and

She deletes the message thread before she can see him typing again. She eats standing up, the food already cooling. The flavors taste more invasive now, as though someone has worn her favorite shirt and left their scent on it. When she finishes, she checks the locks twice before going to bed.

Sleep doesn't come easily. Her mind loops through the fragments of strangeness that have happened through the last twenty-four hours. The fake message, the found charger, the dinner. Each thought folds into the next until it feels like she's hearing the static of an open line. Somewhere beneath it,

Amber's voice whispers reassurance. You're safe. Help is on the way.

She jolts awake, realizing it was her own imagination, or a dream, or both. The room is quiet except for the hum of the air conditioner unit. She checks her phone to find no new messages.

When she wakes to her alarm later, the feeling of pressure hasn't shifted. Leah calls in sick for the first time in years. Miguel's voice on the other end is kind but curious.

"Everything okay?"

"Just over tired," she says.

"Rest up and get better," he says. "We've got coverage."

When she hangs up, she notices her phone screen flicker with a flash of static before returning to normal. She tells herself it's the battery. She charges it, watches the light blink amber, and walks to the window. The parking lot below is almost empty. A single gray sedan sits near the exit. She thinks she recognizes it but can't be sure. She pulls the curtain closed.

By nightfall she's restless again. She makes tea and sits on the couch with her notebook. The pages are neat, rows of recorded calls, timestamps, short notes about training issues. She turns to a blank page and writes down all the things that don't fit. Message to Sam that wasn't mine. Charger moved. Dinner from A.

She stares at the list until the letters blur. Then she closes the notebook and sets it face down.

Her phone buzzes. A text from Amber. *How's your night off? Miss hearing your voice.*

Leah types, *Quiet. Just resting.*

Amber replies instantly. *Good. You deserve rest. The world is loud enough.*

Leah hesitates before responding. *See you tomorrow.*

Can't wait.

Leah sets the phone down and walks to the kitchen. The air feels heavy and dense. She opens the fridge, grabs water, and catches her reflection in the dark window. For a heartbeat, she thinks she sees another shape behind her. Perhaps a trick of light, or memory, or both. She turns back, heart ticking fast. The apartment is empty. It's always empty.

She sits, drinks the water, and laughs once, quietly. Paranoia. That's what Sam would call it. He used to tell her the mind fills silence with ghosts. Maybe he was right.

Across town, Amber sits cross-legged on her bed. The apartment around her is spotless, with all its edges sharp and precise. Her phone glows in her lap, Leah's contact photo shining softly. It's a candid image from the training day, of Leah mid-laugh, unaware of the camera.

Amber taps the screen, scrolling to the saved audio clips. Leah's voice fills the small space, steady, composed, kind.

"Stay calm. Help is coming."

Amber repeats it under her breath, syncing her breathing with Leah's recorded rhythm. The same cadence that anchors the chaos now anchors her. The headset cord wraps around her wrist as she presses the phone close.

She whispers, "You live for those voices. I live for yours."

On the nightstand lies an open notebook. Inside, Leah's phone number is written over and over, each time a little smaller, until the digits blur into a dark smudge. Amber closes her eyes and hits replay. Leah's voice begins again, calm and unbreakable, filling the silence until it sounds like safety.

6

Leah wakes to the sound of her phone vibrating against the nightstand. The noise has threaded itself through her dreams in an echo that becomes real only when she opens her eyes. Morning light leaks through the half-closed blinds, too bright, too soon. Her head feels heavy, and her mouth dry. She picks up the phone to find six missed calls and three messages. All from Sam. She blinks at the screen until the words make sense.

Why won't you answer me?

Are you serious about what you said last night?

I can't keep doing this if you're going to shut down.

Leah sits up slowly, her heart beating too fast. She scrolls through her sent folder. There are messages there she doesn't remember writing, all sent last night, when she was sure she was asleep.

Maybe we're done.

I need quiet, not demands.

Stop calling.

She stares at the messages, the words pale against the white screen, her own number above them. The timestamps are from after midnight. She was definitely asleep by then. A small, absurd hope flares. She didn't send these messages, so it must be some kind of system error, maybe. A glitch. Ghost texts. It happens. Her phone buzzes again. It's Sam.

She hesitates, then answers. "Hey."

His voice comes sharp, already frayed. "Hey? You don't get to talk to me like that and then act like nothing happened."

"I didn't send those messages."

"Leah—"

"I swear, Sam, I was asleep."

He laughs once, short and bitter. "You always have an excuse. It's either work or stress or something with your phone. Do you even hear yourself anymore?"

"I'm telling you the truth."

Silence fills the space between them, and Leah feels it pressing at her ears like a vice. He sighs finally.

"You need to figure out what you want. Because I can't keep guessing. Let me know when you know what you want to do."

The line goes dead.

Leah lowers the phone into her lap. The air feels too still. For a few seconds she sits motionless, waiting for her pulse to slow. Then she opens the messages again, reads them one more time, as if repetition will rewrite what's there. She deletes them, though the act brings no relief.

At the dispatch center, the day begins quietly, almost deceptively so. The calm after too many nights of chaos. Leah's console hums with its low electronic life. The clock on the far wall ticks loudly.

Amber arrives carrying two coffees. Hazelnut syrup. She doesn't ask if Leah wants one; she just sets it down, the same way she always does.

"You look exhausted already," she says. "Rough morning?"

Leah nods, not trusting herself to answer. Amber slides into the next chair, perfectly angled toward her.

"Want to talk about it?"

"Not really."

"Then don't." Amber smiles. "I'm here if you need to."

The first call blinks red. Leah takes it, grateful for the distraction. A woman reports smoke in a warehouse near the interstate. Leah dispatches the Fire service, confirms the cross-streets, stays calm as the woman stumbles over details. Her voice steadies because that's what it knows how to do. When the call ends, her hand trembles faintly. She hides it under the desk.

Amber notices anyway.

"You can lean on me, you know," she says, reaching into her pocket. She sets a small blue stress ball beside Leah's keyboard. "I find this helps."

Leah looks at it, then at her. "You carry one of these?"

"Picked it up at the conference. It helps distract me when things get too much."

Leah rolls the ball once in her palm, and nods her thanks. Bree wanders over from her station, hair pinned messily back.

"We're grabbing drinks tonight. You coming, Leah?"

Leah glances at the shift board. "Maybe. If we finish on time."

Before Bree can respond, Amber leans back in her chair, smiling. "She's had a rough day. Don't fool yourself that she'll make it."

Bree grins. "Rough days are what drinks are good for fixing."

"True," Leah says, smiling. "I'll do my best."

Amber's tone softens, half-apologetic. "I'll make sure you get home safe if you do come out."

Leah laughs under her breath, embarrassed by how warm her face feels. "I can get myself home."

"Of course," Amber says, still smiling. "But it's nice to have someone watching your back, isn't it?"

Bree shrugs, amused. "Mother Hen alert."

Amber doesn't react. She turns back to her console, expression smoothing into something colder.

By midafternoon, any hope of a calm shift dissolves. A pile-up on the highway floods the board with calls. Leah moves through them like muscle memory, taking reports, dispatching units, marking times. The sound of sirens bleeds faintly through the shared radio feed.

Amber mirrors her every move. The two of them sound like one mind split into two bodies. Miguel stops behind them, listening for a moment before speaking.

"That's clean work, both of you."

Leah gives a tired nod. Amber glows under the praise, eyes bright. When the final call clears, Leah leans back, rubbing her eyes. Amber reaches out, lightly brushing the back of her wrist.

"You were so in control then, it was impressive."

Leah pulls her hand away, subtle but firm. "It's my job."

"Doesn't make it easier."

"No." Leah glances toward Miguel's office window, where the blinds hang half-closed. "It doesn't."

The moment stretches, awkward, until Bree returns from the breakroom with two sodas. "Heroes, both of you," she says. "I'm clocking out before the next apocalypse. I think we can safely say drinks are off tonight. I need to sleep!"

Amber smiles thinly. "See you tomorrow."

When Bree's gone, Leah checks the time. "I owe you a thank-you. For earlier. For covering me during that misroute."

Amber's expression softens. "You don't owe me anything. But... if you want, maybe grab dinner? My treat."

Leah hesitates. "Tonight?"

"Just a quick bite. We've got to eat."

Leah hears herself agreeing before she's thought it through.

~

The café near the center is small, half-hidden behind a gas station. Leah has driven past it countless times but never gone inside. The walls are painted the color of clay, and the lights are comfortingly low. Amber sits across from her in the booth, jacket folded neatly beside her. She has ordered wine for herself, iced tea for Leah.

"Thought you could use something non-caffeinated," she says.

Leah smiles faintly. "You notice everything."

Amber shrugs. "It's a habit. I listen for a living."

They talk about work first, moaning about the new routing software, and Bree's tendency to sing when she's tired. They laugh at Miguel's endless spreadsheets. The conversation is easy until it dries up.

Amber tilts her head. "How's Sam?"

Leah takes a slow sip of tea. She doesn't really want to talk about it.

"We're... figuring things out."

Amber's gaze doesn't waver. "He doesn't really get what you do, does he?"

"He worries it takes up too much of my time. Outside of work."

"He wants you to himself?"

Leah frowns slightly. "I think he wants me happy."

Amber's smile is gentle, understanding. "But he doesn't get what you hear every night."

Leah sighs. "No. I guess he doesn't."

"Maybe he's not built to."

The words land with surprising weight. Leah looks down at

her drink. She should defend Sam, say something about the years they've shared. But her throat feels tight, and nothing comes out. Amber reaches across the table, fingertips brushing Leah's wrist. The touch is deliberately light, just enough to draw a line through the air.

"You deserve calm," she says quietly. "Not demands."

Leah pulls back slowly. "You make it sound simple."

"It is simple." Amber's tone is soft but steady. "Sometimes people bring noise into our lives, and sometimes we outgrow the noise."

Leah forces a small laugh. "You'd make a good counselor."

Amber leans back, satisfied. "I just pay attention."

"He's a good man."

"But...?"

"No but. He *is* a good man."

"Just maybe not the one for you?" Amber smiles as though she's stating the obvious.

Later, at home, Leah's apartment smells faintly of jasmine from the candle she had lit the night before. She sets her bag down, hangs her jacket, and checks her phone to find two missed calls from Sam. He's left one voicemail. She stares at the notification. The small red circle feels like a weight pressing on her chest. She opens the message list, thumb hovering above play, then deletes it instead.

Guilt twists low in her stomach. The thought of not having him in her life has lingered all day. She hadn't sent those messages, but the resulting fallout has made her realize how they've drifted. She tells herself she's too tired to fight again. Tomorrow, she'll call. Tomorrow, she'll try to explain what she doesn't quite understand herself.

7

The next evening, when Leah arrives home, her key sticks in the lock. She twists it twice before the latch releases and the door pushes open. She steps inside, dropping her bag beside the shoe rack, and sees a cardboard box on the floor just below the coat hooks, rain-darkened along the edges.

For a long second, she just stares. The return label is smudged but legible. It's Sam's address in tiny blue ink. She kneels, the cardboard cold beneath her fingers, and lifts the lid. Inside, she finds the folded shirts she used to leave at his place after long weekends, a framed photo of them at a hiking trail two summers ago, the glass cracked across the middle. There's also her toothbrush in its case and a single note torn from a notepad. *I can't do this anymore.*

That's all. No apology. No explanation. The words sit heavy in her hands. She reads them again, then again, until they blur into ink stains. The air feels too thick to breathe. Something gives way inside her chest, starting small at first, then breaking wide open. She throws the note. Then the box. The contents scatter in a mess of cloth and glass and the dull thud of things that once belonged to another life. The photo frame hits the floor and finally shatters. She sinks to her knees, sobbing in short, jagged gasps that sound like static in the quiet apartment.

The sound rises and falls until she can't tell if it's her voice or an echo off the walls. She wipes at her face with the back of her hand, smearing tears and mascara into a gray streak across her skin. The knock startles her. Just two soft taps, a pause followed by another knock, louder this time.

She pulls herself up, heart still racing, and opens the door hoping for Sam. Amber stands there holding a paper bag that smells faintly of baking and garlic. Her hair is tied back, jacket unbuttoned, expression perfectly calm.

"I had a feeling you might need company," she says.

Leah blinks, stunned. "How did you know?"

Amber's smile is faint but certain. "You didn't look too happy in work. I just... had a feeling."

Leah's first instinct is to send her away. The mess around her feels too raw, and too private. But her throat burns, and the apartment feels unbearable, and Amber's calm feels like something solid to hold on to.

She steps aside. "Come in. Excuse the mess. I was just having a moment."

Amber moves through the doorway like she's been here before. She sets the bag on the counter, surveys the wreckage without a word, and starts picking things up from the hallway floor. She folds shirts, picks up the frame, sweeps the glass into a napkin.

Leah whispers, "You don't have to do that."

Amber hums softly under her breath, a low tune without melody. "Let me help you. What's all this about?"

Leah sinks onto the couch. Her hands shake when she reaches for the paper napkin Amber offers. "He sent everything back. He said he can't do this anymore."

Amber glances over her shoulder and makes a sympathetic face.

"Then he doesn't deserve you."

She stands again, dropping the glass into the kitchen bin and pours wine into two glasses she finds in the cupboard. "Sometimes people mistake strength for distance." She crosses the room, sets the glass in Leah's hand. "Have a drink."

Leah hesitates, then obeys. The wine burns a little on the way down. Amber sits beside her, close but not too close.

"You give too much to everyone else until there's nothing left for you."

"I thought we were okay," Leah whispers. "He's always been patient."

"Patience isn't love if it comes with conditions." Amber takes the empty glass from her and sets it on the table. "You don't need anyone else. Not really."

Leah laughs through the tears. "That's not true."

Amber's tone softens further. "Maybe not forever. But right now, you need quiet. You need peace. You need to look after your own heart before you can look after someone else's."

The hum she'd been making returns, soft and rhythmic, almost soothing. She stands, collects the folded clothes and arranges them into a neat pile on the armchair. Her movements are efficient, practiced, like someone restoring order to a scene she already understands.

When she's done, she finds a blanket from the couch and drapes it over Leah's shoulders. "Why don't you get some rest. I'll sit with you a while if you want."

Leah closes her eyes for a moment. Her body feels heavy, her mind floating just above exhaustion, and her limbs feel suddenly leaden. Amber's presence fills the silence, calm and unhurried.

"I don't know what I'd do if you weren't here," Leah murmurs.

Amber smiles, though Leah doesn't see it. "You'll never have to find out."

～

The next morning, Leah's alarm feels cruel. She wakes on the couch, with the blanket still tucked around her. The room is spotless. There is no sign of the glass, no clothes, no evidence of the chaos she remembers. Even the wine glasses sit rinsed on the counter, and Amber is gone.

Leah presses a hand to her temple, unsure if she dreamt half of it. The takeout containers are in the trash, folded neatly, as though they'd been washed first. For a moment she considers texting Amber, but the thought makes her feel strangely exposed.

Work will be a distraction, she'll speak to her there. She showers quickly, avoiding her reflection. When she arrives at the center, the building's hum feels louder than usual, almost oppressive.

The day drags. The calls blur together. Leah's voice trembles once during a routine welfare check, and she catches herself too late. Bree frowns and slides a sticky note across the divider. *Take a break.* Leah shakes her head.

"I'm fine," she mouths back. But her hands are unsteady. A moment later Amber appears at her side, as though summoned.

"You okay?"

Leah nods. "Just a bit shaky."

Amber places a hand lightly on her shoulder. "You've been through a lot. It's okay to not be perfect today."

Miguel passes by, scanning the floor. "Everything all right here?"

Amber answers before Leah can. "She's had a rough week. Just needs a little space."

Miguel frowns, sympathetic. "Take fifteen, Leah. Clear your head."

"Thanks." Leah forces a small smile.

When Miguel walks away, Amber leans closer. "See? I've got you."

"You didn't have to say anything."

"I wanted to." Amber's smile doesn't fade. "You're hardly going to speak up for yourself are you. You need to take it easy today."

In the breakroom, Bree sits perched on the counter, swinging her legs.

"You look wiped out," she says as Leah enters. "You sure you're okay?"

"Yeah," Leah lies. "Just...having a few man troubles."

Bree nods. "I heard. Miguel mentioned something."

Leah's stomach drops. "He what?"

Bree shrugs. "He didn't mean it in a bad way. Said you're one of his best, just... human. We all have limits."

Amber appears in the doorway, leaning casually against the frame. "Talking about me behind my back?"

Bree grins. "Always."

Amber's voice is light. "Good. Means you're still breathing."

She crosses the room, plucks a napkin from the dispenser, and starts wiping crumbs off the counter. Her presence changes the air, making it more focused and somehow tighter.

Bree hops down. "We're doing those drinks tomorrow if you want to join."

Leah glances at Amber, whose expression doesn't change. "Maybe," she says.

Amber smiles without looking up. "She needs rest. Don't tempt her."

Bree rolls her eyes. "She needs to get out and enjoy herself. I'll take that maybe." She leaves, muttering good-naturedly under her breath.

When she's gone, Amber says softly, "You shouldn't push yourself to be social. People drain you."

"They help me feel normal."

"Do you want normal?" Amber asks. "Or do you want peace?"

Leah doesn't answer.

By late afternoon, Leah's concentration has thinned to threads. A call comes through from a child whispering that her mother won't wake up. Leah's voice catches on the first word. Bree takes over before anyone has to ask. When the line clears, Leah stares at her trembling hands. She can feel Miguel's eyes on her from across the room. He comes over quietly, lowers his voice.

"Go home," he says. "We'll cover."

"I'm fine," Leah insists, but the denial sounds weak even to her own ears.

"Amber says you haven't slept properly in days."

Leah looks at Amber, who gives a small, concerned shrug.

"She's right," Miguel adds. "Go home, Leah. That's an order."

Leah packs up her things slowly, her mind caught somewhere between gratitude and humiliation. She leaves the floor to the sound of phones ringing, her headset's absence leaving her head oddly light.

That night the apartment feels colder. She doesn't bother turning on the lights. The city's glow slips through the blinds, painting thin lines across the floor. She drops her bag, raids the fridge for leftovers, pours a glass of wine and heads to the lounge, where she collapses onto the couch, and pulls the blanket over her.

Sleep comes fast. The exhaustion finally runs deep enough to drown thought. Somewhere in the haze of half-dream, she hears the door click. A soft rustle follows, footsteps light as breath. Then she hears a low, steady voice, the same tone she's heard a hundred times through static and sirens.

"You're safe now."

A hand touches her arm, warm and deliberate. She wants to open her eyes, but they won't obey. The touch lingers, then moves away. Leah drifts back under, comfort and unease blending until she can't tell where one ends and the other begins.

In the morning, light slices across the living room floor. The blanket still covers her, tucked under her chin. The wine glass from last night's dinner is rinsed and left upside down on the counter. She doesn't remember even drinking it after she poured it, let alone getting up to rinse it.

She remembers the presence in her half-dream and calls out, tentative. "Amber?"

No answer.

She sits up, scanning the room. Everything is in its place. She tells herself it must have been a dream. A byproduct of exhaustion and memory.

She showers, dresses, ties her hair back, and steps outside. The sunlight stings after the dim of the apartment. On the sidewalk, the trash bin lies tipped on its side. At first, she thinks the wind must have done it. Then she sees the mess of soggy papers, torn packaging, and coffee grounds spread across the concrete. And among it, are other, unmistakable, intimate things. Used tissues. The pad she threw away last night, bright against the gray. Her stomach turns.

She glances up and down the street. A neighbor's curtain

shifts. She crouches quickly, gathering the mess with shaking hands, stuffing it back into the bin. The smell is sharp and sour. She works fast, her heart pounding, desperate to finish before anyone sees. When it's done, she stands, and forces herself to laugh quietly.

"Animals," she says aloud. "Just a fox."

She drags the bin against the wall, checking the latch twice. Her hands smell of iron and soap even after she wipes them clean. Inside, she washes them again, scrubbing them with warm water and soap. The world feels slightly off-kilter, like she's half a step behind her own life.

By the time she reaches work, she's already rehearsing explanations she'll never give for her strange behavior. She'll tell them about sleep, about stress. She won't mention how she must have imagined the hand on her arm.

The dispatch center hums, same as always. Amber is already there, headset on, eyes bright. She glances up when Leah enters, a smile flickering.

"Morning," she says. "Sleep okay?"

Leah hesitates. "Much better, I think."

Amber studies her a second longer. "Good. You look more peaceful."

Leah takes her seat, adjusts her screen. The motion steadies her. She tells herself that's all she needs. The structure and routine, the sound of someone else's emergency filling her ears. Something louder than her own thoughts. She doesn't notice the way Amber watches her across the divide, eyes patient, protective, almost tender.

8

Amber's apartment is smaller than Leah's but feels fuller, as though it's lived in by several versions of the same person. The walls are pale, almost white, except where the color has been replaced by sheets of paper. Printouts cover the walls in careful rows. Shift rosters, weekly call schedules, photocopies of dispatch memos. Each page is pinned with perfect alignment, forming a calendar that maps one life in quiet detail.

At the center of the wall above her desk, a photo from the internal newsletter of Leah at her console, headset angled across her cheek, eyes lowered in concentration. The image catches her profile in soft grayscale, the light making her appear almost serene. Beside it, Amber has pinned a mirror photo of herself from a training exercise, cropped so that their faces align. She has trimmed the edges so that Leah's smile meets her own.

Amber sits on the edge of her bed, tying her hair back. The bedspread is pale pink, the same shade as Leah's. On the nightstand lies a twin-frame picture she bought last month, each side holding a copy of those same photographs. She adjusts them, straightens the hinge, and whispers, "Better."

She moves through her morning routine with deliberate

rhythm. Coffee first, measured exactly how she's learning to like it. Exactly as Leah likes it. One scoop, a half-pour of hazelnut syrup, stirred clockwise five times. The scent rises, sweet and clean. She carries the mug to her desk and presses play on her laptop. Leah's voice fills the room from an audio clip saved months ago, the cadence of training instruction.

"I am here with you. Stay calm. Help is on the way."

Amber closes her eyes, repeating the words with her, matching the breath intervals, the tone, the pace. "I am here with you," she murmurs. "Stay calm. Help is on the way."

She sips her coffee between phrases, inhaling on Leah's inhale, exhaling on her exhale. The two voices blend, one real, one recorded, until the difference between them fades.

On her desk, an open notebook shows pages of handwriting, this time, it's Leah's name written again and again in careful loops, sometimes followed by Hunter, sometimes by Klein-Hunter. In the margins, Amber has written phrases she's heard Leah say on calls, fragments of empathy that sound like devotion when taken out of context. *You're safe now. I'm right here. You did so well.* She folds the notebook closed and checks her watch. Time to leave.

The air outside is already warm, the sun sharp against her eyes. The drive to the dispatch center takes twenty minutes, long enough for her thoughts to settle into their usual order. She pictures Leah arriving just before her, moving through the hallway, straightening her badge. She imagines her voice greeting the security guard, low and polite. The small rituals of someone who brings calm wherever she goes.

Amber smiles. She has made sure to learn all those rituals, to use them as proof of how alike they are. When she reaches the lot, Leah's car is already parked under the shade of a tree. A flicker of satisfaction moves through her. She parks two rows behind, far enough not to seem deliberate.

Inside, the center hums with its morning rhythm. Bree laughs loudly at something Miguel says near the coffee station. The sound grates in Amber's ears. She smiles her hellos and keeps walking.

At her console, Leah is adjusting her headset. There's a faint tiredness to her face. It's subtle, like a shadow under the eyes. Amber wants to smooth it away.

"Morning," she says.

Leah turns, smiling faintly. "Hey. Early start again?"

Amber nods. "Couldn't sleep."

"Too much caffeine?"

"Too much quiet," Amber answers, and Leah laughs softly, a sound that feels like reward.

They settle into their chairs. The first tones of the shift sound in a steady rhythm of incoming calls, voices flickering between panic and relief. The morning moves as it always does, in a whirl of practiced, coordinated control. When the lull finally comes, Leah stretches her hands, glancing toward the far wall where the clock ticks past eleven.

"I've been thinking about transferring to Flagstaff."

Amber's hands freeze over her keyboard. "Flagstaff?"

"They need dispatchers there. Smaller department. Quieter. Fewer night shifts."

Amber's smile appears quickly, practiced. "You'd hate it there."

Leah shrugs. "Maybe. But sometimes I think about leaving the noise behind. I'm tired."

"The mountains are cold," Amber says softly. "Lonely, too. You'd miss the rhythm here."

Leah tilts her head. "You sound sure."

Amber meets her gaze, holding it just a moment too long. "Because I know what you're like. You need connection. You'd go mad with silence."

Leah laughs once, uncertain, and turns back to her monitor. "Maybe you're right."

Amber relaxes her grip on the desk. The room feels normal again, but the echo of the idea lingers, like a warning she can't ignore.

Later, when Leah steps away for a break, Amber walks toward Miguel's office. He's leaning over paperwork, reading glasses halfway down his nose.

"Got a minute?" she asks.

He gestures to a chair. "Sure. What's up?"

Amber sits, folding her hands neatly. "It's about Leah."

Miguel looks up. "Something wrong?"

"She's been... different lately. Distracted." Amber's tone is soft, concerned, the language of someone protecting rather than accusing. "She had a hard time after the breakup, and I think it's affecting her more than she's letting on."

Miguel nods slowly. "I figured as much."

"She won't say anything, but I think she's pushing herself too hard. Maybe she could take a few personal days."

He studies her. "You two seem close."

Amber gives a small, modest smile. "I just worry about her."

Miguel sighs. "I'll talk to her. See what she wants."

"Maybe don't mention I said anything," she adds quickly. "I don't want her to feel like people are talking behind her back."

He nods again, thoughtful. "You're a good friend, Amber."

"I just want what's best for her."

She lowers her eyes, pretending to blush. When she leaves the office, she feels a quiet rush of satisfaction. The groundwork is always in how others perceive your kindness.

The afternoon drags into slow routine. Leah seems quieter, glancing at her own phone between calls. Amber pretends not to notice. Bree's chatter fills the gaps, full of her plans for Friday, some new guy she's seeing. The noise of ordinary life. Amber waits until Leah is alone at her station before leaning closer.

"I think Miguel might suggest you take a few days off."

Leah frowns. "Why?"

"He's worried you're over-stretching yourself."

"I'm fine."

Amber shrugs. "Maybe he's right, though. Some proper rest might help."

Leah looks at her, puzzled. "Did you say something to him?"

"Of course not. He notices these things." Amber's expression is all innocence.

Leah studies her for a beat, then sighs.

"Maybe. I'll think about it."

"Good." Amber smiles, letting the moment settle. She turns back to her console, the faintest trace of victory behind her calm.

By evening, the shift winds down. Leah packs her bag slowly, rubbing her temples. Bree waves on her way out, voice bright. "See you after the weekend. Have fun."

Leah smiles tiredly. "I'll try."

Amber lingers. "Need a hand?" She holds a hand out as though to help Leah with her bags.

"I'm fine, thanks."

"I'll walk out with you."

Leah hesitates but doesn't argue. The parking lot glows with the orange wash of sunset when they step outside. Leah unlocks her car, tossing her bag inside.

"See you tomorrow."

Amber nods, standing still as Leah drives away. Only when the taillights vanish does she move, walking to her own car. She doesn't go home immediately. She drives instead toward Leah's neighborhood, her hands loose on the steering wheel, the road familiar now after so many detours. The sun sinks lower, and the first lights begin to blink on across the city.

When she turns onto Leah's street, she parks two houses away, far enough to be hidden behind a row of trees. Leah's building glows softly, the second floor window lit, curtains drawn. The shape of her moving behind them catches Amber's breath in her throat.

She stays there, engine off, hands resting on her lap. She closes her eyes, breathing deeply, imagining Leah moving around her apartment.

"You're not leaving me," she whispers. "Not ever."

Outside, the street quiets to the pulse of crickets and distant traffic. She stays there, watching, until the window in Leah's apartment begins to darken, one light at a time.

It is nearly midnight when she finally returns to her own apartment. The air inside feels cool and stale, as though it's been waiting for her. She turns on a lamp and walks to the wall of printouts. Her fingers trace the latest roster update, where she has Leah's name highlighted in yellow. She circles the weekend date in red pen. Flagstaff conference (optional). Her heart stutters once, quick and sharp. She steps back, and exhales.

"Optional," she says aloud. The word sounds fragile.

On the desk, the twin photo frame catches the lamplight. Leah's image gleams beside her own, the two faces aligned. For a moment, it looks like one person with mirrored halves.

Amber touches the glass.

"You belong here," she murmurs. "Not Flagstaff."

Her phone buzzes with a message. It's Bree, in the group chat. *Drinks Friday, don't flake.* Amber stares at it for a second before putting down the phone. She moves to the kitchen, pours herself water, and sets two glasses on the counter out of habit. She only fills one but leaves the other beside it, empty. She imagines Leah in her own kitchen, getting a glass of water, watching the light from the window. She can see it clearly, as though she's standing right behind her.

Amber sits down, crosses her legs, and closes her eyes. In her mind, she is back at the dispatch center, side by side with Leah. The sound of phones, the rise and fall of voices, the steady repetition of those words that mean everything.

"I'm right here with you," she whispers.

Her breathing slows to match the rhythm she's learned from listening. She opens her eyes again, and her smile returns, soft and certain.

9

The message waits in her inbox before she even takes her coat off.

From: Tom Watkins, HR

Subject: Please report to my office at 09:00.

Leah stares at it, coffee in her hand. Her first thought is that it must be about overtime, or scheduling, maybe, or payroll. Rather than taking time off, as Miguel had suggested, she's doubled down and thrown herself into the work, welcoming the distraction. She's worked double shifts all week, covering sick leave. She tells herself there's nothing unusual about being called in. Still, the phrasing of the email feels clinical. No greeting, no explanation. Just that one request.

She glances across the call floor. Amber is already at her console, headset in place, a faint smile when their eyes meet. Bree waves from her desk. The ordinary rhythm of morning fills the air and Leah forces a small smile back to Amber, sets her mug down, and heads toward the HR corridor.

Tom Watkins' office smells faintly of his aftershave. The blinds are half closed against the rising heat. He sits behind his desk, tie slightly crooked, glasses perched low on his nose. He gestures to the chair opposite.

"Morning, Leah. Thanks for coming in."

"Of course." She sits, smoothing her palms against her knees. "You wanted to see me?"

"Yes." He folds his hands. "I'll get straight to it. We've received an anonymous complaint."

The words stop her. "A complaint?"

He nods once. "About you."

Her pulse skips. "What kind of complaint?"

Tom's voice stays even, professional. "The report describes erratic behavior on shift, emotional outbursts, difficulty maintaining composure, and one incident where you allegedly dropped a live call."

Leah stares at him. "That's not true."

"I'm sure you believe that."

"I don't just believe it, Tom, I know it. I've never dropped a call in ten years. Not once."

He sighs, shuffling papers on his desk. "There's an audio file attached to the report. It appears to be a partial recording from two nights ago."

"I wasn't even on shift two nights ago. Miguel changed my rota. He can confirm."

Tom nods, cautious. "That's helpful. We'll verify it."

"Who filed this?"

He spreads his hands. "It's anonymous, as I said."

Her voice rises before she can stop it. "So anyone can just accuse me of incompetence and I'm the one answering questions?"

"Leah." His tone turns firm. "No one is accusing. We're required to follow up on all internal reports."

She forces herself to breathe. "Can I hear the recording?"

He hesitates, then opens a file on his monitor. The speakers crackle. A woman's voice. Hers, apparently. She sounds calm at first, then breaking mid-sentence. "Ma'am, please... please stay on the line while I—" A click, followed by dead air.

Leah shakes her head. "That's not me."

"It sounds like you."

"It's edited. Or copied from another call." Her words tumble out too quickly. "You know how easy that is. It could be..."

Tom leans back shaking his head. "No one is saying this is disciplinary yet. But I need you to write a statement. Just a summary of what you recall from that shift."

She swallows hard. "There's nothing to recall. I wasn't on the shift."

He nods sympathetically, sliding a form toward her. "Then that's what you'll say. It's just procedure."

She takes the paper with unsteady hands. The lines blur slightly as she reads them.

"Can I go?"

He studies her for a moment, maybe searching for something in her face.

"Yes. And Leah? Try not to take this personally. Sometimes these things resolve themselves."

She forces a smile that feels like glass cracking.

"Sure."

Outside, the hallway seems longer than before. She walks into the breakroom to find Bree already there, sipping from a water bottle. She looks up when Leah enters.

"Hey. Everything okay?"

Leah drops into a chair. "HR just called me in."

Bree frowns. "Why?"

"They've had an anonymous complaint. They said I dropped a call. Two nights ago. But I wasn't even on shift."

Bree's eyes widen. "That's ridiculous."

"I know."

Bree leans forward. "Did they say who reported it?"

"Anonymous."

Bree shakes her head. "You've been here longer than anyone. They'll sort it out."

Amber enters mid-sentence, balancing two coffees.

"Sort what out?"

Leah doesn't look up. "Apparently, I'm unstable now."

"What do you mean?" Amber's smile falters, just slightly.

"Someone reported me for dropping a call, on a shift I wasn't on. Said I was erratic and emotional."

Amber sets one coffee in front of Leah.

"That's absurd."

Bree crosses her arms. "We both know she doesn't drop calls."

Amber nods slowly, as if remembering. "Still... maybe they're just concerned. You've been under pressure. It's not always easy to see ourselves clearly."

Leah looks up sharply.

"You think it's true?"

"I think people make mistakes when they're tired." Amber meets her gaze evenly.

Bree's eyes narrow. "I can't believe you're not backing her."

"I didn't drop a call," Leah says, pushing the coffee aside.

Amber's expression softens.

"I believe you. I just mean... Well, you can't run away from your problems every time something feels unfair."

The words sting more than they should. "Who said anything about running away?"

Amber shrugs, her tone mild. "You've talked about transferring. Maybe part of you already wants to leave."

Leah stands abruptly.

"Excuse me."

Bree watches her go, frowning. "What was that?"

Amber sips her coffee. "Just a dose of honesty. She hasn't been herself lately."

～

The rest of the day blurs. Leah completes her calls on autopilot, voice steady through sheer force of habit. She catches Miguel glancing her way once or twice, and each time she looks back, he pretends to be checking paperwork.

When her shift ends, she doesn't go straight home. Instead, she stays behind, waiting until the floor empties. Then she logs back into the system under her credentials, navigating to the archive interface. The glow of the monitor paints her face pale blue. Every operator's call record is stored here with a timestamp, duration, and outcome. She scrolls to the date Tom mentioned. Her name appears twice. One call correctly marked as completed. The other is listed as abandoned, line dropped.

She checks the shift roster. Her name isn't listed at all for that night. She'd traded with Bree. She pulls the access log and finds that someone used her login from Terminal 6 at 21:03. She never works on terminal 6. Leah leans back, heart pounding. Someone's using her credentials.

She prints the access log, folds the page, and slips it into her pocket. When she turns to leave, the reflection in the monitor catches movement behind her. Amber stands near the door wearing a faint smile that doesn't reach her eyes.

"Working late?" she asks.

Leah jumps. "You scared me."

"Sorry." Amber steps closer, calm as ever. "I thought you left hours ago."

"I just wanted to check something."

Amber nods, gaze flicking to the printer still warm on the tray.

"Working late never looks good after a complaint, you know."

Leah bristles. "I haven't done anything wrong."

"I know." Amber's voice is soft. "But sometimes people only see what they want to see."

Leah holds her stare, then logs off and gets up.

"Goodnight, Amber."

"Night, Leah." Amber smiles again.

At home, the apartment feels smaller, as though the shadows have edges now. She spreads the printed log on her table and traces the lines with her finger. There's no mistake. The login came from another console under her ID. While she wasn't even in the building. She'll show it to Miguel tomorrow, she tells herself. He'll know what to do.

She heats soup and eats with a kind of steady distraction. When she finally crawls into bed, she dreams of ringing phones that no one answers.

Morning comes gray and heavy. Leah wakes before her alarm. The first thing she thinks of is the printout in her bag, folded carefully beside her ID badge.

At the center, the day starts like any other. Bree waves from the vending machine.

"You look better today!"

Leah forces a smile, heading straight for Miguel's office. He looks up from his desk, as though surprised to see her.

"Morning."

"I need to show you something." She slides the page toward him. "This log shows someone used my login while I wasn't even here."

He studies it. "Terminal 6?"

"Yes."

"That's Amber's usual console."

The air thickens. "I know."

Miguel frowns. "You think she...?"

"I don't know what to think. But I wasn't in that night, and I didn't drop that call."

He nods slowly. "I'll look into it. Quietly."

"Thank you."

As she turns to go, he adds, "Leah? Try not to let this consume you. HR will handle it."

She nods, but her hands are trembling as she closes the door.

By lunchtime, the gossip has begun. She can feel the whispers that stop when she walks past, and the furtive glances traded over coffee cups. Bree sits with her at a corner table, keeping her voice low.

"People are idiots," Bree says. "You've done nothing wrong."

Leah picks at her sandwich. "Someone wants me gone."

"Then screw them. We know the truth."

Across the cafeteria, Amber sits with two junior dispatchers, laughing softly at something one says. When she catches Leah's eye, she raises her coffee cup in a silent toast.

"She's enjoying this," Bree mutters.

"Seems to be." Leah looks away. "I can't prove anything yet."

"Yet?"

"I'll find a way."

Bree reaches over, touching her wrist. "Just promise me you won't let this eat you alive."

Leah smiles weakly. "I'm fine."

But she isn't. That evening she drafts an email to HR, attaching her evidence, then stops midway. Tom will see it as defensive. Better to talk in person. Instead, she opens the internal portal and clicks Transfer Request, scrolling to Open Positions. Flagstaff sits at the top of the list. She hesitates only a second before typing her name. When she hits submit, relief and dread intertwine.

The next morning, Miguel stops by her desk.

"I heard from HR. They're accepting your transfer request."

Leah exhales. "That was fast."

"You've earned it." He hesitates. "You sure this is what you want?"

"I need a fresh start."

He nods. "Then you'll have it. Flagstaff's lucky to get you. Unlucky for me, they want you to start straight away. I've agreed, reluctantly. But it's probably best, with everything that's going on here."

"Thanks," is all she can manage.

Bree hugs her when she tells her.

"It's perfect. You'll love it there. Fresh air, fewer calls."

Amber approaches mid-conversation, eyes wide in feigned surprise.

"You're leaving?"

Leah nods. "Just a transfer."

Amber's face softens into a perfect imitation of sadness. "I'm going to miss you so much."

Before Leah can react, she steps forward and hugs her tightly. The gesture lasts too long, and feels too firm. Leah freezes, caught between politeness and discomfort. Around them, other staff glance over, smiling at the display of friendship. When Amber pulls back, she's smiling.

"You'll text me, right?"

"Of course," Leah says automatically.

Amber tilts her head. "Promise?"

"Promise."

Miguel interrupts with a stack of forms for Leah to sign. As she bends to the desk, she can feel Amber's gaze still on her, steady and unblinking.

∿

By evening, the floor is quiet. Leah finishes her last shift, removes her headset, and looks around the room one final time. The hum of computers feels like ocean noise from the beach, constant, familiar, and impossible to forget. Amber waits near the door.

"Walk you out one last time?"

Leah almost refuses, then relents. "Sure."

The sky outside glows orange with the remnants of sunset. The parking lot is half-empty, with a steady heat rising off the asphalt. Leah opens her car door, glancing back. Amber reaches into her pocket.

"I got you something."

She holds out a small keychain bearing a silver compass, simple and elegant.

"So you'll always find your way back."

Leah smiles, touched despite herself. "Thank you."

Amber fastens it to her keyring for her, fingers brushing hers. "Now you'll never get lost."

"Thank you." Leah slides into the driver's seat, and starts the engine before any more hugs can be issued. "Goodbye, Amber."

Amber's smile is calm, unbroken. "Goodbye."

As Leah drives away, she glances once in the mirror. Amber still stands there, motionless in the heat haze, one hand in her pocket. Inside it, a second compass rests in her palm, identical to the one she just gave away. The metal cool against her skin. Amber closes her fingers tight around it and whispers, "You'll find your way back to me. Or I'll find mine to you."

10

The boxes are smaller than Leah expected, though they fill the apartment like an invading tide. She sits cross-legged on the living-room floor surrounded by cardboard, the faint smell of tape and dust rising with every movement. The morning light through the blinds slices the room into thin bands. Each one glows against the stacks of her life from kitchenware to clothes, framed certificates to the mug with the faded Stay Calm slogan that used to sit beside her console.

She picks up the compass keychain from the coffee table. The arrow quivers for a second before finding north, a steady pulse of direction in the stillness. Amber's voice echoes in her head. *So you'll find your way back to me.*

Bree has been there for an hour already, helping her pack. She kneels beside her, wrestling with the tape gun.

"You're bringing that little thing? What's it for?"

"It's a compass. A gift from Amber."

Bree grins. "Of course it is."

Leah smiles faintly. "She means well."

"Sure. But she's a little intense." Bree pulls a strip of tape across a box with a loud rip.

"You know, I think you'll love Flagstaff. It's quiet, clean, and it has actual seasons. And people there tend to sleep through the night."

"I could use a bit of that."

"Peace and quiet." Bree stands, stretching. "The exact opposite of this place."

Leah nods. The phrase peace and quiet repeats in her mind, as if saying it often enough might make it real. They move through the small apartment methodically. Bree packs the kitchen while Leah sorts through old files, tossing duplicates, stacking what she'll keep. The room feels emptier with each box sealed, like the walls are exhaling.

"You sure you don't want me to drive up with you?" Bree asks.

"I'll be fine."

"You don't sound convinced."

"I think I need the drive," Leah says. "Time to clear my head."

Bree watches her for a moment, then shrugs. "Text me when you get there. If you vanish, I'm sending a search party."

Leah laughs softly.

"Deal."

They finish the last box together, pushing it aside with a scrape. The room now looks less like a home and more like a depot. Bree glances around.

"We did it. You ready?"

"Almost." Leah looks toward the bedroom doorway. "I'll meet you at the car."

When Bree leaves, the silence folds back in. Leah walks to the bedroom, scanning what's left. The bed frame, mattress stripped. A single picture frame, face down on the dresser. She picks it up, looks at the photo of her and Sam on the hiking trail, and slips the frame into an open box in the hall labeled

Personal. On her way out of the apartment, she slips the compass into her pocket. The rest will be collected by the removal guys.

She drops in at the dispatch center on her way out of town to sign her final papers. Leah signs out her ID badge for the last time. Her desk is already cleared, and the monitor dark. Someone has tied a balloon to her chair. It's silver, heart-shaped, with Good Luck Leah scrawled across it in permanent marker.

Miguel approaches first. "So, this is really it, huh?"

"For now." She smiles.

He shakes her hand, his grip steady.

"You've been one of the best I've ever supervised. Don't let the noise here follow you."

"I'll try not to."

Bree appears behind him with a paper cup. "One last coffee for the road. It's terrible, as tradition demands."

Leah laughs, accepting it. "I'll miss the terrible coffee."

"Liar."

"Maybe a little."

When the laughter fades, there's a brief lull, like a collective reluctance to let the moment end. Then Amber steps forward. She's holding a small package wrapped in pale paper tied with ribbon.

"I got you something," she says.

Leah hesitates, then takes it. "You didn't have to."

Amber smiles. "Open it."

Inside, beneath layers of careful wrapping, is a framed photograph of the team, with everyone crowded around their consoles, smiling for the camera. Leah recognizes it from the newsletter board. In the center, Amber stands beside her, hand resting lightly on her shoulder.

"So you won't forget us," Amber says.

Leah runs her thumb along the edge of the frame.

"I couldn't if I tried."

Miguel clears his throat, sensing the weight in the air. "We should get a group photo before she escapes."

Phones are lifted, flashes bright against the sterile light. Leah smiles for the camera, her face calm, though her chest feels tight. When it's over, Amber lingers beside her as the others drift away.

"You're really doing this?" Amber says quietly.

"I think it's time."

Amber's eyes hold hers a moment too long. "You'll always have me."

Leah swallows. "Thank you, Amber."

Amber steps closer, arms sliding around her in a sudden, firm embrace. The faint jasmine scent of her shampoo fills Leah's senses. The hug lasts longer than it should. When Amber finally pulls away, her smile has returned, flawless.

"Drive safe," she says. "Text when you get there."

"I will."

By noon, the sun sits high over the desert. The road north stretches in a straight line toward the horizon, broken only by the shimmer of heat. Leah drives with the windows cracked, the dry air sweeping through.

Each mile feels lighter, the city shrinking behind her. She passes the last exit for Phoenix, watching the skyline blur in the rearview mirror until it disappears entirely.

She turns the radio on but finds only static. She cycles through stations until she finds an old song she half remembers. The melody fills the car, steady and familiar. For the first time in months, she allows herself to breathe deeply. There are no ringing phones, no glowing monitors, no endless voices crying out for help. Just road, sky, the steady hum of the engine, and an old, familiar tune.

She glances at the compass now hanging from the keys in the ignition. The needle trembles with the car's vibration. An hour north, the desert gives way to stretches of red rock. The color changes with the light from burnt orange, to rose, to rust. Leah rolls down the window fully and the wind whips through her hair, carrying dust and heat.

She checks the mirror automatically, a habit from years of commuting. A white SUV follows several car lengths back, too far to read the plate. She doesn't think much of it at first, it's just another traveler heading north. But it stays there. For ten minutes, then twenty. When she switches lanes, the SUV does the same. Her pulse quickens. She slows slightly, and it mirrors, maintaining distance. Coincidence, she tells herself. Just coincidence.

At the next exit, she signals and pulls off onto a smaller road, even though it's not her route. The SUV continues straight, disappearing into the blur of heat and distance. Leah exhales slowly, gripping the steering wheel until her knuckles ache.

"You're fine," she whispers. "You're just being silly."

She circles round and pulls back onto the highway, focusing on the open stretch ahead. The mountains rise gradually from the desert, blue in the distance, then green with pines as the road climbs. The air cools. Clouds drift low enough to touch. Leah feels the tension in her shoulders ease, replaced by relief, maybe, or just exhaustion.

By the time she reaches the outskirts of Flagstaff, the sky has turned pale gray of evening. She follows the directions the relocation office sent, turning left past the old water tower, right toward a line of rental cabins surrounded by tall trees. Her new home sits at the end, small but clean, windows facing west.

She parks and sits for a while, letting the engine tick cool.

The silence feels almost physical. She's spent years surrounded by voices, and, for now, there's only her own breath.

Inside, the cabin that will be her new home smells faintly of pine and new paint. Her boxes have already been delivered, and line the wall in the lounge and bedroom. The furniture throughout is sparse. Just a table and two chairs in the kitchen/diner, a small sofa, and a metal framed bed in the bedroom beside a wooden nightstand. She sets her keys on the nightstand, and lays the photo of the dispatch team beside it. The frame catches the afternoon light, reflecting it against the wall.

She unpacks slowly, each movement deliberate. She folds her clothes into drawers. Puts her dishes in cupboards. The pattern of an ordinary life feels like it's beginning again. When the last box is empty, she carries it outside to the recycling bin. The air is cool enough to make her skin prickle. In the distance, wind moves through the trees with a sound like distant waves. She stands out there for a moment and breathes it in. It feels fresh. For the first time, she thinks she might sleep through the night.

The evening settles in quietly. Leah cooks simple pasta, eats by the window, and watches the light fade behind the trees. The horizon glows faintly orange before it dims to violet. Her phone buzzes once. It's a message from Bree. *Made it safe?*

Leah types, *Yes. It's beautiful here.*

Send pics soon.

She smiles, snapping one of the mountain view from her window. Then another of the compass on the table, the silver catching the last bit of sun.

A new message appears a few seconds later. *Looks peaceful. You deserve that.*

Leah hesitates before replying. *Thank you.*

The next message doesn't come from Bree. It's from an

unknown number. Just one sentence. *North always leads home.* Her stomach tightens. She reads it twice, checking the unfamiliar digits. No name, no photo. She tells herself it must be Amber, trying to be cryptic. A friendly joke, nothing more. Still, her fingers tremble as she deletes the message and sets the phone down. Outside, the wind picks up, rattling the branches, as though sensing her disquiet.

Later, she lies in bed listening to the still peacefulness. It's not like the city's quiet. This one has depth, and there's space between the sounds. In the distance, a dog barks. She turns her head toward the nightstand. The compass glints faintly in the light from the streetlamp outside. The needle quivers, just barely. She watches it, half-amused. Cheap nonsense, she thinks. It'll probably break within the week. Leah exhales, forcing a small laugh.

"It's fine," she whispers. "Everything's fine."

She reaches out, turning the compass face-down. The metal is cool under her fingertips. She imagines Amber back in Phoenix, still working the night shift, headset on, guiding another stranger through chaos. The thought is strangely comforting. Her eyes close.

Back in the city, the dispatch center glows under fluorescent light. Amber sits alone at her console after everyone has left, the hum of machines surrounding her. She holds her phone in her lap, scrolling through a photo that Leah texted earlier showing the view of the mountains, the compass on the table.

She zooms in on the compass and smiles. On the desk beside her, another compass lies open, identical to Leah's. Its needle trembles faintly before aligning.

Amber whispers to herself, "I'll always be able to find you."

Then she presses play on her recorder. Leah's voice fills the empty room once more.

"I'm here with you. Stay calm. Help is coming."

Amber closes her eyes, listening until the words become her own.

11

The air in Flagstaff tastes different than the city. It's thin, cool, and pine-sweet. Leah breathes it in as she jogs the trail that cuts behind her cabin, her feet crunching over needles and dirt. It's early. The sunlight is just beginning to spill through the trees, scattering gold across the path. The mountain air sits cold against her lungs, sharp in the best way.

This is the first morning in months she hasn't woken to phantom voices. There are no calls replaying in her head, no echo of panic bleeding into waking thought. Just birds, and the rhythmic sound of her breath. She knows it probably won't last, but for now, she feels free.

She keeps her pace steady, letting the forest absorb her thoughts. The trail winds upward, then dips near a creek that murmurs faintly over stones. Her body feels heavy but clean, the kind of ache that comes from physical effort, not fear.

When she reaches the clearing near the ridge, she stops to stretch, hands on her knees, watching sunlight shift through the branches. A few locals pass her, just dog walkers and another runner. They nod in polite acknowledgment. No one knows her here, and that anonymity feels like safety. For the first time, she can imagine starting over.

The Flagstaff Emergency Dispatch Centre is smaller than Phoenix's. It has half the consoles, fewer people, a quieter energy that hums instead of roars. The walls are painted a soft green that makes Leah think of sea glass. A coffee pot gurgles in the corner.

"Leah Hunter?"

She turns to find a woman in her early forties, short dark hair streaked with silver, sharp eyes softened by warmth.

"Carla Jimenez," the woman says, extending her hand. "Welcome to the calm side of chaos."

Leah smiles. "I like that slogan."

"I'm sure it's on a mug somewhere." Carla gestures for her to follow. "You've got the kind of résumé people here only whisper about. Ten years in Phoenix? That's trench work."

"I loved it," Leah says automatically, then hesitates. "Most of it. But I'm looking forward to the change of pace."

Carla nods, as if she understands more than Leah says.

"We're smaller, but our calls cover the forest and county roads. So it's quieter, yes, but we get our fair share of lost hikers and overexcited campers. Although, nothing like Phoenix's madness."

Leah looks around the room. There are only six consoles, arranged in a gentle arc. The lighting is softer. The air smells faintly of fresh pine, rather than the disinfectant and burnt coffee of Phoenix. A young woman waves from one of the desks.

"Hey! I'm Tanya."

Leah waves back. Carla lowers her voice.

"Tanya Ng. One of our best dispatchers and our unofficial morale officer. She's been here since college. And Jason's the tech wizard. He keeps the systems from melting down."

Jason, a quiet man in his thirties, raises a hand from behind a monitor but doesn't look up.

"Let me show you your station," Carla says.

Leah follows, noticing how her nerves seem to ease with every step. The center feels human-scaled. The voices here are calm, phones ringing in predictable rhythm. No one is rushing, and there are no raised tones.

"This will be you," Carla says, tapping the console closest to the window. "Shift lead. You'll run nights for now, since they're quieter. You've got the calm voice people trust. We heard your reference calls. You have beautiful control."

Leah swallows. "Thank you."

Carla studies her. "We value composure here, but we value honesty more. If you need to step back, take a breather, you say so. Understood?"

"Understood."

Carla grins. "Good. You'll fit right in."

By the second week, Leah knows the rhythm. Morning jog, coffee, a short drive to the center. Her routine becomes muscle memory again. Log in, headset on, voice steady. But here, the emergencies sound smaller, and more manageable.

"Flagstaff Emergency, what's your location?"

A teenager has locked her keys in her car. A hiker with a sprained ankle. A noise complaint about fireworks or rifle shots near the woods. Each call ends with thank yous instead of screaming. She finishes her shifts without trembling hands.

During breaks, Tanya often pulls her into conversation. She has tons of funny stories about mishandled calls, strange tourists, ghost sightings in the old forest cabins. She's young, bright-eyed, with an easy laugh that draws people in.

"You're like a zen version of me," Tanya says one afternoon, munching on trail mix. "I panic, you just breathe."

Leah smiles. "It comes with practice."

"What's your secret?"

"Pretend you're talking someone back from the edge of a cliff," Leah says. "Then talk yourself back too."

Tanya laughs. "That's either really profound or really depressing."

"Maybe both."

Carla joins them briefly, handing out new shift schedules. "Leah, you're leading Friday night. That okay?"

"Perfect," Leah says. And it is. For the first time in years, she doesn't dread walking through a dispatch door.

At home, the cabin feels larger than it is. The windows open to a stretch of pines, their needles whispering when the wind moves. Leah decorates slowly with soft lamps, a throw blanket, a plant she's determined not to kill. She keeps her phone near the window where the reception's strongest.

One evening, after a particularly calm shift, she opens her laptop for her scheduled online therapy session. Her therapist, a woman named Dr. Weller, appears on the screen wearing glasses and a gentle half-smile.

"How's the transition been?"

"Good," Leah says. "Quieter than I expected."

"You sound steadier."

"I feel it." Leah pauses. "Mostly."

Dr. Weller tilts her head. "Still having the flashbacks?"

"Less often. The silence helps."

They talk for a while about routine, and grounding exercises, and fading triggers. Near the end, Dr. Weller says something that stays with her.

"You can't save everyone, Leah. But you can start with yourself."

Leah sits with that after the session ends. The words sound simple, but they carry weight she's not used to accepting. That night she makes a light supper, sits on the balcony, and watches the stars push through the dark. The air smells of resin and woodsmoke from some distant cabin. She tells herself she's beginning again, properly this time.

Late one night on shift, Leah takes a call about a missing hiker. The woman is calm, apologetic, embarrassed to have lost her bearings on the northern trail. Leah guides her gently through landmarks, asking her to describe what she sees, triangulating coordinates while Jason traces the signal.

"Stay on the line with me," Leah says. "You're not alone."

The woman laughs softly. "I feel stupid."

"You'd be surprised how many hikers we get like you. The forest looks different when the light shifts. You're doing fine."

Within fifteen minutes, a ranger locates the woman. Safe. When Leah disconnects, the silence feels earned, not empty. She stares at her hands and finds them steady and calm.

Carla passes by, tapping her shoulder lightly.

"Nice work."

Leah nods. "Thanks."

"Feels good, doesn't it?"

"It does."

Carla smiles. "Told you this place was different."

A week later, an email pings her personal inbox. She hesitates before opening it.

From: Sam Reed

Subject: Just wondering

Hope you're okay. I heard you transferred. I'm sorry for how things ended. Still think about you sometimes. Be safe.

She reads it, then moves the cursor to Delete. Her finger hovers for a heartbeat. Then she clicks. The message disappears. For a moment she feels nothing. No anger, and no nostalgia. Just absence. That, she decides, is progress.

By early August, Leah joins the center's wellness program. Yoga in the staff breakroom, therapy check-ins, guided meditation sessions that Tanya insists are "weirdly effective." Carla encourages it.

"We value quiet in our heads," she says. "You've earned it."

Leah nods. "Trying."

When she talks about her childhood in therapy, the memories feel distant, like someone else's life. The endless caretaking for her mother, the noise of paramedic radios in their small house, the constant emergencies that shaped her need to control chaos.

"I used to think," she tells Dr. Weller. "That if I stayed calm enough, no one could fall apart."

"And what do you think now?"

"That I was wrong."

Dr. Weller smiles. "Good. That's how healing starts."

The nights grow cooler. Leah still jogs every morning under a silver dawn, watching mist curl low over the ground. The forest has become a kind of companion. Each path she learns feels like reclaiming territory, stepping away from fear.

At work, Tanya brings her wildflower bouquets and endless chatter. Jason fixes her computer twice without complaint. Carla invites her to lunch on her off days. Bit by bit, Leah builds something like belonging.

One evening, after a long shift, Tanya tosses her a chocolate bar.

"You're far too serious. Sugar helps."

Leah laughs. "You sound like Bree."

"Who's Bree?"

"Friend from Phoenix."

"You miss it there?"

Leah considers. "Sometimes. But mostly I miss who I was before it all went wrong."

Tanya nods. "Well, whoever she was, she' sounds great. You were kind of a legend here before you arrived."

Leah smiles at that, unexpected warmth rising in her chest.

The following Friday, the dispatch center feels unusually still. Only three calls all evening. One minor crash, one domestic noise report, one bear sighting that turned out to be a large dog.

At midnight, Carla leans on Leah's desk.

"You good?"

"All good."

"Too good. Nights like this make me nervous."

Leah chuckles. "Don't jinx it."

Carla grins. "Right. Keep proving me wrong."

When the shift ends, Leah drives home through the sleeping town. Streetlights blur past like slow fireflies. The drive outside her cabin is empty as ever. She locks the car, climbs the stairs, and pauses before unlocking her door. The quiet feels heavier than usual, almost thick enough to notice. Inside, everything is as she left it. She tells herself she's safe and believes it.

Saturday evening, she takes a walk through the neighborhood. The pines sway overhead, whispering in a language she almost understands. The sun drops low, turning the treetops gold. A family walks a dog ahead of her, their laughter faint through the air. At the corner store, she buys milk and coffee filters. The clerk, a young man with freckles, greets her by name now. She likes that because she likes routine.

The air cools quickly after sunset. She cuts through the lot behind her cabin toward the stairs. That's when she sees a white SUV parked at the curb, engine idling. Her breath catches. She stops mid-step, the plastic bag crinkling in her hand. The headlights glow softly but the interior is shadowed. No visible driver. She tells herself it's nothing. There are hundreds of white SUVs. It's just someone waiting for a friend, a delivery maybe. Still, the sight pins her.

She forces herself forward. The SUV remains still, humming faintly. Halfway up the steps to her door, she looks back. The engine revs once, then the vehicle pulls away, turning the corner without haste. Leah stands on the porch, pulse racing. She stays there long after the taillights vanish, listening to the faint echo of the engine fade into distance. Finally, she unlocks her door and steps inside.

She sets the groceries on the counter and locks the door, laying her keys on the small table beside the door. The cabin feels colder than before. She walks to the window, pulling the curtain aside just enough to peer through. The street is empty again. The night has swallowed everything. She lets the curtain fall, checking the lock on the door once more before sitting on the couch. The clock ticks quietly. Her hands still tremble slightly.

She thinks of the compass on her keyring, of the way its needle quivers sometimes, as if reacting to something unseen.

Leah stands, crosses to the table, and lifts it. The metal is cool in her palm, the arrow steady on north. It never shifts, no matter which direction she points it. She stares at it for a long time.

Outside, the pine trees sway, black shapes against a darker sky. The soft, rhythmic sound they make feels like whispering. Not quite words, but something closer to taunting laughter. Leah places the compass back on the table and sits on the sofa again. The silence stretches, deep and wide. She tells herself the SUV was a stranger. Just coincidence.

She lies down, eyes open to the shifting shadows on the ceiling, and listens to the forest breathe. When she finally slows her breathing, she considers that here, she has almost, almost found peace. But peace, she knows, has a fragile temper.

12

The rain in Flagstaff comes without warning. It begins as a whisper against the pine needles, then thickens until the sound fills Leah's cabin like static. She sits at her small dining table, laptop open, the faint reflection of her face trembling in the screen's glow. It's late, long past midnight, and the only light in the room comes from the desk lamp and the occasional flash of headlights on the quiet road outside.

Her cursor blinks over a login screen for the Operator Support Network: A Forum for Emergency Dispatch Professionals. She hesitates before typing her name. It feels strange, belonging to a space where everyone speaks in shorthand about trauma and endurance, as if those are languages all dispatchers know. The threads scroll past with titles like Can't Sleep After Shift, Coping with Burnout, Worst Calls You Can't Forget. Leah reads for a long time before she adds her own post:

Hi, I'm new to Flagstaff Dispatch. Ten years in Phoenix before this. I used to love my job. I still do, but I can't shake the feeling that part of me stayed behind. How do you stop hearing the voices once you're off shift?

She rereads the words, then hits Post. The response is almost instant. User CalmVoice27: *Still saving everyone but yourself.*

Leah stares at it. The phrasing feels too personal. Too familiar. She refreshes the page. The comment remains. The user's profile is blank with no picture, no location, just the handle and a single line of text as their status: Listening helps.

Her stomach tightens. She clicks on the name, but it leads nowhere. Access restricted. She closes the laptop, the sound sharp in the quiet room. The rain outside grows heavier, pressing against the windows in long, steady lines.

Morning brings sun, almost aggressively bright after the storm. Leah walks to the dispatch center with her jacket unzipped, the air sharp with wet pine. By the time she reaches the building, the unease from the night before has dulled, replaced by the calm rhythm of routine.

Inside, the floor is quiet. Tanya waves from her console.

"Hey, early bird. Carla's bringing doughnuts. You picked the right shift."

Leah smiles. "Best supervisor ever."

Carla appears a moment later with a box under her arm.

"Bribe for good behavior."

The team laughs. For a while, it feels normal again. Leah logs into her station, headset ready, fingers moving over the keyboard. The first hour passes without incident in routine welfare checks, an accidental dial from a construction site, a lost wallet. The soft hum of voices around her becomes almost meditative. Then her screen freezes.

For a heartbeat, she assumes it's lag. But the cursor locks, the timer stalls, and the display fills with white. Then black. A line of text appears across the middle of the screen, faint green against the dark background:

Stay Calm. Help is on the way.

It repeats once. Then again. Then again, each line stacking

over the last until the screen fills entirely with the phrase, a wall of her own words. Leah's throat goes dry. She hits the keyboard, tries to exit, presses escape. Nothing.

"Jason," she calls softly. "Can you come here?"

The technician approaches, chewing gum, calm as always.

"What's up?"

"My terminal's frozen."

He leans over, eyebrows lifting slightly at the screen. "Weird. Haven't seen this before."

"Is it a virus?"

He shakes his head. "Probably just the software update from last night. Sometimes the system loops the standby script. I'll reboot it."

The screen flickers, then resets. The words vanish.

"There," he says. "All good. Don't panic."

Leah manages a weak laugh. "Occupational hazard."

He grins. "You'd be surprised how many dispatchers forget their own advice to stay calm."

When he walks away, she glances at the reflection on her blank monitor. For an instant, she thinks she sees another figure standing behind her, tall, dark hair pulled back. But when she turns, there's only Tanya.

"Everything okay?" Tanya asks.

"System glitch."

"Must be haunted." Tanya grins, then leans close, lowering her voice. "You sure you're not seeing ghosts of old calls?"

Leah smiles, though her palms still sweat. "Maybe."

The day drags on, blissfully uneventful. But when Leah removes her headset for the final time that evening, the silence rings in her ears like it used to. She tells herself she's fine, drives home through the thinning traffic, and lets the radio fill the car.

At her cabin, she makes dinner, sits at her small table again, and reopens her laptop. The forum login glows on the screen, familiar now. She types in her password and checks her notifications. There are no new replies and no private messages. She scrolls through other threads to distract herself, reading confessions from strangers who sound too much like her. Can't sleep. Still hear them. Dreamt I was on shift forever. She exhales slowly, comforted and unsettled all at once.

The rain starts again. A faint crackle fills her laptop speakers. She frowns, adjusts the volume. But there is nothing playing. Then, faintly, through static, she thinks she hears breathing. Soft, slow, and close. She slams the laptop shut. The sound stops instantly. She sits very still, laptop in front of her, heart pounding against her ribs.

Two days later, it happens at work. Leah is mid-shift, handling a domestic disturbance call, her tone steady, voice level. Then the line cuts out. Static replaces the caller's voice.

"Hello?" she says. "Can you repeat that?"

Nothing but faint breathing on the other end.

"Caller, are you safe?"

Silence. Then a whisper, too faint to catch, just air through the receiver. She ends the call, checks the log. The number registers as Withheld. Two minutes later, it happens again. It's a different line, but another silent call. She flags it for review, assuming a technical glitch. But it happens twice more before the shift ends and each time it's the same static, shallow breathing, but no voice.

By the third call, her hands are shaking.

Tanya leans over. "You okay?"

"I keep getting silent calls," Leah says. "I've had four in two hours."

Tanya shrugs. "Pranksters. It happens every few months. Kids think it's funny."

Leah forces a small laugh. "Right. Kids."

"Want me to take the next one?"

"No, it's fine."

But when the next silent call comes, she lets it hang in silence until the system reroutes it automatically.

That night, Leah's apartment feels colder. After dinner, she opens her laptop again. The moment the lid lifts, the camera light flicks on. She notices the small white glow beside the lens. Her breath catches. She isn't recording anything, so there's no reason the camera should activate. The light stays on. She covers it with her hand. The light seeps through her fingers.

Her chair scrapes back as she stands abruptly, slamming the laptop shut. The sound is sharp enough to echo. For a long moment, she just stands there, breathing hard, palms flat on the table. She checks the locks twice before going to bed, the laptop closed tight on the counter. She considers putting it out in the car, but thinks better of it.

The next morning at the dispatch center, she tells Tanya about the camera.

"Probably auto-updating," Tanya says, pouring coffee. "They do that sometimes. Don't freak yourself out."

"I wasn't recording."

"Computers have minds of their own." Tanya nudges her shoulder playfully. "If it makes you feel better, tape over it."

Leah nods, though the reassurance feels thin. At her work console, she focuses on the rhythm of work. Calls come in, calls end. Voices rise and fall. She keeps her breathing slow.

But near the end of her shift, her personal phone buzzes against the desk. She ignores it. Another work call comes through, a false alarm from a gas station. When she finally checks the message, her chest tightens. It's another email from Sam.

From: Sam Reed

Subject: Did you mean to send that photo?

She opens it before she can think. Attached is a single image, grainy and dark, but unmistakable. It's her. Sitting at her laptop. The photo taken from behind, over her shoulder, her own screen visible.

Leah stares at it until her stomach turns. The timestamp is from the previous night, around the exact time she'd been home, laptop open. Her vision narrows. She logs off, grabs her bag, and walks straight out without saying goodbye.

The drive home is a blur of headlights and noise. She keeps checking her mirror, expecting to see a white SUV, though the road behind her stays empty. At home, she bolts the door, leaves the lights on, and sits at her table with the photo open on her phone. She studies every detail, checking the angle, the color of the light, the way her shoulder tilts slightly. It's her. There's no question.

Her phone buzzes again with a message from Sam.

Leah? Are you okay? That picture scared me. Please tell me it's not what it looks like.

She types back quickly. *I didn't send it. I'm sorry.*

Three dots appear, then vanish. No reply. She deletes the thread, but the image remains burned behind her eyes.

The next morning, Carla calls her into the office. "Everything okay?"

Leah hesitates. "Why?"

"IT flagged a few login anomalies from your terminal. Might just be the update again, but Jason wanted me to check in."

Leah's pulse spikes. "Anomalies?"

"Access from offsite IPs, brief but strange. Jason says he'll handle it."

"There's been some weird stuff happening," Leah agrees, then stops herself before she shares too much.

Carla studies her. "You look tired."

"I didn't sleep."

"Take tomorrow off."

"I'm fine."

Carla smiles gently. "That wasn't a suggestion."

Leah forces a nod. As she leaves the office, Tanya waves.

"Movie night still on?"

Leah shakes her head. "Can I take a rain check? I'm shattered."

Back home, she powers up the laptop one last time. The fan whirs. The screen glows blue, then white. She navigates to the dispatcher forum, scrolling to her original post. It's still there. So is the comment. *Still saving everyone but yourself.*

She clicks Report User, but the button doesn't respond. She tries again. Nothing. The cursor flickers, then moves on its own, dragging across the page, selecting her own words, copying them.

The text box opens by itself. The copied sentence pastes. Then a new line appears beneath it, typing letter by letter:

Stay calm. Help is on the way.

Her breath stops. She slams the lid down, heart hammering. The light under the laptop pulses once, then fades.

Hours pass. She doesn't open it again. Instead, she sits on the couch, staring at the blank television, the ticking clock, the faint movement of shadows across the ceiling. Finally, she stands, walks back to the table, and flips the laptop open. The screen lights instantly, her forum profile displayed front and center. She clicks Delete Account.

A pop-up appears. Are you sure you want to delete your profile? This action cannot be undone. She clicks Yes. The screen turns black. For a second, she feels something like relief. It's a physical release, as though she's cut a wire. Then a notification blinks once in the corner of the dark screen before disappearing:

User CalmVoice27 liked your post.

13

The morning begins like any other. Leah arrives at the center before sunrise, the pine trees outside the Flagstaff Dispatch still wet with dew. The air carries that faint mountain chill that makes her lungs feel clean. She walks with her coffee balanced in one hand, badge clipped to her collar, telling herself that today will be ordinary. She will keep her focus. She will be calm.

Inside, the center hums to life. Consoles blink awake one by one. Tanya waves from her desk, hair pulled up in a messy bun. Jason scrolls through diagnostics, muttering to himself. The smell of cheap coffee and powdered creamer hangs in the air, familiar enough to be grounding.

Leah slips into her chair and exhales, letting the headset rest around her neck for a moment. The soft murmur of voices across the room is comforting in its rhythm. She sips her coffee and opens the shift log. No overnight incidents, no equipment failures. Just another Tuesday. Carla's voice cuts through the chatter from the front of the room.

"Morning, everyone. Quick huddle before we start."

The operators gather in a semicircle near the board. Leah joins them, notebook in hand. Carla's energy, as always, feels warm but brisk. She has perfected the tone of a woman who's run too many shifts and learned to disguise exhaustion with optimism.

"Before we review last night's reports," Carla says, smiling, "I want to share some good news. We've got a new transfer joining us from Phoenix."

Leah's pen stops moving.

Carla continues, "She's got plenty of experience in crisis response, strong record, stellar references. Please welcome..."

Leah already knows. Some part of her knew before the name leaves Carla's mouth.

"...Amber Klein."

The room bursts into polite applause. Leah's pulse drops into her stomach. The air shifts, suddenly thick. Her hand tightens around her pen until the plastic creaks. The door opens.

Amber steps in as if she owns the light. Her uniform is flawless, navy shirt pressed, badge gleaming. Her hair is shorter now, cut neatly at her jawline, the shade a little darker. She carries herself with practiced ease, her smile open and dazzling.

"Hey, everyone," she says. "Thanks for having me."

Her gaze moves over the room, quickly assessing, before landing on Leah. That smile deepens, becomes something smaller, private.

"Small world, right?"

The words echo in Leah's head like feedback. Carla beams. " You two already know each other?"

Leah can't find her voice. She nods once, mechanical. "Amber started in Phoenix not long before I left."

"Perfect," Carla says. "That'll make the transition easier."

Amber laughs lightly. "Guess fate wanted us to work together again."

The others chuckle, and Leah forces a small smile she doesn't feel. Her pulse pounds in her ears. When the meeting ends, she gathers her notes, hands trembling just enough to spill a drop of coffee onto the page. She mumbles something about needing the restroom and leaves before anyone notices.

Inside the restroom, Leah braces her hands against the sink and stares at her reflection. The fluorescent light buzzes softly above her. Her face looks pale, the kind of pallor that belongs to fear rather than illness. She watches her own throat move as she whispers, "Not again."

The mirror fogs slightly from her breath. She presses her palms flat to the counter until the trembling stops.

"You're fine," she tells herself quietly. "It's coincidence. Transfers happen. She's just another dispatcher."

But the words sound hollow, because she knows they're not true. She closes her eyes and counts her breathing like she's guiding someone else through a panic call. In for four. Hold for four. Out for six. When she opens them again, she forces a professional expression back into place, shoulders squared, jaw set. By the time she returns to the floor, her face is calm.

Amber is already at her new console, talking easily with Tanya.

"Phoenix was nonstop," she says, smiling. "You guys have it good up here."

Tanya grins. "Don't you ruin us with your work ethic."

Leah slides into her chair, pretending to check the shift schedule. Her stomach twists when she realizes Amber's station is directly across from hers. Amber glances up, her expression bright.

"You run such a calm team, Leah. It's nice to see familiar leadership again."

Leah keeps her tone level. "Glad you're settling in."

Amber tilts her head, studying her.

"You look good. Flagstaff suits you."

Leah doesn't reply. She smiles, adjusts her headset and turns toward her monitor.

The next few hours pass in fragments of ordinary calls, routine chatter, the illusion of normality stretched thin. Leah moves through it automatically, her responses smooth, her tone precise. But every time she looks up, Amber is there. Watching. Smiling. Mirroring her gestures the way she used to, fingers tapping the console in the same rhythm.

When Leah drinks, Amber lifts her own cup. When Leah laughs politely at Tanya's story, Amber's laughter follows half a second later, echoing just out of sync. By noon, Leah's nerves feel raw.

Carla announces lunch. Tanya and Jason head out together. Amber falls into step beside Leah as they walk toward the staff lounge.

"Feels like old times," Amber says.

Leah's voice is flat. "I didn't expect to see you again."

Amber shrugs. "Neither did I. They needed experienced staff. You know how short-handed Phoenix's sister centers are."

"Right."

They enter the lounge, which is a narrow room with vending machines and tired furniture. Leah sits at the end of the table, unwrapping a sandwich. Amber chooses the seat directly across from her.

"You seem better," Amber says softly, almost kindly. "I'm glad."

Leah's appetite evaporates.

"Why are you here, really?"

Amber smiles, unbothered. "Because this is where I'm needed. Fate, maybe?"

Leah stares at her. "Fate doesn't transfer personnel."

Amber laughs. "Always so literal." She leans forward, lowering her voice. "You don't have to be afraid of me."

Leah's pulse kicks up. "I'm not."

Amber's eyes flicker with amusement. "Good. Maybe tell your face that."

The door opens. Tanya pokes her head in.

"Hey, Carla's asking about the new log-in forms."

Amber waves cheerfully. "Already on it."

As she leaves, she touches Leah's shoulder lightly. It's a friendly gesture, nothing overt, but the contact burns like electricity.

When Leah finally finishes her shift, her head aches. The last hours blur into one long stretch of white noise and forced calm. Amber has been effortlessly charming, asking the right questions, laughing at the right moments, impressing Carla with her efficiency. Everyone seems to like her already.

Leah packs her bag slowly, waiting for the others to leave first. Outside, the sky has dimmed to a dull violet. The air smells of rain and asphalt. She walks to her car with her keys clutched tight, scanning the lot out of habit. Across the asphalt, Amber stands beside a small silver sedan, waving cheerfully.

"Night, Leah!"

Leah forces a wave back. "Night."

Amber's smile doesn't falter as she gets into her car. The engine starts with a low hum.

Leah unlocks her door, slides behind the wheel, and sits there a long moment before starting the ignition. Her hands shake against the steering wheel. When she finally drives off, the headlights from the sedan behind her flare briefly before turning in the same direction.

Leah's car pulls onto the main road, tires whispering across wet asphalt. Streetlights flicker through the mist, each one catching her mirrors like a pulse. She tells herself she's imagining it, but every time she checks, the sedan still there, a steady pair of lights following at the same careful distance. She slows. The sedan slows too. At the next intersection, she signals left. The sedan signals left.

Her pulse begins to pound in her throat. When she finally turns onto her own street, the car keeps going, rolling past at an unhurried pace, disappearing around the bend. She exhales shakily, her fingers gripping the wheel until they ache.

Inside her cabin, she doesn't turn on the lights right away. The darkness feels safer, protective. She listens, hears nothing unfamiliar, and then moves to the window. The street outside is empty. The night sits heavy and clean.

She pours a glass of water, sits at the table, and stares at the laptop. For the first time in weeks, she doesn't want to open it. She doesn't want to risk seeing that green text again.

Instead, she pulls out a notepad, the kind she used for field reports back in Phoenix. The paper is rough beneath her hand as she writes:

She's here. She followed me.

She stares at the sentence for a long time before tearing the page out and shredding it. There's no proof. There never is.

The next morning, Leah arrives early again, trying to regain control through routine. The center smells faintly of disinfectant and coffee. Tanya waves from across the room.

"Morning, superstar," Tanya says.

Leah forces a smile. "Morning."

Amber is already there, of course. She's talking to Carla, showing her a folder of transfer documents. When she catches Leah's eye, she smiles. Not wide, not mocking, just enough to acknowledge the connection between them. Carla calls across the room.

"Leah, come here a sec."

Leah's stomach tightens. She walks over, trying to look neutral.

"Amber was just telling me about your old department," Carla says. "She says you trained half the team there."

Amber nods earnestly.

"Leah's calm under pressure. Everyone wanted to be like her."

Carla laughs. "I believe it. I'm lucky to have you both."

Leah manages a polite thank-you and retreats to her console. Her screen blurs for a moment as she stares at it. Amber's voice carries easily across the room, low and melodic, impossible to ignore.

The shift runs smoothly at first. Routine calls, nothing unusual. But each time Leah focuses on her screen, she can feel Amber's presence nearby, and hear the subtle rhythm of her voice in her headset, the same phrasing, the same tone.

"Flagstaff Emergency, what's your location?" The inflection is identical.

When a minor car accident comes through, both women handle separate lines of the same incident. Their voices overlap in eerie unison, echoing the same commands.

Tanya glances between them, amused.

"Creepy how in sync you two are."

Amber grins. "Old habits."

Leah forces a small smile. "Guess so." But her throat feels dry.

Later, during the lull between calls, Tanya nudges her.

"She's kind of amazing, huh? Total pro."

Leah nods, because disagreeing would sound petty. But inside, the tension coils tighter. Amber is too perfect. She's playing a different part here to the one she played in Phoenix. Here, every gesture is rehearsed, every answer charming. It's as if she's rewritten herself for this new audience.

Whenever Leah catches her reflection in the dark monitor glass, Amber's figure is visible in the background, eyes fixed on her. At lunch, Leah tries to eat alone in the breakroom, but Amber appears moments later, balancing a salad and water bottle.

"Mind if I join you?"

Leah considers lying, saying she has a call, a meeting, anything, but the words don't come. Amber sits before she can refuse.

"I missed this."

Leah stares at her fork. "What exactly?"

"The rhythm. The energy. You."

"Amber..."

Amber leans back, crossing her legs neatly.

"Relax. I'm not here to upset you."

"Then why transfer here?"

Amber smiles, eyes bright.

"It's a small world, Leah. Dispatch is an even smaller one. Maybe this is just where I'm supposed to be."

Leah's pulse hammers in her ears. "You could have gone anywhere."

Amber shrugs. "You make it sound like I followed you."

Leah meets her gaze. "Didn't you?"

Amber doesn't blink. "Would it scare you if I had?"

The silence between them stretches until Tanya bursts through the door with a bag of chips, cheerful as ever.

"You two okay?"

Amber's smile returns effortlessly. "Just catching up on old times."

Tanya laughs. "Don't tell me you're ankle deep in Phoenix gossip already."

Leah stands abruptly, her chair scraping.

"I need to check something."

She leaves before either can stop her. In the restroom again, Leah locks the door and grips the sink. The mirror stares back, harsh and unflattering. Her reflection looks older, thinner, like someone carrying invisible weight. She hears the faint sound of the lounge door opening down the hall, and muffled voices from inside, one of them unmistakably Amber's.

She turns on the tap, pretending the noise is just water. For a long time, she stays there, breathing through the panic. You're fine. You're safe. She can't hurt you here. But deep down she knows that isn't true.

That afternoon, Carla stops by her station.

"Hey, how's everything going? You've been quiet today."

Leah forces a smile. "Fine."

"Good. Just checking. Amber says she's thrilled to be working under you again."

"Under me?" Leah echoes.

Carla laughs. "Not literally. Just means she respects you. She said you taught her everything about handling chaos."

Leah nods mechanically, though her stomach churns. Amber is setting a narrative already, and she's reshaping the story. By the end of the shift, Leah feels raw again. Every sound is amplified. The buzz of the lights, the hum of computers, the distant ringing of a phone. When she removes her headset, her neck aches.

Carla calls out, "Good work today, team! Go get some rest."

Amber stands beside the exit, waving goodbye to Tanya and Jason. When Leah approaches, Amber's smile widens.

"Big day, huh?" she says softly. "Feels right being here."

Leah doesn't answer. Amber steps closer, lowering her voice so only Leah can hear.

"I think we both needed a fresh start."

Leah's throat tightens.

"Stay away from me."

Amber tilts her head.

"That's not very welcoming."

"Don't twist this."

Amber's smile never falters. "I'm not the one twisting things."

Leah's breath catches. She glances toward the door where Carla's silhouette is visible through the glass. Then she looks back at Amber. Amber steps aside smoothly, her expression composed.

"See you tomorrow, Leah."

Outside, the evening air is cool, threaded with pine and exhaust fumes. The parking lot gleams with puddles from an earlier rain. Leah walks quickly toward her car, keys clenched tight, her heartbeat loud in her ears. Behind her, she hears Amber's voice.

"Night, Leah!"

She turns. Amber stands by her sedan, waving cheerfully under the streetlight. Her face glows faintly in the pale orange hue. Leah nods stiffly and turns back to her car. Her hand shakes as she unlocks the door. She sits inside for a moment, staring at the steering wheel, trying to slow her breathing.

When she finally starts the engine, her headlights sweep across the lot. Amber's car is still there, motionless. Amber herself stands outside it, still smiling, she waves again. Leah backs out and drives away, refusing to look again, but the reflection in her rearview mirror catches movement, just enough to see the sedan's lights flicker on.

That night, Leah dreams of the Phoenix dispatch floor as a cavern of voices and flashing screens, every console manned by someone who looks like Amber. Their heads turn in unison as she enters. Stay calm, they say together. Help is coming. She wakes before dawn, drenched in sweat, the sound still echoing in her ears.

When she steps to the window, the street below lies empty. Only the wind moves through the trees, bending them toward her window as if listening. She turns away and tells herself that she'll talk to Carla, that she'll explain everything rationally. But part of her already knows how it will sound. She followed me. She's pretending this is coincidence. There will be sympathy, nods, the quiet weight of disbelief, and a look at the HR file that followed her here.

Leah sits on the edge of her bed, the compass gleaming faintly on her nightstand. The needle trembles once, then steadies north. Outside, the first faint light of morning seeps through the clouds.

She whispers, "Stay calm," because the words are habit, because they are the only defense she has left.

14

The morning begins with noise. The dispatch floor hums like a live wire, with phones trilling, voices rising and falling in overlapping cadence, the air thick with coffee and recycled breath. Leah sits at her console, eyes on the call queue. She can feel the pulse of the room through her headset, the quickened rhythm of emergencies overlapping.

"Flagstaff Emergency, what's your location?"

Her voice is smooth, steady. The call is short, it's only a minor accident, easily resolved. She disconnects, logs the time, moves to the next. Across the aisle, Amber mirrors her posture almost perfectly, headset angled the same way, hair tucked behind one ear. The sound of her voice carries faintly over the noise, calm, clear, and identical in tone.

"Stay calm. Help is on the way."

Leah's throat tightens. The shift supervisor walks past, nodding approvingly. Carla's voice cuts through the static.

"Good work, team. Nice control today."

Amber looks up, smiling. "That's because we've got the best leader here."

Leah glances over. Amber's gaze is warm, open, her expression all innocence.

"She's taught me everything I know."

Several of the team laugh. Tanya grins.

"If I had your composure, I'd bottle it and sell it for millions."

Leah forces a tight smile. "Just practice."

But inside, something twists. It feels like the compliment turned knife-edge. Amber's tone is reverent, but the eyes that meet hers say I made you look. The next call comes through and saves her. She dives into it with too much focus, voice clipped and professional, grounding herself in the task until the noise in her chest dulls.

By the time the lunch break arrives, her jaw aches from keeping her tone neutral.

The staff kitchen smells of reheated curry. Leah opens the fridge, scanning for the small Tupperware she packed that morning. It's gone. She checks the shelves twice, then the side counter.

Her name is written clearly on the label. She closes the door and leans against it, pressing her fingers to her temple. Tanya walks in, phone in hand.

"You look like you just lost the lottery."

"Someone took my lunch."

"Oh no. The eternal office crime." Tanya opens the fridge, peering in. "I swear, we need cameras in here."

"It's fine," Leah says quietly. "I'll grab something later."

She's halfway to the vending machine when Amber enters, bright and unhurried, holding a plastic container. "You won't believe this."

Leah stops. Amber lifts the box with a sheepish grin.

"I found your lunch in my bag. I must've grabbed it by mistake when I meant to take mine."

Leah stares at the neat label with her name. Amber laughs softly. Tanya chuckles.

"Mystery solved. At least it wasn't stolen."

Leah manages a thin smile. "Right. Easy mistake."

Amber sets the box down on the counter. "Here you go. Safe and sound."

Her tone is gentle, her movements casual, but Leah can't shake the image of Amber placing it there deliberately, fingers brushing over her name. Amber closes the fridge and glances at her.

"You should eat. You look pale."

Leah nods. "Thanks."

Amber leaves, and the air seems to follow her out, leaving the room thinner and quieter. Tanya leans on the counter, scrolling her phone.

"You're lucky, you know."

Leah frowns. "Lucky?"

"Having someone like Amber around. She's been singing your praises since she got here. Says you were her mentor, her role model."

Leah's stomach turns. "Really."

"Yeah. It's sweet. She's obviously grateful. Most transfers come in like they're competing."

Leah looks down at the countertop, tracing a small scratch with her thumb. "She's... very loyal."

"Exactly." Tanya smiles. "Everyone needs someone like that watching their back."

Leah forces a nod and picks up her water bottle.

"I'll be back in five."

When she steps into the hallway, the sound of laughter from the kitchen follows her like static.

～

That evening, Leah drives home under a bruised sky. The pines sway in the wind like dark dancers, their movement hypnotic. She tells herself the day was ordinary. She tells herself to stop reading into things. But the moment she reaches her cabin door, unease returns, small, immediate, and crawling up her spine before she even knows why.

On the floor on the porch lies a cardboard parcel. She hesitates, crouches, and picks it up. The box is light, faintly floral-scented. She carries it inside and across to the table and slices the tape open with her house key.

Inside, nestled in white tissue paper, is a single white lily. Its petals are unblemished, waxy in the lamplight, a drop of water still clinging to one edge. Beside it lies a folded sheet of paper, typed neatly in black ink.

You're safe now.

Her stomach lurches. The words seem to hum in the air. She checks outside, but the street is empty. No footsteps outside, no sign of delivery. She looks again at the lily. The scent is faint but sharply perfumed.

Her hands tremble as she lifts the box and drops it into the bin. The flower lands softly, face up, petals untouched. She forces the lid down and steps back. The apartment feels colder. She locks the door and checks it twice, then sits on the couch, gripping the armrest until her fingers ache.

She stays that way for nearly an hour, listening to the silence, waiting for a sound. Finally, she stands and checks the windows. All closed. The locks gleam in the faint streetlight. Still, she can't shake the feeling of being watched.

The next morning at work, the world feels both sharper and hazier. Each sound feels too loud, each light too bright. Leah keeps her focus pinned to the console, her voice steady even as her thoughts fray. Halfway through the morning, a floral scent hits her. It's faint at first, then stronger. She glances up.

Amber stands at her console, smiling. She's wearing a crisp white blouse patterned with pale lilies that bloom across the fabric like ghosts.

"New top," she chirps. "You like it?"

Leah's throat closes. She can't speak. Amber tilts her head, waiting.

"You look like you've seen a ghost."

Leah swallows hard. "It's... nice."

Amber's smile widens. "Thanks. I thought it was calming. You're always talking about calm."

She turns back to her console, humming softly under her breath. Leah stares at the pattern, those same curved petals, the same pale green stems, until the room seems to spin around her. Her stomach knots. She presses her headset tight against her ears, forcing her attention back to the calls, the noise, anything that isn't that blouse.

That evening, Leah sits at her dining table in near-darkness, the only light coming from the laptop in front of her. The screen shows her call logs, with numbers, times, and outcomes in endless rows of order that should soothe her but don't.

She scrolls down, fingers slow, eyes unfocused. She can't help feeling the camera is watching her. Her pulse stutters. She quickly attaches a strip of tape over the lens. She shakes her head, taps a key, the screen flaring bright again. But the feeling lingers, cold and certain.

Somewhere inside her head, Amber's voice whispers, soft, familiar, and impossible to block out.

Stay calm, Leah. You're safe now.

The sound vibrates beneath her skin. She closes the laptop, the click echoing loudly in the quiet room. She knows already that she won't sleep.

～

The next morning, Leah wakes to the sound of rain. It comes down in soft sheets, steady and rhythmic, tapping against the windowpane like fingers. She lies still for a while, listening. It should be soothing. It isn't.

She rises, showers, dresses. Her clothes feel too tight, her own reflection in the bathroom mirror too sharply angled. The white blouse she chooses looks plain, neutral, harmless. She wears her hair up, the way Carla prefers, looking neat, professional, and invisible.

The drive to work feels longer than usual. The road is slick with pine needles and runoff. Each stoplight turns red just before she reaches it, as if the city itself wants her to pause, to think. But she doesn't want to think.

By the time she arrives, the dispatch center hums with early-shift chatter. Tanya waves from across the room, holding a paper cup of coffee like an offering.

"Carla's in one of her moods," she says, laughing. "Be glad you're going on nights."

Leah nods, smiling faintly, but her stomach twists when she sees Amber already at her console. She's early, as usual. Amber's blouse today is different but familiar. It's ivory silk, patterned faintly with gray vines. The lilies are subtler, almost hidden, but Leah's eyes find them instantly. Amber turns, as if sensing her gaze.

"Morning," she says, her tone bright.

Leah forces a greeting. "Morning."

"You look tired," Amber adds softly. "Rough night?"

"Couldn't sleep."

Amber nods sympathetically. "You should try lavender oil. I used to get terrible insomnia. Then again..." Her smile widens slightly. "It helps to know you're safe."

Leah blinks. "What?"

Amber shrugs, still smiling. "Just something I heard you say once."

Leah stares at her, waiting for a hint of irony, but Amber's face remains serene. She turns back to her screen, the reflection of green text flickering faintly across her glasses.

Mid-morning, Carla calls for a quick meeting. The team gathers near the whiteboard as she runs through the week's updates. Amber stands beside her, relaxed and confident, contributing small remarks that make the group laugh.

Leah tries to focus on Carla's voice, but her attention drifts to Amber's neatly manicured hands, resting lightly on the edge of the desk. The same hands that once touched her shoulder, the same calm voice that whispered reassurance in her ear when everything began to fall apart.

Carla's tone shifts, cheerful again.

"Before we go, I just want to acknowledge Leah for maintaining composure under pressure this month. Great leadership as always."

Leah feels a small flush of embarrassment, murmurs thanks. Amber claps softly, smiling.

"She's amazing. Everything I know, I learned from her."

The words draw polite laughter. Tanya nudges Leah's arm.

"See? You've got a fan club."

Leah nods, forcing a laugh she doesn't feel. The noise around her becomes too bright, too loud. Amber's compliment lands like an invisible bruise. Carla dismisses them, and the operators drift back to their desks. Amber leans close as she passes.

"You're blushing," she murmurs. "It suits you."

Leah stiffens. "Don't."

Amber's voice lowers to a whisper. "You don't like attention. I forgot."

She walks away before Leah can answer.

Later, during break, Leah escapes to the kitchen again. She sits alone with a cup of coffee, staring at the rain sliding down the window. Tanya joins her a moment later, dropping into the seat opposite.

"You okay?"

"I'm fine."

"You sure? You've been jumpy lately." Tanya sips her coffee, watching her. "Amber was telling me you two went through some rough calls back in Phoenix. That kind of stuff sticks."

Leah looks up sharply. "What did she say?"

"Nothing bad. Just that you used to mentor her. She said you were the calmest person she'd ever known."

Leah exhales slowly. "Right."

"I think she really looks up to you."

Leah almost laughs at that, but the sound dies before it reaches her throat. "Maybe too much."

Tanya grins. "You're being modest. She's harmless."

The word stings. Harmless.

"Anyway," Tanya continues, "Carla's been talking about recommending you for shift coordinator. Amber said she'd support it. You've got good allies here."

Leah's fingers tighten around her cup. "Allies," she repeats.

"Yeah. You should be proud."

Leah nods, but her pulse thrums like static.

When Tanya leaves, Leah stays behind, staring at her untouched coffee. The rain outside has thickened, drumming harder against the glass. She imagines it washing everything clean, the way water can strip paint, erase tracks. She whispers to herself, "Stay calm," as if the words still hold power.

The evening drags. Calls blur into one another, endless background noise that feels both distant and too close. Leah's concentration slips, though. Twice she catches herself staring at nothing, headset silent, her own breathing too loud in her ears. At one point, Amber touches her shoulder lightly.

"You should take five."

"I'm fine."

"Carla won't mind."

"I said I'm fine."

Amber's eyes linger on her, full of pity that feels theatrical.

"Of course. You always are."

Leah turns back to her screen, jaw tight, hands trembling slightly on the keyboard.

By the time her shift ends, the air feels heavier, pressing down like humidity before a storm. She gathers her bag quickly, avoiding eye contact.

"Heading home?" Tanya calls.

"Yeah. Long day."

Amber's voice follows, gentle. "Drive safe."

Leah doesn't look back.

At home, the apartment feels wrong the moment she steps inside. The air is too still, too scented. There's a faint floral note that is sweet, heavy, and unmistakable. Her gaze darts to the counter. The bin lid is closed, but the smell of lilies lingers as if the flower never left.

She moves through the apartment slowly, checking windows, doors, and locks. Everything is as it should be. In the bedroom, she notices something new. Her framed photo of the dispatch team has been moved slightly, angled differently on the shelf. She stares at it, trying to remember if she'd touched it herself. The photo glints faintly in the lamplight, showing everyone smiling, Amber's hand resting on her shoulder.

The image seems to watch her. Leah steps back, heart thudding. She tells herself she's tired. That she's imagining it. Still, she takes the photo down and slides it into a drawer, face down. The apartment feels smaller afterward, as if removing it hasn't helped but made the shadows closer.

Later, she sits on the couch with her laptop open, scrolling through her call logs again. The list scrolls endlessly downward, each entry a small anchor of routine. But her eyes keep catching on a pattern. There's a repeated phrase in the notes section, lines she doesn't remember typing: Caller reassured. Told to stay calm.

She checks the timestamps. Some belong to calls she didn't handle. Her pulse quickens. She double-checks the operator ID. It's hers. L.H. The entries repeat across multiple nights.

She opens one at random. The recording begins as normal with a faint male voice reporting an accident, panic rising, but when the playback reaches her own response, her voice sounds wrong. It's not her tone, and not her phrasing. It's Amber's.

The voice says calmly "Stay calm. You're safe now."

Leah slams the lid shut, breath catching. The sound echoes in her head, looping, flattening into mechanical rhythm. She grips the laptop until her knuckles whiten, as if she could crush the memory out of existence. Then, slowly, she stands and walks to the kitchen. She fills a glass of water, drinks it, sets it down. She looks out of the window and just for an instant, she thinks she sees movement of a shape outside in the rain, blurred but human. When she blinks, it's gone. She pulls the curtains closed and locks the latch.

The next day, Leah arrives early, determined to confront Amber, to demand some kind of explanation, even if it makes her look paranoid. But when she walks in, the atmosphere is already buzzing with laughter. Carla is at her desk, Tanya beside her. Amber stands near the coffee machine, pouring a cup for each of them. The three of them look up as Leah enters.

"Morning, sleepyhead," Carla says warmly. "We were just saying how lucky we are to have this dream team."

Amber hands Leah a cup. "I made your coffee how you like it."

Leah takes it automatically, throat dry. "You didn't have to."

"I wanted to," Amber smiles.

Tanya pats her arm.

"See? She looks out for you."

Leah tries to smile but can't. The room spins faintly, and the scent of lilies seems to rise from the cup, faint but cloying.

Carla frowns. "You okay?"

"I... yeah. I'm just tired."

Amber tilts her head. "You should rest more. I worry about you."

Leah's pulse quickens. "Don't."

Amber's brow furrows in gentle confusion. "Don't what?"

Leah opens her mouth, but the words die. Carla and Tanya exchange puzzled looks.

"I just meant," Leah says quietly. "You don't have to worry."

Amber smiles. "Of course I do."

That evening, Leah sits alone in her cabin again, laptop dark, curtains drawn. The silence feels heavier than before, dense with things unsaid. She closes her eyes, pressing her palms against her temples, trying to will the noise away. Not the voices from the day, but the echoes, the whispers, the memory of Amber's voice in her ear. It doesn't leave. It grows softer, closer.

Stay calm. You're safe now.

Her eyes snap open. The sound isn't in her head this time. It's in the room. It's faint, tinny, coming from somewhere near the laptop. She reaches for it with shaking hands. The lid opens and the screen glows to life. The words appear slowly, one line at a time. *Stay Calm. Help is on the way.* Then another line beneath it. *You're safe now.* The cursor blinks once, then freezes.

Leah slams it shut, her pulse hammering in her throat. The words still echo in her mind, soft and relentless, as if someone is whispering them through the walls. She sits in the dark until the first light of dawn bleeds through the curtains, unable to move, afraid that any sound she makes will answer back.

15

The storm arrives in Flagstaff like a wall. Rain hits the windows in sheets, drumming hard enough to blur the parking lot into a smear of silver. Over the pines, the sky sits black and low, pulsing with distant lightning. Inside the Dispatch Centre, the room braces itself around the sound.

Leah is already in her chair when the first wave of thunder rolls through. She wears the headset high on her crown, cord coiled neatly, posture set. The call board populates in bursts. There are power lines down on the north of town, a couple of minor crashes, alarms tripped by surges. The tone for medical priority cuts through a chorus of lower alerts. She breathes once and answers.

"Flagstaff Emergency. Your location."

A caller coughs, frantic and winded. Tree through a kitchen window. Glass everywhere. A deep cut on a forearm that keeps bleeding. Leah's fingers move without conscious thought. She maps the address, signals the nearest unit, speaks in a gentle pace that keeps the caller with her. She tells her to put pressure on the wound with a clean towel. Sit on the floor away from the window. Help is on the way. The storm's voice presses on the glass, rain thrashing like a crowd.

Across the aisle, Amber settles into the station that faces Leah's. She looks composed, hair pinned tight, uniform collar crisp. Her voice filters through the room, low and steady, handling her own incident while Leah wraps the call. They do not need to look at each other to keep the rhythm. The habit is deeper than preference. It is muscle and memory.

Carla steps to the front rail with a clipboard and a phone tucked at her shoulder.

"We are on full storm protocol," she calls, not raising her voice but cutting through the noise anyway. "Jason, lock the update channel to my console. Leah, you are flood-response lead. Amber, you have family shelter calls. Tanya, you take road closures. We need triage and clear reporting."

There is no time to answer. The phones do that for them.

A county reservoir overflow flags red on Leah's screen. The drainage map blooms into lines and blue shading. She pulls the flood deck without thinking, showing sandbag points, evacuation triggers, low crossing warnings. She starts the group channel that will stay open until the surge breaks. Public Works, Fire, Patrol, two park rangers, and the volunteer coordinator all click in, their voices coming and going like lights in a storm.

"Flood channel open," Leah says. "Switch to plain language. No codes."

"Copy," comes back from four directions at once.

The first road closure lands. Tanya logs it and pings the message board. The second and third closures follow, then more. A transformer pops somewhere north. The building lights flicker once as if startled, they dim, then hold. The call board refreshes again. A cluster of pins appears along the creek that runs under the highway. Leah narrows the view and marks the low tunnel that always floods first. She signals a patrol unit to block it before someone tries to drive through the water.

A scream cuts across air on another line. Amber says, "I am here," without raising her voice. "Tell me the street. Tell me the number." She speaks as if the words are a rope and she is throwing it to someone in the dark.

Leah hears only the shape of it. There is no time to listen for content. Another alert opens and she is already moving. The spillway is overtopping at mile marker thirty-one. She requests barricades for the far lane and a ranger for the footpath. Public Works comes back with a breathless confirmation. On the shared channel, a sergeant asks for a repeat. Leah repeats without sighing. The reverb in the room smooths to one sound. The storm, the board, the voice, the rhythm. She lives here.

A child cries on Amber's line. "Mama, the water is coming in under the door." The words arrive thin and high, picked up by a phone that keeps cutting in and out. "Daddy is stuck outside with the car."

Lightning flashes and thunder hits a breath later. The center's lights flicker again, longer this time, enough for Leah to see her own reflection on her dark secondary screen. When the power steadies, the reflection vanishes, replaced by a new red flag. A basement full of water. An elderly couple with no sump pump and no way to reach the main breaker safely. Leah requests Fire swift response and tags the case as a rapid check. The queue for that channel is already building. She marks priority and moves to the next.

On the family call, the audio drops for a full second. Amber says, "Stay with me," and the line returns. A second dropout, longer this time. She glances at Jason, who is already on his feet with a cable in hand and eyes set with stubborn focus.

"Switch that family to the redundant trunk," he says.

Amber's hand moves. The board blinks. Her screen shows

the call jump to a backup route, then stabilize. She speaks again, slower than before, as if the storm can hear her and will calm if she does.

"You are doing so well. I will stay with you until the firefighters arrive."

Leah hears the cadence and finds that her body matches it without conscious intent. It shortens her sentences. It steadies her breath. She does not look up. She does not need to see Amber to know where the rhythm is.

Carla moves like a conductor, not rushing but holding everything to tempo.

"Jason, good save. Tanya, publish the updated sandbag locations again and pin the post. Leah, your channel is clean and clear. Keep the river markers updated."

"Yes," Leah says. The answer is a shape more than a word. A light on her map turns amber. A flood sensor at the creek's bend tips to warning. She calls the ranger to move people off the footbridge. He answers with his voice too close to the wind.

The hours stretch and collapse. The storm makes that happen. Time falls into the work until the work is all there is. Leah holds the flood map in one part of her head and the emergency service rosters in another. She pings the volunteer lead to send six people to the senior center with bottled water and blankets. She tags the road update with a caution about downed trees. She speaks in that measured calm that has nothing to do with feeling. She does not let herself scan for a white blouse or a pattern of lilies. She keeps her eyes on the work.

The family line wavers again and then holds. Amber mouths a thank you to Jason and shifts her audio level slightly.

"I hear you," she says. "You are inside a hallway now. Go to the back room. Keep the sandbags at the bottom of the door. Sit on the floor away from the window. Tell me what you can see."

Thunder rolls long and low. In the brief quiet after, Leah hears the smallest sound through the room mic. A child counting breaths. It hits her like a sensation more than a fact. She will not think about childhood tonight. She sets a flag on the flood map and moves to the next task.

A patrol unit calls in a stalled car at the low tunnel that Leah closed fifteen minutes ago. The barricade arrived late. Someone moved it. Leah bites her lip once, hard enough to feel the sting, and marks the detour on the shared view.

The storm's heart shifts east. The intensity dips and returns in a new pattern that is more line than circle. The worst of the winds are over. The water is not. It climbs stairs and pushes at doors. It finds basements and sinks them. The board throws a new cluster of pins in a neighborhood two miles from the river. Leah toggles to the sewer map and recognizes the reason. Old lines with bad slope and poor uphill drains. She codes for additional crews.

At the back of the room, someone groans at a news alert. Carla holds up a hand and says nothing. The hum continues. The discipline holds. Still, the family call does not end. It narrows. It rests in the small shape of reassurance that can carry people across five minutes that feel like an hour. "The fire crew is on your street," Amber says. "Listen for their voices. They will knock. They will call your name. Do you hear the siren now?"

A weak "Yes" comes back through the line and the entire room seems to relax.

Leah logs a resource request for a shelter bus. She tags two addresses as priority pick-ups. She keeps her breath even until her chest stops aching. Her headset speaker hisses and clears. She adjusts the gain and continues.

A sharp crack splits the air. For a fraction of a second, every screen in the room tilts toward black. The power drops, catches, then surges higher than before. An alarm chimes from the server rack. Jason swears under his breath and disappears behind the equipment wall.

On Amber's screen, the family line goes to empty.

"No," she says softly. She moves before the word is fully out, switching to manual routing. Her fingers find keys Leah knows by touch. The line does not return. She opens the old list for legacy backups. It is a page almost no one uses anymore. She launches the analog bridge as if it belongs in this century. The call snaps back into her headset with a sound like a gasp.

"I have you," she says. She speaks into the space that had opened and filled again. "I am here."

Carla lifts a hand of congratulation. "Nice work."

The firefighters confirm entry into the house. The family is lifted, one adult, one child, one dog, one cat in a carrier. The operator notes scroll.

"You two make a great team," Carla says, not as a line for effect but as a statement of observed fact.

Leah does not look at Amber right away. She keeps her eyes on the map and marks a school as closed for the foreseeable due to roof damage. When she finally looks up, it is not to meet Amber's gaze but to take in the room. It is different for a beat. Softer. The hostility she has been braced against is not there in this moment. There is only the work, and the way two voices can hold a county up while the water tries to push it down.

The board shifts to yellow as the surge moves on. The hours that follow are more cleanup than containment. They are the part where patience returns as a virtue rather than a posture. Leah moves through it with care. She reschedules crews, answers calm questions that still carry adrenaline. She makes lists for morning. She drinks the coffee that has been sitting beside her for half an hour and grimaces at the taste.

When the final high-priority case closes, the room goes quieter in a way that is not silence but relief. People roll their shoulders and stretch their necks. Tanya tosses a pack of crackers at Jason, who catches it without looking. Leah removes her headset and sets it gently on the desk. Her ears ring with the absence of voices. The storm beats softer on the glass.

Amber stands and turns toward her. For a moment they face each other across the aisle like actors who have just finished a scene that carried them somewhere they did not expect to go.

"Thank you," Leah says. Her voice comes out rougher than she intends. "For the manual bridge. You saved that call."

Amber shakes her head. "You kept the map. You kept the room." She steps closer, not invading, but near enough that Leah can see the texture of her makeup. Her voice drops into a register that is almost intimate. "You are always safe when I am beside you."

The words land between them like a weight wrapped in velvet. Leah feels the gratitude and the warning at the same time. She nods once, slow, because rejecting the line will trigger something and accepting it will invite something else. There is no good answer.

Carla claps her hands once.

"Canteen," she says. "Ten minutes. Then we write this up."

The team moves as if pulled by a tide. Leah finds that she is moving too.

The staff canteen has fogged windows and a tile floor that never looks clean. The air smells of damp sweaters and the metal tang of the old coffee machine. People talk softly and laughter breaks and fades. A few operators lean their foreheads on their wrists and sit like that, eyes closed, letting their nervous systems climb back down. Leah stands near the counter, pouring herself a water. Her hands feel steady for the first time all afternoon. When she looks up, Tanya is there with a generous smile and a chocolate bar that has started melting in a pocket.

"For blood sugar," Tanya says. "Also for morale."

Leah smiles, real enough to register in her cheeks. "Thank you."

They sit at the small table by the vending machines and the low talk of the team makes a soft wall around them.

"You were brilliant," Tanya says. "That flood channel sat straight through three hours of chaos. Zero confusion. Zero ego. I wish I'd recorded it so I could shove it in the face of every trainee who thinks they can multitask without a plan."

Leah sips her water. The cool loosens something in her throat. "It felt a bit like Phoenix," she says, and hears the ache slide under the words.

"Yeah," Tanya says. "But more remote."

Leah nods once and looks into the glass. Tanya lowers her voice.

"You and Amber were kind of scary together. In a good way. It was like the room narrowed to you two."

Leah keeps her eyes on the glass of water so she will not be caught in whatever look is on her face.

"We have history," she says. "We learned the same patterns."

"I can see that," Tanya says. She hesitates, chewing the edge of the wrapper. "I know she unnerves you sometimes. You told me that. But today... I don't know. It felt like she had your back."

Leah exhales. "That is what makes this hard."

"Because it is true and not true at the same time?"

"Yes."

Tanya taps the table softly. "Maybe she just wants your approval. You are the person who taught her how to do this that well. Maybe that is all it is."

Leah wants to believe that. She feels the wanting as a tenderness, a small pull toward relief.

"Maybe," she says.

The room grows quieter as people finish tea and stand. Carla calls something across the canteen about forms and timestamps. Jason jokes about inventing an umbrella for servers. The storm rolls away from the building and toward the next county, and the windows have stopped rattling.

Leah sets her empty glass in the sink and stands slowly. Tanya stands with her, and they walk back toward the floor together. At the door, Tanya squeezes Leah's arm.

"Good work, boss."

Leah smiles, small and tired. "You too."

She watches Tanya head to her station, then turns down the small corridor that leads to the lockers. The hall is dimmer here, lights flickering a little under the strain of the day. She opens her locker and exhales when the smell of dry paper and soap rises up. She takes out her sweater and phone from the locker, grateful of the smell of the clean fabric and the warmth it will bring.

From the main room, she hears a line of laughter and a soft voice that she recognizes without effort. Amber again, charming in the aftermath. Leah closes her locker and rests her forehead against the cool metal for one second. Then she straightens, composes her face, and walks back into the room where the aftercare of crisis is still work.

She does not know yet that the rain will not stop before midnight, and that she will arrive home soaked through the sleeves. She does not know yet that when she sets her keys on the table, a small silver circle will glint there. For now, there is only the canteen aftertaste of tap water and the echo of a sentence that is both rescue and trap. You are always safe when I am beside you. She carries the line like a weight in her pocket as she returns to her console and opens the report template, ready to write the story the storm will leave behind.

The rain hasn't stopped. It trails her home like a shadow, chasing her headlights up the mountain road, relentless and fine as static. The wipers sweep across the windshield in mechanical rhythm, thud, pause, thud. Leah grips the steering wheel tighter each time the lightning flares.

She tells herself she's just tired, just coming down from the adrenaline of a twelve-hour storm shift. The rain will pass. Everything passes.

By the time she reaches her cabin, the drive is half-flooded. She splashes through it with her bag clutched to her chest, hair soaked to her scalp before she even reaches the stairs. The building hums faintly from the backup generator; its yellow glow seems weaker than usual.

Inside, she drops her keys into the bowl by the door and leans against the wall, eyes closed, the smell of wet pine thick in her nose. The silence after the storm isn't silence at all. It's a ringing, the leftover echo of voices through the headset, of frightened callers, radios, Amber's steady tone saying I am here. You are doing so well. You're safe now. Leah exhales slowly, but the words stay lodged somewhere deep.

She kicks off her soaked shoes, pulls her hair free from its clip, and goes to the kitchen. The clock on the microwave blinks 00:00. There's obviously been a power loss. She'll reset it later. When she turns toward the table, she freezes. There, in the center sits the compass. Her breath catches. The small disk gleams under the lamplight, lid open, needle trembling faintly but pointing north all the same. A faint smear of rainwater surrounds it, as if it had just been placed there.

Leah's throat goes dry. She took it off her keys as soon as Amber had arrived in town and put it in the drawer beside the table. She hadn't thought about it since. Now, her hand lifts toward it before she can stop herself. The metal is cold against her fingertips. She flips it shut and stares at the engraved back seeing the familiar, small, looping script. *Find your way back.*

Amber's voice echoes in memory, sweet and low: *So you'll always find your way back.*

Leah drops the compass into the drawer beside the table and slams it shut. The sound is too loud in the still cabin. Her pulse drums in her ears as she locks every window and checks the door chain.

It has to be coincidence. Maybe she unpacked it without remembering. Maybe it slid out of a box. Maybe she's exhausted enough to be losing track of what's real again.

By the time she sits down, her phone buzzes with a message from Tanya.

Power finally back. Still raining. Hope you made it home safe.

Leah types back slowly.

I did. Thanks. Longest shift ever.

Another buzz follows almost instantly.

You handled it like a pro. Amber's still here helping Jason with the servers. She's a machine.

Leah stares at the message until the words blur. She imagines Amber in that dim back room, standing close to Jason, head tilted just right, eyes half-shut in that calm, almost holy focus she wears like a second skin. She types a reply.

She's good under pressure.

But before she can send it, she deletes it. And types again.

That's great. She knows the system well.

She sends it and then puts the phone face down. Through the window, the rain keeps falling. The streetlights outside flicker, casting slow-moving shadows across the road. Her heart is still hammering, and her stomach feels uneasy. She tries to tell herself she's fine. That the compass means nothing. That Amber's words during the storm, *you're safe when I'm beside you*, were just habit, the same kind of comfort any operator might give after a hard shift. But her mind keeps circling the memory of the way Amber had looked at her when she said it. Her expression had been soft and certain, as if the whole room existed for their connection alone.

Leah stands abruptly, needing movement, needing sound, anything to distract her from these worries. She puts on music, low. It's some old acoustic playlist from her phone. The first song crackles before settling into gentle guitar chords. It helps, for a moment. The noise fills the apartment, and turns the silence into something human again. Until she hears another sound layered beneath it.

A faint tap. She turns off the music and the tap repeats its irregular pattern, like fingertips against glass. Her eyes flick to the window, but there's nothing out there but rain. Then she realizes the sound isn't coming from outside. It's coming from the desk drawer. Her stomach tightens and she steps forward slowly.

The tapping continues, soft and rhythmic, as if something inside the drawer is shifting. She hesitates, then pulls it open, leaning back in case it's some kind of creature trapped in there. The compass lies still. It's closed, but the needle twitches, vibrating faintly against the metal like it's alive. Leah slams the drawer shut again and the sound stops.

She backs away, hand pressed to her mouth.

"You're tired," she whispers. "You're overtired."

Her voice trembles. She grabs her phone, scrolling through contacts until she reaches Tanya's name, hovering her thumb over the call button.

Then she stops. What would she say? That she has a possessed compass in her drawer? That it somehow made its way out onto the table? That she's losing it, again?

She locks the screen and sets the phone down. The silence returns.

~

The next day, Leah arrives at work earlier than usual, still unsettled but determined to act like nothing's wrong. She's slept maybe three hours. The coffee she bought on the way in burns her throat, but its doing its job.

Amber is already there. Of course she is. She's at her console, humming softly, hair loose for once, giving her an almost girlish look. When she sees Leah, her face brightens.

"You made it through the storm," she says. "I was worried about you on those roads."

Leah forces a smile. "I'm fine."

Amber tilts her head. "You didn't reply last night."

"I fell asleep."

It's a lie. She'd seen Amber's message and left it unread. She doesn't want to encourage any further conversation with her.

"Good. You needed it." Amber's eyes flick to Leah's cup. "Too much coffee, though. It'll make you jittery."

Leah nods, pretending not to feel the small prickle of irritation. "Thanks for the tip."

Carla enters, clipboard under one arm.

"Morning, team. Good work yesterday. Regional command sent their thanks. Zero fatalities in our district, which is always a win."

Applause breaks across the room. Tanya whoops softly, Jason grins. Leah smiles, but her stomach knots. Amber looks at her over the console, that same measured calm back in place.

"We did well," she says quietly, like a shared secret.

Leah nods, trying to summon gratitude but feeling something else entirely.

By lunchtime, the day has settled back into its usual quiet routine. The team scatters to the canteen, all of them exhausted but lighter now that the crisis has passed. Leah joins Tanya at the corner table, stirring her soup absently.

"You sure you're okay?" Tanya asks. "You look frazzled."

Leah hesitates. "Yeah. Just tired. Storms always unsettle me."

"You look it. You should take a day off. Go to the spa. I can cover your calls."

Leah shakes her head. "Keeping busy helps."

"Amber told Carla how hard you always worked back in Phoenix." Tanya grins. "She's like your personal PR manager."

Leah forces a small laugh. "She's... dedicated."

"Yeah. Kind of intense, but in a good way."

Leah doesn't reply. She glances toward the water cooler, where Amber stands refilling her bottle, back turned, posture relaxed. Even from here, Leah can hear her humming again in that same soft pattern, rhythmic but somehow careful. Something inside her chest hitches. Tanya follows her gaze.

"She really looks up to you, you know. Says she learned everything from you."

Leah's spoon stills. "She's said that before."

"It's a compliment."

"Maybe." Leah keeps her eyes on the table. "Sometimes it feels like she's reminding me of something I forgot."

Tanya frowns slightly. "What do you mean?"

Leah shakes her head. "Never mind."

"Leah..."

"Really. It's nothing."

Tanya hesitates, then nods. "Okay. Just... Don't bottle everything up. We're all still getting to know each other here. But we can help each other through things."

Leah nods, grateful but detached. She can't explain the feeling that every gesture, every word Amber speaks, seems perfectly designed to blur the edge between gratitude and unease.

~

That night, Leah returns home later than usual. The rain stopped hours ago, but the air still smells like wet earth and electricity. She switches on the lamp, drops her bag, and walks straight to the table. The drawer is still closed. She hesitates, then pulls it open.

The compass sits exactly where she left it, still and quiet. She lifts it carefully and holds it in her palm. The metal feels warm now, as if it has been touched recently. She studies it for a long time before setting it down again.

As soon as she puts it down, her phone buzzes with a message from an unknown number.

Always find your way back.

Her heart lurches. She looks down to see the compass needle shift, pointing not north this time, but slightly left toward the window. She turns her head, pulse thudding.

Outside, across the road, stands a figure beneath a streetlight. The glow blurs the outline, and they're standing too far away to make out any features clearly. But the stance, the angle of the shoulders, the stillness all tells her it's Amber.

Leah blinks, and the figure is gone. The compass lies on the table, the needle trembling between directions. She drops it back in the drawer, closes it, turns off the lamp, and sits in the dark, staring out of the window.

She tells herself she's imagining it. That exhaustion makes ghosts of the living. But deep down, she knows better. The storm might have passed, but something else has settled in its wake. Something quiet, constant, patient as breath. And in the darkness, Leah swears she can still hear Amber's voice like a whisper threaded through the memory of thunder.

You're always safe when I'm beside you.

16

The sound wakes her before she knows she's awake. A scrape, faint and irregular, like metal brushing stone. Leah's eyes snap open. For a second, she can't place the sound. The cabin is dark, a light wind whispering through the trees outside. Then the sound comes again. It's a slow drag just outside the window, too close to be wind. She holds her breath, straining to listen. Another scrape, softer now. Then a thud, low and damp, like a shoe sinking into wet soil.

She sits up slowly, the sheet tangled around her legs. The clock reads 2:14 a.m. The power light on the router blinks, steady and green. She reaches for her phone, but the screen stays black. Her battery must be dead. For a moment, she sits perfectly still. The world beyond the window is all shadow and movement. The curtains shift in the draft, a subtle motion that makes her heart hammer harder.

Finally, she slides out of bed, bare feet soundless on the floor. She moves toward the window and peels the curtain back an inch. Beyond the cold glass, the faint outline of her balcony railing and the stretch of ground below, glistening with water. At first she sees nothing. Then her eyes adjust to the dark and she sees what might be footprints.

There are dark, heavy impressions in the soil beneath her balcony, too large and clean to be animal tracks. The mud is wet, reflecting the faint streetlight from across the road. Whoever made them came close. Right to the edge of her cabin. She swallows hard and listens again, but the only sound now is the steady drip from the eaves and the quiet wheeze of the refrigerator. The scraping has stopped.

Leah closes the curtain quickly, locking the window latch before stepping back. Her skin prickles with the sense of being watched, even though she can't see anyone. She forces herself to breathe. It's nothing, she tells herself. Someone cutting through the back path. A repair worker, maybe. But her heart won't slow down.

She pulls on her robe and walks through the cabin, checking the locks even though she knows they are all secure. In the kitchen, she stands for a long time, staring at the table where the compass lies shut in the drawer below. The thought of opening it feels unbearable, as if doing so will confirm something she doesn't want confirmed. Instead, she goes to the couch, curls up under a blanket, and dozes fitfully until dawn.

By morning, the footprints are still there. Leah stands on the porch with a mug of coffee warming her hands, looking down at them. There are five prints, deep and deliberate. Someone stood right beneath her window. The tread is clearly from heavy soled shoes, maybe boots. She feels a wave of nausea.

Later, at work, she can't stop replaying the sound in the night, the footprints, the certainty that someone had been there. The dispatch center hums around her with its normal efficiency. Tanya hums along to the radio in the corner, Jason complains about the printer. Everything feels ordinary, except Leah's pulse won't match the rhythm of the room.

Carla notices. "You're quiet this morning."

"Didn't sleep well again."

"Bumps in the night?"

"Something like that."

Amber passes behind them just then, her perfume faint and floral. She's carrying two coffees. She sets one beside Leah's desk.

"Extra strong," she says softly. "You look like you need it."

"Thanks." Leah forces a smile.

Amber lowers her voice. "You okay?"

"I think someone was outside my cabin last night."

She says it to watch for a reaction. Anything that will betray Amber. Her expression changes instantly, but it's sympathetic and serious.

"Did you call the police?"

"Not yet. They didn't do anything."

"You should tell them anyway." Her tone is gentle but firm. "And get cameras. Even a cheap one you can monitor on your phone. Just to be safe."

Just to be safe. The phrase hits Leah like déjà vu.

"I'll think about it."

Amber touches her shoulder lightly, then moves away to her own console. The touch lingers long after she's gone.

Leah calls the police after her shift. The operator transfers her to a local patrol officer who agrees to come by that afternoon.

When Officer Daniels arrives, he's polite but distracted. He's middle-aged, raincoat still damp, eyes flicking between his notepad and the muddy ground.

"Footprints, you said?"

"Right there." She points beneath the porch. The afternoon's rain has washed the edges away, but the deeper impressions still show. Daniels crouches down, shining a flashlight.

"No clear tread left. Could've been anyone passing through. Animals sometimes leave weird marks in soft soil."

"They were shoes," Leah insists. "Proper human footprints. I saw them before the rain."

He straightens, smiling the way people do when they think they're soothing you.

"There's no sign of attempted entry. No damage to the locks or windows. Probably nothing to worry about."

She crosses her arms. "Probably isn't good enough."

"I'll make a note in the system," he says, scribbling. "But without any actual act of harm, it's hard to take it further. Could be wildlife. Maybe a neighbor out late."

Leah exhales sharply. "At two in the morning?"

He shrugs. "You'd be surprised. We get all sorts of calls after dark. Shadows look like people. Floodlights distort things."

Her jaw tightens. "I know what I saw."

He gives her a sympathetic nod. "If you notice anything else, call us again. I'll mark it as a welfare check."

When he leaves, she stands in the doorway, anger and fear knotted together. She feels dismissed, like a nuisance.

～

At the dispatch center the next morning, Amber greets her with that same practiced concern.

"Everything okay with the police?"

Leah stiffens. "You were right. They think it was wildlife."

"That must be frustrating." Amber frowns, her expression softening in just the right way.

"It is."

Amber leans closer, voice low.

"You're doing the right thing. Just stay alert. People underestimate how vulnerable we are living alone."

Leah glances at her. "You sound like you've been through this."

Amber's smile is faint.

"You'd be surprised what people ignore until it's too late."

For a second, something in her tone chills Leah. It's too knowing, almost too calm. Then Amber straightens, cheerful again.

"Anyway, if you want, I can bring over one of my spare cameras. I used them back in Phoenix. They're easy to set up."

Leah hesitates. "That's... nice of you. But I'll buy my own."

Amber's eyes narrow briefly before she laughs it off.

"Of course. Just offering."

She walks away, humming under her breath. Leah stares after her, unease creeping up her spine.

That night, Leah returns home to find the cabin oddly silent. Even the trees are still and quiet. The air feels heavier, too, as though someone's been here and only just left. She tells herself she's imagining it. But still, she moves through the rooms slowly, scanning for anything out of place. Everything looks normal. Until she reaches the bedroom.

Her dresser top is the same as ever, except for one glaring absence. The framed photo of her and Sam. She freezes. The photo had sat there since she moved in, as a kind of reminder of all she'd left behind. Sam's arm around her shoulders, both of them smiling, sunlight behind them. Now, the photograph is gone.

She searches the drawers, the nightstand, even under the bed. Nothing. Just blank wood. Leah's heart pounds. She goes to the kitchen, scanning for any other missing items. The dish towel she left draped over the oven handle is folded neatly.

Did she do that? She didn't remember folding it. Her pulse rises.

She snatches her phone, opens the photo gallery, scrolling back to find the picture that had been in the missing frame. When she finds it, her breath catches, because now, even in the digital version, the image looks subtly altered. The background remains, and she looks the same, but Sam's face is darker, and blurred slightly. Her thumb hovers above the screen. She blinks, and looks again. But the image still looks different. As though Sam is fading from it.

It's the phone glitching, she tells herself. It has to be. But she can't shake the feeling that something, or someone, is rewriting the lines of her life.

~

By the next day, Leah's exhaustion has hollowed her out. She loses track of her thoughts, sentences trailing mid-conversation. Tanya notices first.

"You look wrecked," she says gently during break. "Are you not sleeping at all?"

Leah shakes her head. "Not really."

"You really should take time off."

"I can't. I need to be here."

Tanya frowns. "Amber said you've been jumpy lately."

Leah stiffens. "Amber said that?"

"Yeah. She's worried about you." Tanya hesitates. "She told Carla she might stop by your place, just to make sure you're okay."

A sharp pulse of panic hits Leah's stomach. "She what?"

"I think she means well."

Leah forces a smile that feels brittle. "She always means well."

She finishes her coffee quickly and goes back to her desk. The hum of the dispatch room feels louder than usual, almost mocking. Every few minutes, she catches Amber glancing over at her with soft, assessing looks that seem caring to everyone else but feel like surveillance to Leah. She tries to ignore it, focusing on the calls, but her headset hums faintly between connections. Once, she thinks she hears breathing on the line before the call even connects. Her fingers tremble on the keyboard.

When her shift finally ends, Leah walks to her car in the cold night air. The parking lot glistens from earlier rain. She unlocks her door, keys jangling, breath fogging the air.

Then she stops. Across the lot, under a streetlight, stands Amber. Her hands are in her pockets, her posture casual. The yellow light paints her face in soft relief, making her look calm, almost tender. When Leah meets her eyes, Amber smiles. Faint, but knowing.

Leah's breath catches. She blinks. Amber raises a hand, waves with her fingers, and disappears into the shadows until only the rain remains, whispering across the asphalt.

Leah slides into her car, locks the doors, and grips the steering wheel. She whispers to herself, voice trembling, "Stay calm. You're safe."

But she doesn't believe it. She sits in the car until the heater fogs the glass, hands locked on the wheel, eyes fixed on the empty space where Amber stood a moment ago. The lot looks ordinary again. The streetlight hums. A moth circles the glow, tapping it with frantic wings. Leah waits for the feeling to pass but it does not pass.

She drives home on autopilot, the dash clock ticking forward in steady minutes that feel off, as if time itself is shrugging.

Inside, she does what she always does when fear runs high. She locks the doors and windows, draws the curtains, and then she cleans. Dishes stacked right-side, counters wiped even though they are already clean. She empties the bin and takes the bag to the outside bin though it is only half full. She uses the chance to check around the cabin. There's nothing there.

Back in the cabin she pauses at the table drawer. The urge to check the compass rises like a trick in the throat. She does not open it. She turns the deadbolt twice on the front door and sits on the couch, pulling the blanket up around her.

Sleep comes late and thin. She wakes to gray light and a buzzing phone. The display shows 7:42. The oven clock, still flashing from the outage, insists it is perpetually midnight. She taps the screen to silence the alarm and drags herself up.

At the center, the morning feels too bright, fluorescent lights biting at her eyes. Tanya greets her with a muffin, holding it up like a trophy.

"You need sugar."

Leah thanks her, tears the top off, and tastes nothing. "Busy night?"

"Quiet," Tanya says, dropping into her chair. "False alarm at the lakes, couple of minor wrecks, a raccoon invasion. The usual."

Carla appears with a tablet. "Leah, quick word? My office."

Leah follows, heart slipping a beat. Carla closes the door and gestures to the chair.

"I know you filed that report about footprints. Officer Daniels logged a welfare check. He doesn't see cause for more."

Leah nods once. "He thought it was wildlife."

"Could be." Carla's voice is gentle. "I know how that sounds. I don't want you to feel dismissed."

"I did feel dismissed," Leah says, before she can choose a softer word.

Carla holds her gaze. "I also need you to know I take you

seriously. If anything else happens, call it in. Call me. Call 911. Use our chain. Don't navigate it alone."

Leah swallows. "Okay."

Carla hesitates. "There is one more thing. Amber mentioned she's concerned about you. Not in a report way. In a human way."

Leah's stomach hardens. "What did she say?"

"That you have been carrying a lot. That the storm week was hard. She asked if we could lighten your lead duties for a few shifts."

Leah keeps her hands flat on her knees. "Did you agree?"

"For two nights." Carla waits. "You look angry."

"I am tired," Leah says, honest and careful. "I do not need a chaperone."

"Not what this is," Carla says. "Think of it as a reset. You have earned it."

Leah nods once, because arguing will confirm a story she does not want told. She leaves the office with her face arranged in professional calm. Amber is at the coffee machine, pouring with one hand while scrolling her phone with the other. She looks up as if she has been waiting for this specific moment.

"Everything okay?" Amber asks.

"Fine," Leah says.

"Carla told me she's giving you a break," Amber says softly. "I am glad. You never stop."

Leah steps past her toward the sink. "I do not need you to speak for me."

Amber tilts her head, some small, pleased light passing through her eyes.

"Of course you don't. I was just looking out for you."

"Don't," Leah says, and hears the crack in her voice.

Amber lowers hers. "Leah, it scares me that you think the world is against you."

Leah puts the empty cup in the sink and returns to her station without answering. The headset goes on. The call board blinks. She becomes the voice people hear when they need to borrow a nervous system. It is the one place she can still trust herself.

Midmorning, the printer stutters and ejects a maintenance sheet that no one requested. Jason swears and yanks the tray. Someone brings doughnuts. The room settles into its practiced rhythm. Leah's phone, face down beside her keyboard, buzzes once. She ignores it. It buzzes again and again. Finally, during a lull, she looks. There are three messages, all from a withheld number. *Did you sleep last night? I worry when you don't answer. You could be safe and calm if you let me help.*

She deletes them and places the phone screen-down again. When she glances up, Amber is watching her with the expression other people would call concern. Leah recognizes the shape beneath it. Possession wears the mask of care better than anything else.

At lunch in the staff lounge, Tanya sits across from her, elbows on the table.

"Do not throw your yogurt at me," she says. "But I think you should actually let Amber set up one of her cameras. Temporarily. She has the gear. It would make you feel better."

Leah shakes her head. "No."

"She is offering for free."

"That is why I am saying no."

Tanya frowns. "You think she is trying to control you."

Leah chooses her words. "I think the line between support and control is where she lingers best."

Tanya leans back, chewing that. "I have not seen anything but her being useful."

"I know." Leah presses her thumb to the edge of her plastic spoon until it bows. "That is the problem."

The door swings open. Amber enters with two coffees balanced on a cardboard tray. She sets one beside Leah without being asked.

"Extra hot," she says. "It is cold in here."

Leah does not touch it. "Please stop."

Amber pauses, hand still near the cup, then draws back with a soft smile that says she is patient. That she can wait Leah out.

"You do not have to push me away to feel strong," she says. "We both know the work gets easier when we are together."

Tanya looks between them, confused at the static she can sense but not decode. Amber holds Leah's gaze one second too long, then walks out with her own cup, as if she is the one who has been wounded.

"See?" Tanya says quietly. "Trying."

Leah rubs her temple. "Very trying."

The afternoon settles into a quiet calm in the center, although Leah feels unsettled. She keeps losing track of small things. She sets her pens in a line and ends up with three when she had five. Her keycard is not in the pocket where it usually lives, then appears in her bag under the folded scarf she has not worn this week and doesn't remember putting in there. Twice, her calls drop mid-sentence, the dial tone cutting her off the moment she reaches a critical instruction. Jason blames the storm-spooked trunk. She nods, but her stomach refuses to obey logic.

On break, she calls Officer Daniels from the corridor outside the lockers. The phone rings six times before he answers.

"Daniels."

"This is Leah Hunter," she says. "From the cabin off Pine Ridge. We spoke about the footprints."

"Yes, ma'am. Any new developments?"

"A framed photo is missing from my bedroom dresser. No

sign of entry. And my phone is acting strange, I keep getting messages from a withheld number."

He exhales a long, practiced exhale. "That sounds like a couple of separate issues. There's not much I can do about the messages unless they're threatening. Are they?"

"Not exactly," Leah replies. "But they're unsettling."

"Would you like to report the theft of the uh... framed picture?"

"I'm not saying it's a theft," Leah says, heat rising in her face. "But it is intrusion. And targeting."

"I can dispatch a patrol for a courtesy visit," he says. "But we are limited in what we can do for you at this stage. If you have concerns for your immediate safety, call 911."

"I am 911," Leah says, too sharp.

Silence, then the softer tone he reserves for people on the edge. "Understood. Document everything. Photos, times. Have you considered installing cameras?"

She ends the call politely and leans her forehead against the cool wall tile. Behind her, the dispatch floor glows with that aquarium light, people moving in soft lines, all those lives crossing. She goes back in because she knows no other way to go.

~

Evening brings a lull that feels like a trick. The board clears of any calls and Carla calls the team to the rail for a five-minute debrief.

"Good discipline," she says. "Next week we start the winter storm table-top. Leah, you and Amber will co-lead."

Leah's mouth dries. "Carla," she begins, but Carla is already shifting to scheduling, her optimism a force field. Amber smiles as if this were a gift.

"We do our best work together," she says to the room, warm enough to be loved. Heads nod. The story is writing itself without Leah's permission. On the walk back to their stations, Amber falls into step at Leah's side.

"I am glad we have the table-top together," she says softly. "You and I can build something no one else can."

"Stop saying stuff like that. There is no 'we'," Leah answers, barely above a whisper.

Amber's smile does not change. "You are tired. You will feel better after sleep."

The last two hours grind real slow. A stranded motorist. A carbon monoxide alarm sounding an alert that turns out to be a dead battery. A caller who does not speak English who refuses translation and hangs up. Leah's headset hisses once like it wants to whisper something and she pulls it away, pulse spiking. When she puts it back on, her ears feel too warm, as if her own body is trying to step out of a sound it does not like.

At the end of the shift, she lingers at her console to avoid the corridor where goodbyes happen. Tanya pops by with a grin and a yawn.

"Text me if you can't sleep. Or if your raccoon comes back."

"I will," Leah says, not bothering to argue the raccoon.

Carla squeezes her shoulder as she passes.

"You did good today. Let the small things slide. They are not the real story."

Leah nods. She wants to say the small things are exactly the story. That is how this works. That is how you lose the room, the house, the mind. She says nothing. She waits until the last pair of footsteps fades and the room sits in afterglow. The building's hum recedes. She gathers her bag, finds the keycard where it should be, then frowns. The badge reel it's attached to is not the one she owns. The reel is identical but newer, the plastic not scuffed. Her name card sits behind the clear front exactly as she left it, but the clip turns smoother, and quieter. It's not hers. Her scalp prickles.

She looks around the empty floor and hears only the air handler. She swaps the reel for her spare from the locker and leaves the wrong one on the desk, face down.

The hallway smells like mop water and the exit door feels heavier than usual. Outside, the lot is three-quarters empty and wet, the asphalt shining with evening condensation. Her breath fogs as she walks. Tiny needles of cold find the thin skin at her wrists. She tells herself to focus on simple things. One step, then the next. A key in a hand. A lock in a door.

Her car unlocks with a soft chirp. She slides in and shuts the door. The quiet wraps around her hard enough to creak the air in her ears. She does not start the engine. She presses her palms to the wheel and rests her forehead there, eyes closed, counting to eight and back to four the way the therapist taught her. Somewhere beyond the glass a late bus sighs at the curb. Somewhere closer a night bird makes a sound like a hinge. She lifts her head, reaches for the ignition, and freezes.

Across the lot, under the far streetlight, Amber stands in a dark coat. The light holds her in a pale circle. She stands very still, hands at her sides, chin lifted. The distance is not far and somehow impossible. Leah knows the stance the way she knows her own hands. Leah's breath catches in the small space. She reaches to lock the doors out of reflex even though they are already locked. Her heart pounds hard enough to tighten the skin under her ribs.

Amber does not move. She is not threatening. She is not approaching, nor acknowledging. She is only there, present, the way a star is there even when you look away. Finally, she lifts one hand and the gesture is small, almost shy, a wave designed to read as kindness. Leah cannot tell how long they hold the tableau. Ten seconds. A minute. Time folds on itself, making a pocket around the light.

In the corner of Leah's eye, something flickers. She glances down. The small drawer in the center console has shifted open by a fraction, as if from a jolt. She reaches to push it closed and sees, tucked inside, the gleam of the compass charm. She did not bring it with her. She did not put it here. Yet it rests against the felt, cool and sure. She looks up again. The streetlight still glows but the space under it is empty now.

Her throat clicks when she swallows. She pulls the compass free with shaking fingers. The lid opens with its familiar soft pull. The needle floats, trembles, settles north, then tilts a degree right as if listening. She closes the lid and sets the compass on the passenger seat as if it were a sleeping creature she does not want to wake. She starts the engine. The radio sputters to a station she doesn't recognize, a woman speaking in a low voice about traffic on a road Leah does not drive. She turns it off. The heater blows and the windows clear to a cold transparency.

She drives home with both hands on the wheel, the compass shifting with each turn like a small animal adjusting for balance. At a red light she glances sideways and the lid has turned so that the engraved words face her. *Find your way back.*

She parks under her cabin's dead pine, carries the compass inside against her better judgment, and places it on the table where the drawer hides the emptiness she cannot fill. She locks the door, checks the chain, checks the windows.

In bed she lies on her side and watches the slice of light under the bedroom door. It does not change. A car passes outside and the headlights make a slow rectangle across the ceiling and go. She waits for sleep and gets a memory instead. Amber's face quiet and certain in the circle of light, the wave small and proprietary, the look you give something that you own.

Leah closes her eyes and whispers because it is the only thing that keeps her breath level.

"Stay calm." The words fall flat in the dark. She tries a different line. "You are safe now." The sentence tastes like metal. She swallows it and stares at the clock until the numbers stop sticking and start moving.

She will tell Carla again. She will make Officer Daniels come back. She will document every small thing. She will not be alone with this shape that keeps stepping into her sightlines and then out again, leaving only a scent and a smudge and a proof that refuses to hold still.

In the morning, she will find the photo of her and Sam not in the bedroom where it belongs but propped against the kettle, the glass wiped clean, the frame misaligned by a single crooked screw. In the afternoon, a call will drop just as she reaches the phrase that saves people. In the evening, Tanya will say she looks better and she will mean it, but Leah won't feel it.

Now, in the car-echo stillness of her apartment, Leah holds onto a single image of a streetlight, a circle, a smile that is almost tender, and the knowledge that tenderness and threat can wear the same face and the same coat and stand in the same spot and wave.

17

As Leah and Amber leave the dispatch center just after midnight, the air smells of ozone and wet asphalt, the rain a fine, steady mist that slicks the pavement and blurs the glow of the parking lot lights.

Leah pulls her jacket tighter. Her body fizzes with leftover adrenaline from the shift. They'd had three domestic disturbances, a chemical spill on the interstate, and a missing hiker found hypothermic but alive. The room had been a pressure cooker of static and fatigue. Now, out in the open, the silence feels disorienting.

Amber walks beside her, umbrella tilted to share the cover. The two women move in uneasy synchrony, steps echoing through puddles.

"We should go get something to eat," Amber says after a moment, her voice even and soft. "You barely touched your dinner at break."

Leah hesitates. She wants to go home, to the comfort of silence and routine. But she's too tired to argue, and the thought of sitting alone in her apartment makes her stomach twist.

"Fine. But let's go somewhere close."

Amber smiles, just barely. "There's a diner near the highway."

They get into Leah's car, Amber insisting she's fine riding passenger, even though her own sedan sits two rows away. The wipers beat a rhythmic pulse as Leah pulls out, headlights cutting through mist. The road curves north, following the dark outline of pine forest.

For several miles, neither of them speaks. The quiet between them feels almost truce-like. Leah can sense Amber's watchfulness, but tonight it's muted, almost companionable.

"You handled that domestic call well," Amber says finally. "The one with the kids hiding in the closet."

Leah nods, eyes on the road. "Thanks."

Amber tilts her head. "You're much calmer when it matters. It's what I learned from you."

Leah doesn't reply. She's learned that some compliments are traps, meant to soften you before the next cut.

They approach a junction where the rain thickens, fat drops hammering the windshield. Lightning flashes in the distance, illuminating the low clouds. Leah tightens her grip on the steering wheel.

Her phone buzzes in the console with an alert from the regional system. She glances at the screen. Emergency: vehicle rollover on Highway 89, mile marker 243. Possible entrapment. Multiple injuries.

Leah instinctively feels the pull, even though she's off duty. "That's close," she murmurs.

Amber leans in, scanning the location. "Two miles from here."

"They'll have units en route."

Amber's voice sharpens. "We're closer than anyone else."

Leah hesitates. It's not their job to respond in person. Dispatchers stay behind the lines, they're the voice, not the body. But her heart is already pounding in the old rhythm, the one that comes when a call turns critical.

Amber reads her hesitation and leans forward, calm but commanding.

"We can help to stabilize things until first responders arrive."

Leah exhales hard, fighting logic and instinct. "Right. Two miles."

Amber smiles faintly, satisfaction flickering in her eyes. "You drive. I'll guide."

They turn onto the narrow road leading toward the highway. The trees blur past, branches thrashing in the wind. The rain grows heavier, turning into the kind that swallows headlights. When they round the next bend, flashing hazard lights pierce the darkness. One car has stopped at an odd angle on the shoulder. Beyond it, an SUV lies upside down in the ditch, one headlight still burning into the sky.

Leah pulls onto the gravel verge, tires sliding slightly. The world narrows to light and rain and noise. She grabs her phone, calling the center. "Flagstaff Dispatch, this is Leah Hunter, off duty. I'm at the rollover on 89, mile 243. One vehicle overturned, visible entrapment, possible child involved. Request EMS and PD."

The line crackles, Tanya's voice cutting in. "Copy, Leah. Stay clear if it's unsafe."

Amber's door slams before Leah can answer. She's already running into the rain. Leah curses under her breath and follows. The mud grabs at her shoes, cold and slick. The overturned SUV groans as the wind pushes against it. Steam hisses from the radiator. Through the shattered passenger window, a woman's voice cuts through the storm, ragged and panicked.

"Help! My son! He's stuck."

Leah crouches beside the frame, trying to see inside. The woman's face is bloodied, eyes wide with shock.

"Ma'am, stay still," Leah says, her voice steady from years of training. "We've called for help. Paramedics are coming."

The woman sobs, clutching at the air. "He's in the back. Please..."

Amber appears on the other side, kneeling in the mud. "I can reach him."

"Wait," Leah starts, but Amber's already sliding through the broken rear window, her movements precise and unhurried. Leah steadies the woman, pressing a wadded scarf against a cut on her forehead.

"You're doing great," Leah murmurs. "Keep breathing for me, okay?"

The woman's hands shake. "I can't hear him..."

"That's a good thing," Leah reassures her.

Amber's voice comes from inside the car, calm and detached. "The boy's breathing. He's in the car seat. I need space."

Leah's hands tremble as she adjusts her grip on the scarf. The air smells of oil and rain. Sirens wail faintly in the distance, still miles out. Amber's face appears through the shattered glass.

"I need you to hold the seat steady while I cut the strap."

Leah nods, moving closer. The child whimpers, a thin sound that claws at her chest. Amber's hand moves in steady rhythm, voice low.

"It's okay, sweetheart. Stay calm."

Stay calm. The words echo. They always echo.

Leah's breath comes shallow as she steadies the car seat frame. Amber's eyes meet hers briefly, looking serene, in control, almost radiant. Leah feels something inside her constrict, but she's not sure if it's envy or dread or both.

The strap snaps free. Amber lifts the boy carefully, holding him against her chest. He's crying now, alive, terrified. Leah's relief is sharp and dizzying.

She turns to the mother. "He's okay. She's got him."

The woman sags forward, sobbing. "Thank God. Thank you."

Amber slides out of the wreck, kneeling in the mud, rocking the child. Her voice is almost tender. "You're safe now. You did so well."

Leah grabs her phone, still live to the dispatch center. "Tanya, update. We've got one adult female, one male child, conscious, was trapped, now freed. Vehicle stabilized. We need EMS, code three."

Static. Then Tanya's voice, faint and fractured. "Copy. Signal weak. Repeat..."

Leah adjusts her grip, water running down her wrist.

"Say again, center?" Nothing but hiss. Amber looks up.

"Give it to me."

Leah hesitates, then hands her the phone. Amber steps away, phone in hand and speaks, her tone perfectly modulated.

"Flagstaff Dispatch, this is an on-scene responder. Two patients stable but need immediate medical transport. EMS code 3. Coordinates sent. Confirm."

The response comes instantly, Tanya's tone brisk: "Copy, unit en route."

Amber lowers the phone, passing it back with a small smile.

"You must have been too far from the signal window."

Leah nods numbly, aware of the way her own hands shake. She feels like a spectator in her own skin, as though Amber has stepped into her role and worn it better. Headlights bloom against the rain. Two patrol cars pull up, followed by an ambulance. Officer Daniels climbs out, rain beading on his jacket. He spots Amber cradling the boy and strides over.

"You're a lifesaver," he says, voice full of genuine admiration.

Amber gives a modest shrug. "Just did what needed doing."

Leah stands beside the wreck, mud streaked up her jeans,

hair plastered to her forehead. The words she wants to speak knot in her throat. Daniels barely looks at her.

The EMTs move in, taking the child first, then the mother. Amber helps guide the stretcher, efficient and calm. Leah's heart hammers as she backs away, watching her own world invert as the one where she's always the voice of control, now turns to her watching someone else perform her part flawlessly.

When the ambulance doors close, Daniels claps Amber on the shoulder.

"You handled that like a pro. You in emergency medicine?"

Amber smiles. "Dispatch. But we do what we can."

Leah stares at the ground. The mud beneath her boots is slick and black, swallowing the rain. Daniels glances her way.

"You with her?"

Leah forces a nod. "Yes."

Amber looks over, eyes soft.

"Leah kept the mother conscious and calm," she says, her tone measured. "It helped."

It helped. Not you saved her. Not we did it. Just it helped. Leah nods once, throat dry. Daniels tips his hat.

"You two can head somewhere dry. We'll take it from here."

Amber thanks him, already walking back to the car. Leah follows, feeling weightless, disconnected from her own limbs. The rain has softened to drizzle, but the world still feels loud with the sirens, the chatter, the hiss of tires.

At the car, Amber wipes her hands on a towel, her movements calm, deliberate. She looks at Leah as the door slams shut.

"You froze," she says quietly. "It's okay. Not everyone can handle being inside the scene."

Leah stares at her, words failing. Amber's voice drops lower, almost kind.

"That's why people like me are needed."

Leah doesn't remember the drive home. One moment she's on the highway, wipers swiping the last of the rain from the windshield, the next she's outside her cabin, engine off, the world silent again.

Inside, everything looks the same. She sheds her wet jacket and sits on the sofa without turning on the lights. The quiet hums in her ears. Her phone buzzes on the table. Another withheld number. Her stomach twists as she opens it.

Good work tonight, hero.

Attached is a photo of her kneeling beside the injured woman, taken from behind, grainy but unmistakably her. Her breath catches. She looks toward the window. Outside, a siren wails somewhere far away, fading into nothing. She looks back at the phone just as the screen goes black. She doesn't wake it again. Instead, Leah sets the phone down, staring at her hands trembling. She whispers to the empty room, a barely audible "Stay calm."

But she cannot.

Dawn finally appears, thin as smoke. It creeps though Leah's window like an envoy of peace. She sits at the table, hands wrapped around a mug she has just refilled, staring at the compass beside her phone. The lid is open, the needle trembling faintly.

She hasn't slept. The image on her phone burns behind her eyelids whenever she blinks. The image of herself kneeling in the mud, the woman's blood staining her hands, Amber in the background framed by flashing lights. Whoever took the photo had stood close enough to touch her. But it wasn't Amber.

When her alarm buzzes for the morning shift, she kills it quickly. Her body feels heavy, detached. She showers without heat, dresses without thought. In the mirror, her reflection looks drained, colorless. The lack of sleep is really drawing the life out of her.

By the time she reaches the dispatch center, the rain has thickened into a cold mist that clings to her clothes. The fluorescent light inside stings her eyes. Tanya waves from her station.

"You okay? How was it being on scene last night? Mad, right?"

Leah blinks. "Yeah, it was intense."

"Can't believe you were first on scene. Carla said you and Amber were incredible."

Leah's stomach tightens. "She said that?"

"Yeah. The chief even mentioned it in briefing. Said it was crazy how calm you sounded under pressure." Tanya grins, proud. "That audio clip will be used for training. The way you called in the exact details, the update. Exactly what was needed."

Leah feels her throat close. "That was... Amber."

Tanya tilts her head. "No, it was your call. Your cadence. I took the call from you, remember?"

Leah can't breathe. Her mind flicks through fragments of last night: her shaking hands, Amber's steady tone, the way Daniels had thanked her like she was the only one who mattered.

"I need to check something," Leah murmurs.

She walks to her station, logs into the system, and pulls the file from the crash report. She clicks play. Amber's voice fills the headset, clear and calm.

"Flagstaff Dispatch, this is an on-scene responder. Two patients stable but need immediate medical transport. EMS code 3. Coordinates sent. Confirm."

Leah's own breath hitches at the sound. It isn't just similar. It's identical. The same pitch, the same intonation, even the same subtle catch at the end of each line. Tanya's right. It *is* her. Except she knows it isn't. Her hands shake as she removes the headset. Carla walks over, smiling warmly.

"I just wanted to thank you personally. What you did last night, that composure under pressure, that's the kind of leadership this department needs."

Leah opens her mouth, but nothing comes out. Amber passes behind them, setting a folder on Carla's desk.

"You're too kind. Leah kept her cool through all of it. She's a natural."

Carla laughs softly.

"You're both assets. Maybe we should run a joint crisis workshop."

Amber's smile flickers, polite and bright. "We'd love that."

Leah feels the ground tilt.

"Carla," she says quietly. "Can I speak to you? Alone?"

Carla nods and gestures toward her office.

Inside, Leah closes the door, lowering her voice. "That recording. It isn't me. The voice sounds like me, but it's not."

Carla frowns, confused. "What do you mean?"

"Amber took over the call. She was the one who asked for the support. But she made herself sound just like me."

Carla sighs, rubbing her temple. "It was a bad line. You and Amber do sound very different. What does it matter?"

"Yes, but..."

"She probably didn't mean anything by it," Carla interrupts gently. "You both handled yourselves beautifully. Don't overthink it."

Leah's chest tightens. "I'm not overthinking. It just feels like she's manipulating things."

Carla's tone softens further.

"Leah, I know you've been under strain. The last few weeks

have been difficult. Maybe it would help to take a couple of personal days. Get some distance."

Leah shakes her head. "You don't understand. She's doing this on purpose."

Carla leans forward. "I think you're tired. Go home. Rest. I'll handle the scheduling."

Leah leaves without another word. The air outside feels heavier, pressing down like water. She doesn't go home right away. Instead, she drives aimlessly through the city until she finds herself on the edge of town, the pines closing in on either side of the road. The rain has stopped, but the world still glistens, silver and wet.

Back at her cabin, a bird caws loudly from the trees as she slams her car door. The normalcy of it feels almost cruel. She unlocks the front door, flicks on the light, and freezes.

The framed photo of her and Sam is sitting perfectly centered on the table, the glass cleaned of dust. Her breath catches. She walks closer, afraid to touch it. The frame looks identical, but when she peers at the picture, something feels wrong. Sam's smile looks off, slightly blurred, as if someone had pressed a thumb against his face before the image set on the paper.

On the table beside it sits a folded piece of paper. She unfolds it with trembling hands. Typed words. No signature. *It's good to see you doing what you were meant for. You're safe now.*

The phrase sits like ice against her skin. Her knees nearly buckle. She stumbles toward the couch and sits, heart hammering. Her phone rings, startling her. She snatches it up.

"Hello?"

Static fills the line, then a faint voice, like a mechanical whisper threaded through white noise.

"Stay calm. Help is coming."

Her stomach drops. "Who is this?"

The static grows louder. The whisper repeats, identical in tone, like a recording of herself.

"Stay calm. Help is coming."

She ends the call and hurls the phone onto the table. Her whole body trembles. She crosses to the sofa, grabs the blanket, and settles down with it wrapped around her, gently muttering to herself that it will be okay, that's she is fine. You're safe.

Morning comes in shades of bright sunshine. Leah wakes on the couch, neck stiff, head pounding. She doesn't remember falling asleep. The note from last night lies folded neatly on the table, though she's certain she left it open.

Her phone buzzes with a message from Tanya.

Hey, we're debriefing the crash for the weekly highlight reel. Carla wants you and Amber there to narrate.

Leah stares at the words until they blur. Her hands move automatically, typing back.

I can't. Not today.

Three dots appear, then vanish. No reply. She sets the phone face down and presses her palms to her eyes. The room sways. Her mind replays Amber's line from the crash site. *You froze. That's why people like me are needed.*

The phrase keeps looping, fusing with the one from the message. *Help is coming.*

18

After two days of rest, which contained no rest, Leah steps back into the dispatch center with a sense of trepidation and relief in one. In the break room, the wall monitor in the corner runs a local news loop with the sound off. Closed captions crawl under a blurred clip of Highway Eighty Nine. The camera shakes, then steadies on the overturned SUV. The image cuts to a figure kneeling in the rain beside the wreck. The figure's head is bent. Hands are steady. The caption names her. Calm dispatcher turns hero.

Applause breaks and rises like a brief gust as the team notice Leah's arrival. Tanya whistles once, sharp and delighted. Jason taps his pen against the desk in a drumroll that refuses to end. Carla smiles in a way that makes her look younger. She says something about courage. She says something about composure under pressure. She nods toward Leah.

Leah pretends to busy herself with her monitor. Her mouth feels dry and her hands are too warm. She is grateful and she is embarrassed. She knows what the footage does not show. The trembling that lives just under control. The taste of metal in her mouth when the call seemed to have failed. The moment when everything narrowed to a single voice behind her, calmly organizing the help needed. And that voice did not belong to her.

Amber stands near the coffee machine with her cup held in both hands. Her smile is small and perfect. When Leah looks up, Amber steps forward and touches her elbow with two fingers. The gesture is intimate enough to read as support and light enough to pass as nothing.

"You looked so brave out there," Amber says.

Leah's answer is a careful thank you. The words sit at the back of her tongue. She cannot swallow them and she cannot spit them out. The monitor rolls the clip again. Calm dispatcher turns hero. The caption chooses a role for her and refuses to let go.

The room returns to work. Phones ring. Radios crackle. A printer coughs out a maintenance sheet and Jason curses under his breath. Carla moves through the stations with her usual unhurried efficiency. Tanya squeezes Leah's shoulder in a quick friendly grip and says something about cake and celebration. The normal rhythm tries to reassert itself.

Leah's phone buzzes once on the desk. She glances down. The caller ID startles her. Sam Reed. A text appears before she can decide whether to open it.

Saw you on the news. I am in town. Can we talk?

Her chest tightens. Months have passed since the last message. Last time she heard from him was before the cryptic messages, before the silent calls. Before the compass and the lilies and the long nights of hearing her own voice thrown back at her from an empty room while footsteps thud outside. Sam's name looks like something pulled out of another life and left in her current one by mistake.

She does not type. She just stares until the letters blur. The little bubble that signals a second message appears. Then vanishes. Then returns.

I should have said this a long time ago. I am sorry for how I left. I want to see you. Coffee. Ten minutes.

Amber is suddenly there again, not quite at Leah's shoulder and not quite away. She reads faces well. She reads screens too when people let their guard down. Her voice softens.

"You don't owe him anything," she says.

Leah keeps her eyes on the message.

"Maybe I owe myself closure," she replies.

Amber's mouth moves in a shape that could be a sympathetic smile and could be a frown. The shape resolves as a smile.

"Of course," she says. "Do what you need."

Leah looks down again. Her hands feel unfamiliar, as if they belong to a version of her who slept full nights and believed the future was a straight road. She types a short reply.

Okay. Downtown. At three?

For the rest of the shift Leah does the work like it is a path she knows by touch. She speaks the phrases she has spoken for years. She keeps pace with the room. She does not look at Amber. She does not look at the screen where the clip still loops every twenty minutes. She does not think about Sam until the clock reads two forty and Carla says to go already and stop pretending to be irreplaceable.

Outside, downtown Flagstaff wears late autumn like a coat. The air is cold and sweet. Sunlight slips across the brick storefronts and the bare branches that line the street. Leah chooses a small cafe that faces the square. Inside, the windows are clouded at the corners, and the smell of espresso and cinnamon feels like shelter.

Sam is already sitting there with his back to the wall. He stands when she enters and for a moment, she sees the shape of the man she loved before everything went wrong. Taller than she remembers. Paler than she remembers. Eyes a little older. He smiles and the smile tries to bridge the distance.

"You look good," he says. The words sound like a question he is afraid to ask.

"You too," Leah answers. It is not quite true, but she wants to be kind.

They sit. His hands fiddle with the mug in front of him. He clears his throat as if he rehearsed something and lost his place.

"I saw the footage," he says. "That's who you are. The calm in the storm."

Heat rises under her skin. She remembers the rain and the mud. Remembers Amber's voice cutting clean through the static when hers could not. She half smiles and cannot tell if it is visible.

"It was a team effort," she says.

He nods as if that proves his point. He keeps looking at her like he is trying to memorize new edges. He tells her he left Phoenix two months ago. He tells her the road trip brought him through Flagstaff by chance. He tells her he has been thinking about the way they split for so long that the thinking turned into a false apology he whispered to himself while brushing his teeth.

She listens. The coffee smells great. The café hums with small conversations and the distant grind of beans. For a few minutes she almost forgets why her heart is beating too fast. Sam asks after her work. She answers in careful terms. Then the conversation shifts toward the present and lands on the thing neither of them can avoid. Amber.

"She transferred," Leah says. "From Phoenix. She won't leave me alone."

Sam's eyes darken. He leans in. "She's obsessed. You need distance."

Leah lets the words sit. They look true and they look useless. She thinks of locks and cameras and the way authority smiles when it wants you to go home and sleep the crazy off. Distance is an idea that can exist in the same room as the person who refuses to give it. Distance is a word that loses meaning when the other person calls it devotion.

He reaches across the table but does not touch her hand. He stops short, as if he knows contact would turn the conversation into something it shouldn't become.

"Have dinner with me tonight," he says. "Just dinner. I'll leave after if that's what you want."

Leah looks into the dark surface of her cup. The desire for normal human attention feels like hunger after an illness. A small part of her wants to say yes because yes sounds like health, like refusing to let one person infect every corner of her life.

She nods. "Okay."

Relief softens his face. He laughs quietly, and the sound is the first unbroken thing in the room. He thanks her. He asks where. She suggests a place near her apartment. Somewhere with soft lighting and staff who know her face. He agrees. They settle on eight.

Leah relaxes into the shape of a plan that feels almost normal, until the bell over the café door rings and cold air slips inside. She doesn't turn immediately. She knows the shape of the moment by the way Sam's eyes shift over her shoulder. By the small tightening low in her stomach that fires whenever a certain perfume enters a room.

Amber stands at the counter. She orders tea with honey in a voice that could soothe pain, thanks the barista by name, because she always learns names, and turns with the cup in her hand. Her gaze lands on Leah as if the encounter were arranged for her benefit.

"Leah," she says warmly. Then, to Sam, "You must be Sam, right?"

Sam stands politely. They shake hands and he sits. Amber slips into the conversation as though she has been invited.

"It's good you reached out to her. Closure is something you can still give to those you've hurt."

Her tone is pure barbed grace. It is the tone of someone who has already positioned all the chairs so they angle toward her. Leah's pulse spikes. She wants to say *not here*. She wants to say *later*. She wants to say *leave*. Instead, she says, "We were just leaving."

He frowns, but quickly shapes it to a nod. He looks like a person who wants to show he understands. He takes a big swig of his drink and stands again.

"I'll just pop to the toilet," Leah says, as they make for the door.

Out front, Amber smiles at Sam as if they are old friends who have met by accident. They look almost casual, almost friendly, just the shadows of two people waiting for a third.

"...first snow came early this year," Amber is saying. She wraps both hands around her tea, lowers her voice. "Leah can be careless with herself when she's tired. I worry."

Sam's jaw tightens. "She doesn't need saving."

"Everyone needs saving from something," Amber replies softly. The conviction in the words is absolute.

Leah arrives beside them just as the sentence settles. Amber turns toward her like light turns to a mirror. She lifts her cup in a mock salute.

"I should get back to my shift," she says. Then she smiles at Sam. "Nice to meet you finally. I've heard so much."

The words are framed as courtesy, but they land as insult with a hint of possession. Sam frowns.

"Likewise," he mutters.

"Walk me to my car?" Leah says, linking his arm and turning him away from Amber's gaze.

They walk, leaving Amber standing in front of the café, a look of disdain on her face.

"Thank you," Sam says quietly as they walk. "For meeting me. For... trying."

Leah doesn't answer, she just squeezes his arm. Her head aches. Her thoughts keep sliding toward Amber without meaning to. They reach her car in the small pay lot a block away. Sam hesitates.

"You'll text me the address of the restaurant?"

"I will."

He gives a rueful smile. "Eight o'clock, then."

She nods. "Eight."

He squeezes her shoulder once, brief and harmless, then heads for his own car parked along the street. Leah unlocks her door and slides inside. She exhales, long and shaky, before starting the engine.

Sam strides towards his car and clicks the lock and climbs in. As he drives away, Amber stands in front of the café with her cup in her hand and watches the car turn at the end of the block. She drops the unfinished tea in the bin, wipes her hands and smiles.

"Help is on the way," she mutters.

Leah opens the door to the dispatch center and steps into the soft thrum that always steadies her. She retrieves a binder, prints two pages of notes, and sits at the spare console to type a clean summary for Carla. Her fingers move quickly recapping flood triggers, mutual aid timings, the three minute gap between the first call and the manual bridge. She writes until the words stop shaking in her hands. Tanya leans into the doorway with her scarf looped twice around her throat. Her cheeks are pink from the cold. She gives Leah a quick smile that slips toward worry.

"You good?"

"I will be once I've done this," Leah says.

Tanya nods. She pulls a rubber band from her wrist and ties her hair back without looking.

"We are doing the debrief next week instead. Carla said to tell you to go home as soon as you're done."

Leah glances at the clock. She thinks about the cafe, about the feel of early snow in the air, about Sam saying eight like it might belong to them both for one more night. She'd forgotten they were even meant to have a debrief. She closes her document and prints the last page.

"Only two more hours until home time," Tanya says cheerfully, as Leah settles at her own console and reaches for her headset. "You got any plans tonight?"

"Dinner with an old friend," Leah says, and feels the strange normality of it.

"Sounds lovely," Tanya smiles.

The line clicks open on a rush of air and tires.

"911," she says. "What's your emergency?"

A man answers, breathless, voice pitched too high. "Hi... hi, I'm on the eastbound... uh, it's the main road near the mall? Just past the last light?"

Leah's fingers find the map grid, cursor hovering. "Okay. Tell me exactly what you see."

"There was a car way up in front of me," he says. "It looks like it hit the slush and just spun. Did a full spin, I think. It went sideways into the snowbank, nose first. It's still there. I'm past it now. I couldn't stop."

On her screen the road lights up, a thin line cutting across the winter grid. Snow has been thickening for the last hour. She marks the approximate stretch.

"Are you still in motion?" she asks.

"Yeah. Yeah, I couldn't hit the brakes, I've got my kids in the car and there's someone right behind me. I slowed, I swear, but it's slick and..."

"You did the right thing by keeping control of your vehicle," Leah says. The line needs to hear that. "We'll get help to the crash site. I just need a little more information."

He sucks in a breath that clicks against the phone. "Okay."

"How many vehicles were involved?"

"Just one that I saw. A dark sedan? Maybe gray, maybe blue. It all looks the same right now. It skidded across both lanes and slammed into the snow on the shoulder. Not crazy fast but... it was hard. The front end crunched."

"Did you see if it was blocking traffic?"

"No, it's off to the side. In the ditch, kind of. People are still getting by. Slowing down, though."

She tags a single-vehicle collision, not blocking, potential injuries. Her cursor moves almost on its own.

"Did you see the driver?" she asks.

"Sort of," he says. "I mean, I saw someone in the driver's seat when it spun. And when I looked in my mirror after, there was already somebody at the car. On the driver's side."

Leah sits a little straighter. "Someone outside the vehicle?"

"Yeah. On the snow. On the driver's side. Looked like they were trying to get the door open."

"Okay." She adds a note: *bystander at scene.* "Can you tell if they were involved in the crash, or if they stopped to help?"

"I don't know. It happened fast. I just saw... a shape. Coat.

173

Maybe dark hair? They were right up against the car. Looked like they were trying to help, you know? Get to the driver."

He sounds like he's trying to convince himself. She hears that tone a lot.

"Do you see any other vehicles stopped?" she asks.

A pause. Wind. The rhythmic thump of wipers. He must be checking his mirrors.

"No. No, it looks like everyone's just... slowing down and going around. It's still coming down pretty hard here."

Leah glances at the storm radar in the corner of her screen. The band of snow over the city has turned a deeper shade. Roads are lit up with minor collisions, the little red pins accumulating like a rash on the area.

"Okay. So you're no longer on scene, correct?" She keeps the wording precise. Liability lives in imprecision.

"Right. I'm, uh... I'm maybe half a mile past now."

"Are you able to pull over somewhere safe and stay on the line?"

He hesitates. She can imagine the view through his windshield of the whitened road, two small faces in the back seat watching every decision he makes.

"I mean, I can pull into the gas station up ahead," he says. "But I don't think I can walk back. Not with the kids. And cars are sliding a little even at low speed. I don't want to cause another accident."

Leah nods, though he can't see it. "That's okay. I don't want you walking on the roadway in these conditions. Staying safe is important." The words are part of the script, but they are also true. She flags EMS and patrol for response, drops a pin on the approximate location.

"Do you remember anything else about the vehicle?" she asks. "Two-door? Four-door? Any damage you could see?"

"It was a four-door, I think. Mid-size. The front end hit the bank. The back might've lifted, just for a second. I saw the headlights go wild when it spun."

"Did you see airbags deployed?"

"I... I think so? There was a puff, like white, but that could've been snow. It all kind of exploded at once."

"That's okay," Leah says. "You're doing fine."

He blows out a shaky breath. She can almost see his grip shifting on the wheel.

"Did you see any flames? Smoke?"

"No. No fire. Just the car, and another person by the driver's door. They were leaning in." His voice thins. "I figured they'd call."

She types: *caller believes another witness on scene may be assisting driver.*

"Can you tell me what lane the car was in when it left the roadway?" she asks.

"Left lane," he says. "It fishtailed across into the oncoming side for a second, then spun back toward the shoulder on our side. Like the snow just... grabbed it."

She pictures the arc, the uncontrolled spin, the crunch. The way sound changes when something stops moving the way it's supposed to.

"Okay, I've got units on the way," she says. "They'll check the vehicle and anyone inside. You said you're heading to a gas station?"

"Yes. It's the first one after the light."

"Good. When you get there, I want you to park in a safe spot and stay with your kids. If an officer needs more information, they may call this number. Is that okay?"

"Yeah. Yeah, that's fine."

She hears a small voice in the background. A child, muffled, asking a question.

"Is that your child?" Leah asks.

"Yeah. My daughter. She saw it too." His voice sharpens. "She asked why we didn't stop."

It lands between them, heavy in the space the call occupies.

Leah takes a breath. "What did you tell her?"

"That it wasn't safe," he says. "That someone else was there. That we called instead. I don't know if she believes me."

Leah looks at the incident feed, at the cluster of minor crashes blooming with the storm. In training they talk about scene safety, about not becoming a second casualty. In reality, the line between caution and abandonment lives in the caller's chest.

"You did what you could from where you were," she says. "You let us know. That matters."

He's quiet for a moment. The wipers keep a steady beat.

"Will you... let me know if they're okay?" he asks.

She hates that part. "I don't have access to patient updates," she says gently. "But we're sending Fire and EMS. They'll be there as quickly as they can."

"Right," he says. "Right."

"Can you see any part of the crash site from where you are now?" she asks, a final check.

"No. I'm in the parking lot. It's just snow and taillights."

She enters the final notes, sets the call to close.

"Okay," she says. "You're safe where you are. You did the right thing calling us. Is there anything else you want to tell me about what you saw?"

He hesitates. She can almost hear him rewinding the moment in his head.

"The person at the door," he says. "I just keep seeing that. The way they were pressed up against the driver's side, like... like they were trying to pull it open."

"Could you see their face?" Leah asks.

"No. Just... a dark coat. Maybe gloves. They were close. Almost too close."

Her cursor hovers. *Too close* could mean anything. Panic. Urgency. Something else.

"Okay," she says. "I've noted a bystander at the vehicle. Responding units will check on everybody there. If you remember anything else later tonight, you can always call back."

"Yeah," he says. "Okay. Thank you."

"Drive carefully," she says. "Goodnight."

The line clicks off. The call logs itself into the system, one pin among many on the storm map.

Leah pulls her headset away from one ear and listens to the room. Tanya laughs softly at something Bree says in the next row. A printer coughs out a run of paper. Somewhere a chair squeaks as someone shifts their weight. Outside, the snow thickens against the glass.

On her screen, the incident line retreats into the queue. Single-vehicle collision, unknown injuries, units en route. Ordinary words for what could be anything. She thinks of the child in the back seat asking why they didn't stop. Thinks of the man's voice catching on the image of a stranger leaning into a driver's side door. People don't stop for a hundred reasons, whether that's kids, weather, fear of doing the wrong thing. They stop for a hundred reasons too. She has heard them all: *I didn't want them to be alone. I couldn't just drive past. I thought someone else would call.*

She wonders, briefly, if the person at the car will call in. Most do. They want someone to witness their witnessing.

"Everything okay?" Tanya asks, swiveling half around, headset pushed down around her neck.

"Traffic spin-out," Leah says. "Units on the way."

Tanya grimaces. "Snow's chewing people up tonight."

Leah nods, but her mind is still stuck on the phrase *too close*.

She pictures a dark figure at a car door in the snow, pressed in against the glass. Helping or hurting? From this distance, from this room, it all looks the same.

She clears the call from her active screen and opens the next available line.

When the shift ends, she grabs her coat and heads for the door before anyone else can speak to her. At the lobby she stops to text Sam the address for the restaurant. She adds:

Just popping home to change. Be there by eight.

The message hangs in the pale blue of the screen before it shows as sent. She pockets the phone and pushes through the door.

Snow is falling now in heavy flurries. It softens the edges of the parked cars and lays a white film on the blacktop. Leah crosses the street with her head slightly bent. The lot is nearly empty. Cold air works its way under her coat and up her sleeves. She rubs her arms once and starts toward her car.

Leah opens her car door and slides in. The engine catches. Warm air begins to move and the windshield clears in a slow arc. When she looks back, the streetlight hums over a patch of wet pavement. She's half-expecting to see Amber there, but tonight the halo of light stands empty.

She pulls into traffic and turns toward home to change before dinner. By the time she reaches her cabin the snow has begun to stick. She parks and climbs the steps with the feeling that the world is rearranging itself half a second before she arrives at each place.

19

The restaurant smells of garlic, basil, and rain-soaked coats. Candles flicker along the narrow line of tables, catching in half-filled wine glasses and throwing small halos against the walls. Leah sits near the window, where condensation fogs the glass and turns the street outside into a blur of gold and gray.

The waiter brings water. She thanks him and folds the napkin in her lap, smoothing its edges over and over to still her hands. A violin track hums through hidden speakers, soft and careful. Around her, couples talk in low voices that swell and break against one another like overlapping tides. She glances at the door each time it opens.

The hostess greets new arrivals with a smile too bright for this muted hour. Leah's eyes flick automatically toward them, expecting to see Sam, with his familiar height, rough coat, his hand lifting in a small wave of apology for being a few minutes late. But each time it's someone else. A young couple with snow melting in their hair. Two women in wool coats laughing over an inside joke. An older man taking a table for one.

The candle beside her flickers, then steadies. She checks the time again. Ten minutes past eight.

She rereads the last message on her phone. *Be there by eight.*

It sits there, clean and final, the way things always do before they stop meaning what they once meant. Outside, the rain begins again, light and uneven. It streaks down the window in thin rivulets, catching the neon reflection from the sign across the street. Leah traces one finger along the condensation and watches it break the reflected color into fragments.

Twenty minutes pass. The waitress checks in gently. "Would you like a drink while you wait?"

Leah smiles the way she's learned to, both polite and practiced.

"I'll wait a little longer."

The waitress nods and moves away. The sound of conversation swells. Laughter bursts from a nearby table, sharp and sudden, and Leah's body tenses before she can stop it. The sound merges in her mind with another noise. The echo of static through a headset, the rise and fall of panic, the cadence of voices she can't see. She forces herself to focus on her hands, on the simple act of breathing. Thirty minutes now. She types another message.

Everything okay?

It delivers instantly. The small gray ticks beside the words sits like a held breath. But they don't turn to blue. She locks her phone and places it beside the candle. The flame dances across its black surface, like a flicker of false life. The waiter approaches again, hesitant.

"Would you like me to start your order?"

She shakes her head. "I'll give it a few more minutes."

He nods, expression soft with sympathy, and moves toward the bar. Leah exhales. The air feels thick, and far too warm. Her chair creaks when she leans back. Time stretches. The laughter from other tables grows unbearable, like a wave of sound that feels directed at her, though she knows it isn't. She wishes she could mute the room, silence it like an open line after a call ends.

The door opens again. The bell above it chimes, a bright metallic note that cuts through the hum. Leah looks up, and her heart sinks. Amber stands at the entrance, coat damp from the rain, hair pulled into a loose knot that drips faintly against the collar. She scans the room with that deliberate calm she wears like armor. Then she steps toward the counter.

"Takeaway for Klein," she says brightly.

Leah's stomach drops. Amber turns, and their eyes meet. Her expression shifts instantly as the poised neutrality melts into concern. She crosses the room before Leah can look away.

"Leah? You okay?"

Leah forces a small smile. Her throat feels tight.

"Sam was supposed to meet me. He's running late."

Amber glances at the empty table, her brow creasing in what looks like genuine sympathy. "That's awful. Do you want company? I've ordered a takeout, but I'm sure they'll let me eat in."

"Oh, no, it's fine..."

But Amber is already signaling to the waiter. "Can I eat mine here, please? And get a menu for my friend. She's been stood up." She says it as if the decision has already been made.

The waiter smiles, nodding. "Of course."

Leah hesitates, caught between resistance and exhaustion.

"You really don't have to."

Amber sits opposite her with easy confidence, shrugging off her coat. "I know. But nobody should eat alone."

The menu arrives. Leah stares at hers without reading. Amber glances at her. "You always order something simple, don't you? Let me guess. Spaghetti arrabbiata?"

Leah blinks. "How would you know that?"

Amber laughs. "You told me it was your favorite back in Phoenix. I remember because you said you liked the heat."

Leah manages another smile. "Right."

They order pasta and a glass of red wine each. The waiter departs, leaving them cocooned in soft candlelight.

Amber rests her elbows on the table, chin balanced on her hand.

"You were so good with that mother on the highway, by the way. I know I already said it, but you were. Watching you work reminded me why I wanted to do this job."

Leah looks down at her glass. "I keep replaying it. The sounds, her face, her panic for the kid."

"That's normal," Amber says gently. "You absorb everyone's pain. It's what makes you so good. But it's also what makes you fragile."

Leah frowns. "Fragile?"

Amber's tone softens further. "You care too much. People like you always get hurt."

Leah studies her reflection in the wine, faint and red. Checks her watch, and then checks the door again.

"Maybe something happened to him," she says quietly. "Sam wouldn't just not turn up."

Amber tilts her head. "Maybe he got cold feet again. If he cared, he'd be here. Or at least call."

Leah flinches as though the words have touched something raw. She lifts the glass and takes a sip to hide her face. The wine burns slightly at the back of her throat.

"I keep thinking I should call the hospitals," Leah murmurs.

Amber reaches across the table, fingers brushing Leah's wrist. "Leah. Listen to me. You've done enough chasing people who don't stay."

Leah freezes. Amber's hand lingers for a beat too long, warm against her skin. Then she withdraws and sits back, her expression closed.

"You don't need anyone who disappears when things get hard," Amber says softly. "You need someone who stays."

Leah exhales slowly. The wine has blurred the edges of her thoughts, turned them soft and pliable.

"You shouldn't have stayed," she murmurs. "You should've let me eat alone."

Amber smiles faintly, her voice barely above a whisper. "I'll never do that."

The words sit between them like a promise and a warning.

Dinner arrives. The scent of garlic and tomato fills the air. They eat in silence for a few minutes, the clatter of cutlery blending with the muted laughter from nearby tables. Leah forces herself to swallow, though every bite tastes of dust.

Amber keeps the conversation light with stories from the dispatch center, harmless gossip, small compliments about Leah's calmness under pressure. It's soothing in a strange, artificial way, like a lullaby hummed in a dark room. Leah finds herself responding, nodding, almost laughing once. The sound feels foreign coming from her mouth.

Halfway through the meal, Amber reaches for the wine bottle and refills Leah's glass without asking.

"You need to stop punishing yourself," she says gently. "Sam has obviously chosen to walk away again. That isn't on you."

Leah stares at the tablecloth, tracing the red ring her glass has left.

"It's just not like him. He wouldn't just walk away without a message or a call. Something's wrong."

Amber's eyes soften. "If something was wrong, surely we'd know by now."

Leah opens her mouth to argue but closes it again. The logic is too simple, too final. They finish eating. The waiter clears the plates, leaving the candle burning low and steady. Amber insists on paying, sliding her card across before Leah can reach for her purse.

"My treat," she says. "You've had a rubbish night."

Leah protests weakly. "You really don't have to."

"I want to." Amber signs the receipt with a practiced flick of the wrist. "Consider it a celebration. You're still standing after everything."

The phrase lands heavily. Leah nods, unsure what to say.

Outside, the rain has stopped. The air smells of wet pavement and pine. The streetlights cast thin halos on the road. Amber falls into step beside her as they walk toward the parking lot.

"I'll walk you to your car," Amber says.

Leah shakes her head. "You don't need to."

Amber smiles. "I want to. Text me when you get home, okay?"

Leah doesn't answer. She's too tired to argue anymore. At her car, Amber pauses.

"Promise me," she says softly. "You'll text."

Leah nods once, unlocking the door. The small sound of the latch clicks like punctuation.

"I will."

Amber steps back. "Good. And get some sleep."

Leah slides into the driver's seat, the engine coughing to life. Amber stands just outside the glow of the streetlight, hands clasped loosely, watching. Her figure is a dark outline against the damp brick of the restaurant wall. For a moment, Leah feels grateful for the company, for the silence that followed. Then guilt rises, sharp and sudden. Sam should have been here.

She pulls away slowly, headlights sweeping across the lot. In the rear-view mirror, Amber doesn't move until the car rounds the corner and the restaurant disappears from sight.

At home, the cabin feels cold. Leah hangs up her coat and stands in the middle of the room, waiting for her mind to catch up with her body. She shivers, upping the thermostat to boost the heating. She sits on the sofa, phone still in her hand. The wine's warmth fades quickly, leaving her hollow and heavy.

She opens her messages, but there are no new texts. The thread with Sam sits frozen at her last unread message: *Everything okay?* She's pretty sure everything is not okay. She types another message, then deletes it. There's nothing left to say that doesn't sound like pleading.

Suddenly, the phone vibrates in her hand. She startles. Finally, a message. But it's not from Sam. It's from Amber.

You're home safe now. Get some sleep.

Leah stares at the screen. The words blur slightly as her eyes sting. She reads them again. You're safe now. The same phrase Amber used on frightened callers, on panicked victims, on her. She sets the phone face down on the coffee table. The soft glow fades. The silence returns.

Outside, a siren wails in the distance, rising and falling until it's swallowed by the night. Leah lies back on the sofa, eyes fixed on the ceiling. The shadows ripple faintly as car lights pass outside. She closes her eyes. The wine, the warmth, the exhaustion all blur together.

For a moment, she imagines Sam walking through the restaurant door, smiling, and apologizing for being late. Then the image fades, replaced by the memory of Amber's voice.

You don't need people who disappear when things get hard.

The phrase loops softly in her mind, soothing and terrible. When she finally drifts toward sleep, her dreams are a troubled mess of memories of Sam from better times, and that awful feeling of betrayal creeping over her now.

20

The morning after the first heavy snowstorm arrives bright and brittle. Light catches on every surface from the branches of the pines to the handrail on Leah's porch, turning Leah's cabin clearing into something sharp-edged and clean, as if the night has erased all imperfections and replaced them with silence.

She stands on her porch a moment, inhaling the cold. Snow blankets the ground in an unbroken sheet, except for the narrow trail she uses for running. It winds behind the cabin into the trees, a path she hasn't taken in weeks.

She starts down it now, her breath lifting in pale ribbons. The snow crunches beneath her shoes, rhythmic and crisp. Running feels unfamiliar at first, and her muscles are slow to remember the pattern, but the movement brings its own quiet relief. Each step cuts a clean print into the surface. Each inhale burns a little. The forest is stripped down to essentials, thick trunks, shadows, and light.

For the first time in a long while, she senses a margin opening around her thoughts. Not peace, but enough space to breathe. The trail bends toward a stream that runs half-frozen under a lattice of ice. Leah slows there, letting her heart settle.

Snow has drifted against fallen logs, smoothing their edges. Deer prints pockmark the far bank. A squirrel darts across the trail, tail flicking, the only thing in the whole landscape that seems in a hurry.

She wipes sweat from her forehead, letting her breath even out. Then her eye catches something out of place. Across the pristine sweep of snow, cutting parallel to her own path, runs a set of footprints, deep, deliberate, a single pair, each step spaced with calm precision. They lead from the direction of the road, move across the trail, and disappear into the trees behind her cabin. Leah stares at them.

Every print is sharply defined. No melt, no drift softening the edges. Whoever made them walked through sometime after the snow stopped in the early hours, and not too long before she came outside.

A pulse of cold works its way up her spine. She crouches beside one of the prints, brushing the air just above the impression. The depth suggests a full adult weight. Not a jogger. Not a hiker. The direction, heading toward her cabin rather than away, knots her stomach. She straightens and scans the trees.

Nothing moves. There's no sound except the groan of distant branches releasing last night's ice. She tells herself the obvious explanation. There was someone walking the trails after the storm, maybe curious, maybe lost. Footprints mean only that a person passed through. But the trail behind her cabin isn't well known. It's not marked. Only locals use it. And even the locals stay home after the first real snow. She knows this. Everyone knows this. Her neck prickles.

She starts back toward the cabin at a faster pace, breath tightening, heartbeat thudding against her ribs. The snow seems louder under her shoes, each crack pushing her forward. By the time she reaches her porch, her hands are trembling with adrenaline. She fiddles her key into the lock, and freezes. The cabin door isn't fully shut. But she definitely locked it before leaving for her run.

She listens. Hears nothing but the steady hush of the forest. Leah pushes the door open with the back of her knuckles, bracing herself. The hinges creak in a sound she usually finds comforting but today scrapes at her nerves. The interior looks normal at first glance. The wood stove cold but neat. Curtains half drawn. Dishes clean and stacked. But the space feels... misaligned. As if someone moved through it with careful purpose, touching nothing but leaving something behind.

She steps inside, every sense sharpened. The floor shows no obvious sign of footprints from outside. No shed snow, no drops of melted ice. Whoever entered was careful. The first wrong thing is in the lounge. The blanket she'd draped over the arm of the couch is now neatly folded on the seat of the sofa.

She moves to the bedroom. The mirror on her dresser has been tilted a fraction to the right. Enough that her reflection cuts off mid-shoulder. The bedspread is creased as though someone sat there. Did she sit there to pull her running shoes on? She doesn't think so.

And on her dresser, the framed photo of her and Sam that she turned face down last night, now stands upright again, but now it faces the wall. Her breath shivers. She doesn't touch anything.

She moves to the table in the lounge, opens the drawer where she'd left the compass, and sees what she already guessed would be. The compass is gone. Someone took it. She steps backward until her shoulder meets the doorframe. Her phone feels clumsy in her shaking hands.

Officer Daniels arrives twenty minutes later, the crunch of his boots on snow sounding louder than necessary. His patrol SUV idles beside the cabin, steam rising from the exhaust in thick pulses. He stands in the doorway, hands on his belt, taking in the room with a practiced, detached calm.

"You're sure you didn't leave it this way?" he asks.

Leah's voice comes out sharper than she intends.

"Do I look like someone who doesn't know how I leave my own house?"

He raises both palms. "Just covering the basics."

"There was someone here. They moved things, and they took something."

Daniels surveys the cabin again. "You said there's no sign of forced entry?"

"No."

"No broken lock. No pry marks."

"No. See for yourself."

He checks the front door jamb, taps the lock with his pencil and scratches a note in his pad, then shifts into the neutral voice of someone already sliding the complaint into an unimportant category.

"Could be someone has a copy of the key. Previous tenant. Ex. Neighbor. Hard to say."

"It wasn't a neighbor," she snaps.

He gives her a slow nod, the kind meant to look respectful but feels dismissive.

"Alright. I'll file it as unlawful entry, but without evidence of any harm, there's not much else we can do."

Leah clenches her jaw. "You said that last time."

He clears his throat. "Well... you might consider some deterrents. A security camera. Motion lights. Even a dog. Sometimes that's all it takes."

She stares. "A dog."

"Just a suggestion," he says mildly. He hands her the clipboard with the half-filled report. "Sign here. We'll keep it on file."

Leah signs without reading. Daniels thanks her and steps back into the cold, offering the same hollow reassurance as always.

"We'll keep an eye on things."

The door closes. Silence settles over the cabin, deeper and colder than before. Leah turns slowly, taking in the folded blanket, the tilted mirror, the inward-facing photo, the empty drawer. Every detail has her shape in it. Her gaze drifts to the window above the sink. Outside, the surface of the snow is flawless except for the one thin trail of footprints leading from the woods to her porch. She should have mentioned those to Daniels. It wouldn't have made a difference. She exhales, steadying herself.

She'll install a security system tonight. Cameras, alarms, motion sensors, all of it. She'll line this place with teeth. Whatever crossed her threshold last night won't do it unnoticed again. Not ever.

At the dispatch center, the buzz of conversation washes over her like static. She moves through it mechanically, headset on, voice calm, tone perfect. The rhythm of routine steadies her hands, even when her mind drifts back to the rearranged objects waiting at home.

During her break, she spots Amber standing near the vending machine with Tanya. They're laughing softly, heads tilted toward each other. Tanya's laughter sounds uncertain, like it's performing for the sake of harmony. Leah starts walking toward them and Amber's voice drops mid-sentence. Tanya glances up, her smile faltering.

"Hey," Leah says carefully.

Tanya straightens. "We were just talking about... uh... the training schedule."

Amber smiles. "Tanya was telling me she might switch shifts."

Leah looks from one to the other. Tanya's eyes flick away.

"Yeah. Maybe," Tanya says quietly.

Leah can hear the distance in her tone. The same tone people use when they're trying to stay neutral in a story they don't fully understand.

Amber checks her watch. "Anyway, we should get back."

Leah watches her walk away. Tanya lingers a moment, then gives a small apologetic shrug before following. The silence that follows hums like feedback through Leah's headset.

Evening falls with another flurry of snow. The parking lot outside the dispatch building glistens where ice crusts the previous day's fall. Leah pulls her coat tighter and heads for her car, relief washing over her at the thought of being home. But as she nears her vehicle, she stops dead. Amber stands beside the driver's side door, hand resting lightly on the handle.

Leah's keys rattle in her hand.

"What are you doing?"

Amber startles and steps back, laughing nervously. "Oh! I thought it was mine."

Leah looks past her to the next row. Amber's sedan sits there, unmistakable, clean, silver, the same decal on the rear window. Leah's mouth is dry.

"Yours is over there."

Amber follows her gaze, then smiles. "Wow. You're right. Long day, I guess."

The explanation hangs between them like a fragile web. Leah frowns, her pulse hammering in her throat. "Please don't touch my car again."

Amber's smile doesn't waver.

"Of course. I'm sorry. I was just distracted."

She turns and walks toward her own vehicle, unhurried, posture graceful. Leah watches her until the engine starts and the taillights fade into the dusk. Only then does she get in her own car, locking the doors the instant they close. Her hands shake as she grips the steering wheel.

By the time she gets home, her nerves feel shredded. The drive up the mountain road had felt longer than usual, every bend a place her thoughts could tighten. She parks beneath the pines, breath held without realising it, and steps out into the brittle cold.

A man is standing on her porch.

He's bent over the side window, gloved hands working at something near the frame. For a split-second Leah's vision tunnels. The tilt of his shoulders, the way he braces himself against the siding, all of it too close to the silhouette that has lived behind her eyes for days.

"Hey!" Her voice cracks the air. "Step away from the house!"

The man startles, turning with both hands raised. He's in his late forties, maybe early fifties, bundled against the cold, tool belt visible under his jacket.

"Whoa, whoa, easy," he says quickly. "Leah Hunter?"

She stops halfway up the path, pulse thudding against her ribs. "Who are you?"

"Security install," he says, tapping the badge clipped to his coat. "Marcus Gray. You booked the emergency slot this morning."

It takes her a breath or two to remember the call. The urgent voice she'd used. The immediate opening he'd offered. Her shoulders sag as the adrenaline drains.

"I'm sorry," she says, exhaling shakily. "I... just had a break-in."

"No apology needed." Marcus steps down one porch step,

still giving her space. "Judging by your reaction, you really do need this system."

A thin, embarrassed laugh slips out of her. "Yeah. Apparently, I do."

He waves her forward. "Come on. I've already mounted the sensors. Just need you to install the app so I can sync things."

Inside, the cabin feels smaller with a stranger in it, but Marcus moves with the easy calm of someone who's done this a hundred times. He hands her a printed card with a QR code.

"Scan that. It'll pull the app straight up."

Leah does. Her phone vibrates as the download begins.

"Once it opens," Marcus says, gesturing to her screen. "Hit 'Pair System.' You'll see each unit pop up. You've got a door sensor, window sensor, back latch, motion unit in the hallway. You can name them however you like."

Icons appear one by one. She taps, confirms, taps again. The system chirps quietly from the porch.

"You'll get alerts for any activity," he says. "Even if it's just the wind rattling something loose. And you can activate the live camera feed here..." He touches her screen lightly, guiding her to the button. A small loading circle spins. The porch comes into view. Clear. Empty.

Leah swallows. "Good."

Marcus nods, satisfied. "You're set. Full control from your phone. If anyone so much as breathes near this place, you'll know."

He gathers his tools and zips his jacket. "I'll leave you to settle in. If you need anything adjusted, just call the number on the card."

She walks him to the door, the cold air rushing in again.

"Thank you," she says softly.

He gives her a kind, worn smile. "Stay safe out here, alright?"

"I will," she says, though she's not sure she believes it.

When his truck crunches down the snowy road and disappears between the trees, Leah locks the new deadbolt, checks the app, and only then does she let herself breathe.

～

The next morning she wakes to the buzz of her phone. An alert from the new security app. Motion detected at 2:43 a.m. Her pulse spikes. She opens the app and scrolls through the captured images. The first few are empty frames, with no more than shifting shadows, and passing headlights. Then one stops her breath. A still frame from the camera above her window. A figure stands outside in the snow. Hooded and motionless.

The timestamp matches the minute she woke in the night from what she thought was a dream of someone whispering her name. Her fingers tremble as she zooms in. The face is obscured by the hood, but the outline, the slope of the shoulders and the tilt of the head is unmistakable. She's sure it's Amber.

Leah's chest tightens until it hurts to breathe. She dials the police. Officer Daniels returns by afternoon, boots leaving a scatter of melted snow by her doorway. His expression is patient and rehearsed, the look of someone preparing to deliver bad news very gently. Leah hands him her phone without a word. The still image fills the screen of a figure below her window, half-turned toward the camera. Hood up. Shoulder-length hair catching faint silver. The outline of someone who should not be there. Daniels studies it a little longer, squinting as he zooms in. Then he exhales.

"Hard to make out," he says. "Low-light cameras do that. Could be anyone."

Leah feels her pulse spike. "It's not anyone. Look at the hair. Look at the build. It's Amber."

He doesn't even write the name down. "Could also be a neighbor. Delivery driver. Someone lost."

"She was outside my window at two in the morning." Leah's voice frays. "She wasn't delivering anything."

Daniels closes his notebook, which feels like a door shutting. "Look, I get that you're scared. And I'm not saying nothing happened. I'm saying I can't ID a suspect from a motion-trigger still."

"You *can*," she insists. "You just won't."

He sighs through his nose. "What I have is an image of a person near your cabin. Not breaking in, not damaging property, not attempting entry. That isn't a criminal offence."

Leah sighs, frustrated. "She's stalking me."

"Maybe," Daniels says, keeping his tone level. "But unless she threatens you, or you get a clearer shot of her trespassing, all I can do is note the concern."

"No crime until she kills me, right?" The words come before she can stop them.

His lip curls. "Don't say that."

"It's true."

"It's not helpful," he says. "Look. You've done the right thing getting cameras up. We can increase patrol presence on your road for a few days. But if you're feeling unsafe, you should think about staying somewhere else. Or maybe seeing if there's a family member, a friend, someone who can be here with you."

Leah's stomach knots. "I don't have family nearby."

"A friend then," Daniels says. "Someone you trust."

The absurdity of it hits like a blow. The *only* person who has tried to insert herself into Leah's life that way is the same person she's terrified of. Daniels misses the shift in her expression. He taps the top of the clipboard.

"You've got my card. Call if she shows up again, or if the camera catches a clearer image."

"She *did* show up again," Leah whispers. "You're looking at it."

He softens, but only in the way tired people soften.

"I know you're shaken. Try to get some rest. Stress can make patterns look more dangerous than they are."

That sentence lodges in her ribs like a splinter. He leaves with a professional nod, boots crunching through the snow as he crosses the clearing. His SUV reverses down the drive until the lights vanish into the trees.

Leah stands in the doorway long after he's gone, cold air moving around her legs. The clearing is white, silent, impossibly still. The porch camera, new, bright, and unblinking, reflects faintly in the window beside her.

By evening, she sits on the couch with the lights off. Outside, the snow glows blue under the cabin's motion light. The forest crowds close, a wall of shadow and breath. She holds her phone in both hands. The security app rests under her thumb. Every few minutes she opens it, checks the live feed, checks all of the angles.

In the dark bedroom, she sets her phone on the nightstand where she can grab it in a single movement. When she finally lies down, the silence feels weighted, as though something is pressing its ear to the walls, listening back.

Somewhere outside, a car engine hums faintly... then cuts off. Leah holds her breath. A soft sound follows A whisper of movement against glass. Trees in the wind, she tells herself. But she doesn't believe it. Not tonight. She reaches for her phone again. It won't hurt to check the cameras one more time.

21

Snow covers the parking lot in thin, patchy layers, glinting under the pale morning sun. The wind carries a bitter chill that cuts through even Leah's thick coat as she hurries across the tarmac toward the dispatch building. Her breath comes out in short, visible bursts. She is late.

Her badge trembles in her hand as she scans in. The door releases with a faint click, and the warm air inside rushes against her frozen cheeks. The control room is alive with low conversation and electronic noise. The same rhythm that once steadied her, now seems too loud, and too sharp. Screens glow across the long rows of desks. Tanya glances up briefly, then back down, her greeting cautious. Carla's voice cuts through the din.

"Leah, can I see you a moment?"

Leah turns. Carla stands near her office door, arms folded, expression carefully neutral.

"Of course," Leah says, voice flat.

Carla gestures for her to follow. Leah hangs her coat on the back of her chair, eyes scanning the room. Amber sits two rows over, headset off, chatting quietly with Tanya. When Leah's gaze meets hers, Amber smiles a soft, warm, almost apologetic smile. Leah looks away without returning it.

Inside the office, Carla closes the door and gestures to the chair opposite her desk. The blinds are half drawn, the morning light slanting across a stack of papers. The scent of coffee fills the room.

"Leah," Carla begins, "I know you've had a difficult few weeks. I just wanted to check in."

Leah forces a smile. "I'm fine. Just tired."

Carla nods slowly. "I understand. But we've had a few... concerns raised."

Leah's stomach tightens. "Concerns?"

"Some of your coworkers have noticed changes in your behavior. You've seemed distracted. Upset. Apparently, you were heard crying in the break room after shift."

"That's not true," Leah stops, realizing how defensive she sounds. "I just needed a minute. It was a long night."

Carla folds her hands on the desk. "It's not about one incident. There's a pattern. People are worried."

Leah stares at her. "People?"

"Amber came to me first," Carla says gently. "She said she's been trying to support you, but she's concerned you're under too much strain."

Leah lets out a hollow laugh. "Of course she came to you first."

Carla sighs. "She cares about you. We all do."

Leah's voice sharpens. "No, she doesn't. She's been doing this on purpose. Turning everyone against me. Rearranging things in my apartment. Following me."

Carla's expression shifts to sympathy. It's that pitying look Leah has come to hate.

"Leah, there's no evidence of that. Officer Daniels said they couldn't substantiate anything."

Leah stands abruptly. "You think I'm making it up?"

"I think you need rest," Carla says quietly. "That's why HR asked to speak with you. This isn't a disciplinary. It's a wellness meeting."

Leah laughs again, brittle and sharp. "A wellness meeting?"

"Please, Leah," Carla says, standing too. "They just want to talk. For your own good."

Leah hesitates, pulse hammering. Then, knowing it's pointless to argue, she nods.

The HR office smells of printer toner and coffee gone cold. Mr. Hinton, the HR officer, sits at the head of the table, glasses perched low on his nose. Carla sits to his left, arms crossed loosely. Amber is already there. Her hair is neatly pinned, uniform immaculate. She offers Leah a small, nervous smile as Leah enters.

"Hey. I'm glad you came."

Leah stops at the threshold. "I didn't have any choice, since you've obviously told them I'm not fit for duty."

Amber's smile falters. "That's not fair. I just said I was worried about you. You've been through so much."

Hinton gestures toward the chair. "Leah, please, sit down. This isn't an interrogation. We're just checking in on your wellbeing."

Leah sits, stiff-backed. Her hands rest in her lap, knuckles white. Hinton opens a folder.

"We've received several reports of erratic behavior, late arrivals, emotional distress during shifts, an altercation in the parking lot last week."

Leah cuts in. "That wasn't an altercation. Amber was trying to get into my car." She turns to Amber. "Tell them what you've done. What you've been doing."

Amber looks at her with wide, glistening eyes. "Leah, I haven't done anything. I've tried to be there for you."

"You've been in my cabin."

Amber's voice drops to a whisper, full of gentle concern. "I think you really believe that. But I swear, I haven't."

Leah's throat tightens. "You stole my compass."

Carla exchanges a look with Hinton. "Compass?"

"It was a gift. It's gone."

Amber leans forward slightly. "It was a gift from me. Why would I take it back? Maybe you misplaced it. You've had a lot on your mind."

Leah slams her palm against the table. "Stop talking like that!"

The sound echoes. The room stills. Amber flinches back, eyes watering.

"I'm sorry," she murmurs. "I didn't mean to upset you."

Leah stares at her, breathing hard. The image of the woman standing outside her window in the security footage flashes in her mind. She knows it was Amber. She knows it. But the way everyone in this room looks at her, pitying, careful, and afraid, makes her doubt even that.

Mr. Hinton clears his throat. "Leah, we're not here to judge. We just want to help you find support. Maybe some time off, maybe professional counselling?"

"I don't need counselling," she snaps. "I need you to believe me."

"Believing you means what, exactly?" Hinton asks gently.

"That she's dangerous."

Amber's voice breaks. "I'm not dangerous. I'm trying to help you."

Leah pushes back from the table, chair scraping hard against the floor. "You're lying."

Carla stands. "Leah, please. Sit down."

Leah looks around the table. Three faces. Three pairs of eyes that no longer see her as capable, rational, or trustworthy. Amber leans forward, her tone measured.

"She's been struggling for a while. Even back in Phoenix, it was getting to her."

Leah rounds on her. "You wanted this. You wanted to break me."

Amber shakes her head. "That isn't true."

Carla moves between them. "Let's all sit down."

Leah remains standing.

"She's been following me. She was outside my apartment. I have pictures."

Hinton speaks calmly, the practiced voice of a man who has handled breakdowns before.

"We've reviewed your previous reports to the police, Leah. The evidence was inconclusive."

Leah laughs once, short and bitter. "Inconclusive. Of course."

Amber's voice softens. "I just want you to get help. We all do."

Leah's vision tunnels. The room tilts slightly, sound fading to a low hum. Carla's hand is on her arm, steady but firm.

"Leah," she says, "you're not in trouble. But you need rest. We're placing you on medical leave, effective immediately."

Leah pulls her arm free. "You can't do that."

"It's for your safety."

Amber steps closer, voice trembling just enough to sound sincere. "I'll sign as your workplace contact, okay? So, if you need anything, I can..."

"Don't you dare."

Amber's expression folds into sorrow. "Someone has to make sure you're alright."

Leah stares at her. For a moment, she cannot tell whether the tears in Amber's eyes are real or just part of the performance. Mr. Hinton slides a form across the table.

"You'll need to attend a psychiatric evaluation before you can return to work. Standard procedure."

Leah stares at the paper. Her name sits at the top in black print, next to the words Employee Mental Health Review. Her signature trembles as she scrawls it. She doesn't even know why she signs. Perhaps to end the moment. Perhaps because fighting seems pointless. When she looks up again, Amber is watching her with quiet triumph hidden behind sympathy.

Carla drives her home. The ride is silent. Leah sits in the passenger seat, staring out the window at the blur of pine trees and snowbanks. Her reflection in the glass looks too pale, almost transparent. At one point Carla tries to speak. "You'll feel better after a few days. I've seen people come back stronger."

Leah doesn't respond. When they reach her cabin, Carla hesitates.

"Do you want me to come in?"

Leah shakes her head. "No. Thank you."

Carla nods and leaves. Leah watches her car disappear down the road before climbing the steps.

Inside, the cabin feels dark and confined. She closes the door and locks it. She walks room to room checking every window twice. She shuts the blinds, switches the light on, and crosses to the table where her laptop glows softly, screen saver flickering. She stares at it for several seconds before moving. She unplugs the power cable. The light dies instantly. She places the laptop in the drawer, and disconnects the router, the blue lights fading to nothing.

Then she slides down the wall until she is sitting on the floor, knees pulled to her chest. She presses her palms against her ears, trying to block the sound of her thoughts. For a moment it works. Then another sound creeps in. It's the faint hum of an engine outside. She holds her breath. The sound is steady, low, distant. A car idling somewhere near the curb.

She crawls toward the window and peeks through a narrow gap in the blinds. A silver sedan sits beneath the streetlamp. Headlights off. The outline of a figure in the driver's seat, motionless. Leah's breath fogs the glass. She can't see the face, but she doesn't need to. She lets the blinds fall back into place. The sound of the engine continues, soft and patient.

She slides to the floor again, pulling the blanket from the sofa around her shoulders. Her body shakes. She presses her hand against her chest, trying to feel her own heartbeat, to remind herself she is still here, still real. Her eyes sting, tears slipping silently down her face.

Outside, the car finally shifts into gear. The engine fades. But Leah keeps listening long after the sound is gone. She imagines footsteps on the porch, circling slow and deliberate. But she doesn't move to check. She's too tired.

22

The light in Leah's cabin is dim, filtered through half-closed blinds. She sits cross-legged on the floor, the rug buried under papers, printed messages, and scribbled notes. A map of northern Arizona spreads before her, its creases torn from overuse. Yellow highlighter traces the roads between the café and the small Italian restaurant where she was supposed to meet Sam. Each loop of ink is frantic, layered, as if circling could force the truth to appear.

She stares at the map for a long time before picking up a pen. Her handwriting shakes as she writes another note in the corner. Sam's car: blue Toyota. Route 180. Seen last?

Her phone buzzes once beside her. Not a message but a notification reminder for her therapy appointment. She swipes it away. The silence returns, heavy and absolute.

She has left ten voicemails since Monday. All the same. *Sam, please call me. Just tell me you're okay.*

She has texted more times than she can count. *Where are you? Did something happen? You said eight. I was there. You could just text. Tell me you're alive.* But every message remains unread.

She even tried calling his office, the number he once gave

her for emergencies. The automated voice had been cold, detached. "This line is no longer in service."

Her search history is a blur of phrases like missing adult Arizona, road accidents Flagstaff, unidentified male found. Each link leads nowhere. No mention of Sam. No trace. The lack of answers feels like proof of something darker.

By Thursday evening, her reflection in the dark window looks like a stranger's. Her eyes are hollow, her skin dull under the lamplight. The world has narrowed to a single, unbearable question. *Where is he?*

Friday morning, she dials the non-emergency police number. Her thumb hesitates before pressing Call. The line clicks, then a familiar voice answers.

"Flagstaff PD, Officer Daniels."

Leah's throat tightens. "It's Leah Hunter. We've spoken before."

There's a pause, then a professional but weary tone. "What can I do for you, Ms. Hunter?"

"It's my boyfriend. Ex-boyfriend. Sam. I think he's missing."

"When did you last see him?"

"Almost a week ago."

"You've reported this already?"

"No. Not yet. I thought he'd get in touch, but it's been almost a week."

Daniels sighs softly. "He's an ex, you say? Maybe he just needs space."

"Not like this," she says quickly. "He wouldn't just disappear. He was supposed to meet me for dinner. He never showed."

"Did you argue?"

"No."

"Have you checked with family or friends?"

"He doesn't have family here. I've called everyone I can think of. His phone's off. His car's gone."

Daniels' tone remains even. "It's only been a few days. People go off-grid sometimes. He might just need a break."

Leah presses the phone tighter to her ear. "You don't understand. He wouldn't do this to me."

He exhales, the sound full of patience that borders on pity. "You'll have to come in and file an official missing person report. Until then, there's not much we can do."

"But what if..."

The call disconnects.

She stares at the phone, frozen. Her voice comes out as a whisper. "What if he's gone?"

The next few days dissolve into repetition. Leah refreshes missing person databases, scrolling through lists of names, faces, and case numbers. None of them are Sam. She calls local hospitals. "No, ma'am, no one by that name." She checks every news bulletin. No accidents on the main highways. No unidentified victims. Each absence of information becomes another confirmation that something is wrong.

The cabin grows colder. The blinds stay drawn. Sleep comes in bursts. Sometimes she dreams she is back in the restaurant, candles flickering, Sam walking through the door with that crooked smile. She wakes each time imagining the sound of her phone buzzing, but there is never a message.

At the dispatch center, Tanya looks across at the empty seat before her shift starts. Leah's desk remains untouched, the headset neatly coiled, mug turned outward just as she always left it. She unlocks her own station, glancing around.

"Anyone heard from Leah?"

Amber, seated a few rows down, looks up briefly. "We're not supposed to contact her while she's on medical leave."

Tanya frowns. "I thought she was supposed to come back this week."

Amber shrugs lightly. "Maybe she's not ready."

But the faint crease between her brows betrays something else that looks to Tanya more like control, than concern. During lunch, Tanya sends a text.

You okay? Do you need anything?

Hours pass before Leah replies.

Sam is gone. I know she knows something.

Tanya stares at the message, her thumb hovering over the screen. The word 'she' makes her stomach drop. Does Leah mean Amber? She's been so adamant that Amber is trying to hurt her. Across the room, Amber is speaking to Carla in low tones, voice too soft to hear. When Tanya looks at her, Amber smiles, with that same effortless warmth she always has. Tanya forces a nod and turns away. She types a reply to Leah.

Ask her outright, then. It's the only way.

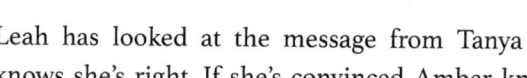

Leah has looked at the message from Tanya for hours. She knows she's right. If she's convinced Amber knows something, she'll have to confront her. Worrying about Sam is driving her closer to the brink of madness with every passing hour. She calls Amber that evening. The first call rings through to voicemail. She tries again. And again.

Each time, Amber's recorded voice plays, her voice sounding calm, professional, and perfectly polite.

"Hi, this is Amber Klein. Leave a message and I'll get back to you."

Leah's own voice sounds strange as she speaks.

"If you've heard from him, tell me. Please."

The next message is sharper.

"I know you're ignoring me. I know you know what's happened to him."

No reply.

When they finally cross paths outside the dispatch center two days later, the winter sun hangs low behind the clouds, the air brittle with cold. Leah steps into Amber's path before she can reach her car.

"Why won't you answer me?"

Amber's posture remains composed. "Because you're scaring people, Leah."

"I'm trying to find Sam."

Amber's expression softens just enough to look sincere. "Go home. You're not thinking clearly. Don't make me press charges for harassment."

Then she turns and walks away, shoes crunching on the snow. Leah stands there, numb, her breath forming white clouds that vanish too quickly.

That night, Leah drives aimlessly through the outskirts of town, headlights cutting through flurries of snow. She checks every parking lot, every layby, every roadside motel. On a loop past the old grocery store, she sees a blue Toyota parked under a flickering streetlight. Her stomach flips. She pulls over, heart hammering, and steps out into the cold. The snow crunches under her boots as she approaches. The car is the same make, the same model, even the same small dent on the front bumper. Around the back, though, is evidence of another accident. More serious, sure, and probably means the car's undrivable, but not enough to harm the driver.

She presses a hand to the glass and peers inside. It's empty inside. No jacket on the seat. No coffee cup in the holder. She whispers to herself, "Something's happened." Her voice catches. "She knows." The words hang in the air like frost. She scribbles a note, telling Sam to call her if he comes back to pick up his car, tucks it under the wiper, and leaves.

Two more days pass. She calls the police again. Daniels is curt this time. "We've noted your concern, Ms. Hunter. Still no record of an accident or missing person by that name."

"His car is in the lot at the grocery store. It's been in an accident."

"And yet, we have no record of an accident. There was one out on the main drag a while ago, but when patrols got there, the car was gone. We can assume it was his, and that it was fine to drive, and that he was unhurt, or he would have reported to hospital. Like I said before. He's an Ex. Maybe just give him some space."

"You're not looking."

"Ma'am, we've checked databases across the state."

"What about Amber Klein?"

"What about her?"

Leah grips the phone so tightly her knuckles whiten. "She's involved. She knows where he is."

Daniels sighs. "Do you have any proof to go with that allegation?"

Her silence is enough of an answer.

"Call again if you have new information," he says before hanging up.

The tone beeps long and final. Leah lowers the phone slowly. Her fingers tremble. She turns toward the map still spread across the floor. The roads blur together under the light. She circles another stretch of highway, pressing the pen too hard, the paper tearing beneath the ink. The room is silent except for the scratching sound of the pen.

She picks up her phone and calls Sam again, even though she knows he will not answer. His voicemail plays. "Hey, it's Sam. Leave a message." She listens to the sound of his voice until the recording ends. Then she presses redial. And again. And again. Her eyes burn, tears blurring her vision of the map beside her. Every road is circled now, a web of desperate ink connecting nowhere to nowhere.

She sits in the center of it all, phone still pressed to her ear, listening to the ghost of a voice that will never answer.

23

Leah wakes unsure of the time. The cabin is dark, the blinds and curtains still closed. For a moment she lies still, eyes half-open, adjusting. Her body feels heavy, as if she has been asleep for days. She pushes herself upright, twists the blinds open a crack and blinks against the weak light filtering through. Every movement feels slow, deliberate, like she is underwater.

When she finally stands, she notices a note slid under the door. She crosses the room and slowly reaches for it, picking it up and unfolding it with trembling fingers.

I thought you could use some supplies and a little pick me up. A.

Amber The sound that escapes her is half laugh, half sob.

She steps backward until she bumps into the table, her knees giving slightly. She drops the note on the table, staggers forward and unlocks the door, throwing it open, half-expecting Amber to be standing there, waiting for her.

On the doorstep sits a canvas tote bag, and a carboard box stacked with groceries. She bends to pick up the box, and carries it inside. There are tins of soup and beans. A bottle of wine. Fresh bread. Ceral and milk.

She returns to the door for the canvas tote. Inside is a new notebook, a paperback novel about forgiveness, and another note on clean stationery. *For when you can think again.* The handwriting is small and rounded. Familiar.

She sets the bag down carefully and looks toward the porch camera fixed above the door. The small red light that usually blinks once every few seconds is dark. She calls the security firm, who promise to send an engineer.

The next few days blur into one another. Leah no longer opens her curtains. The outside world feels like a set of eyes pressed to the glass. Tanya's messages pile up unanswered.

You okay? Call me. Please. I'm worried.

Leah reads them all, but doesn't reply. She can't. There's nothing to say.

At night she moves through the apartment like a ghost, lights off, listening. The air smells faintly of lilies. The same scent that clings to Amber's uniform. But she's sure she's imagining it. Sometimes she swears she hears a car outside, an engine idling low. But when she looks, the street is empty.

Two days later, another package arrives. A smaller box this time, left beside the mat. Inside is loose tea, vitamins, another loaf of bread. No note. The smell of the bread makes her stomach twist. She hurls the box across the room. The sound of glass jars breaking fills the kitchen.

Later, she picks up the loaf, tears off a slice, and eats it standing in the dark. The taste is soft, almost sweet. She cries as she swallows, crumbs sticking to her lips.

"Stop helping me," she whispers into the dark.

Her voice echoes faintly off the cupboards.

Amber sits in her car, diagonally across the road from Leah's cabin. Snowflakes cling to her windshield, catching in the wipers before sliding away. She's parked beneath a tree, engine idling, the heater humming faintly. The dashboard light casts her face in a pale glow. Her eyes are fixed on Leah's window. Amber smiles faintly.

She leans her head back against the seat, closing her eyes, and the memory begins to replay, uninvited, as it always does.

She's in a run-down house on the outskirts of Albuquerque. Paint peeling from the walls, the roof sagging. A rusted car in the yard. Inside, the sickly, familiar smell of sour milk and cigarettes. A woman lies passed out on the couch, one arm dangling toward the carpet. A younger Amber, maybe eight years old, kneels beside her, scooping spilled cereal back into a bowl with trembling fingers.

Her voice is small. "It's okay, Mom. I'll fix it."

The television mutters in the background. A baby cries somewhere down the hall. Amber sets the bowl on the counter and wipes her hands on her shirt. She moves to the bedroom, where her little brother sits on the floor surrounded by scattered blocks.

"Shh," she whispers, gathering him into her arms. "It's okay. Don't wake her."

Later, when the knock at the door comes, loud and official, Amber hides in the closet, clutching her brother's toy truck. Through the crack in the door, she watches the man in uniform kneel and speak gently to the boy.

Her brother's voice is high and scared. "Where's Amber?"

She stays quiet, pressing her hand over her mouth. When the door closes and the car drives away, she crawls out, the toy truck still in her hand. The house is silent except for the ticking clock on the wall. From that day, she repeats the same words over and over to herself, the rhythm like prayer. If I keep things calm, no one gets hurt.

Now, in the present, Amber sits in her car watching Leah's window.

"She needs order," she murmurs. Her voice is calm, as if speaking to an invisible operator. "Structure. Someone to keep her safe." Her fingers drum softly on the steering wheel. "I know what happens when chaos wins."

She thinks of the dispatch floor, and the clean lines of screens, the steady hum of calm under pressure. It is the only world that has ever made sense to her. And Leah was its voice. The one who made everything quiet.

Amber glances up again. Leah's silhouette passes behind the curtain. She smiles. Almost there.

Inside, Leah documents everything. Every movement, every object. She takes photos of her cupboards, notes the exact position of the mugs. Each time she opens a drawer, she writes it down When she wakes in the night, she checks her notebook, flipping pages to remind herself that she isn't imagining it. But the act of writing it down makes her feel even less sure.

The notes multiply. December 18, 3:17 a.m. — smell of perfume near door. December 19, 5:40 p.m. — curtain moved slightly to the left. December 20 — another parcel on the porch. The records make her feel trapped inside her own evidence.

That evening, there's a knock at the door. The sound is gentle but deliberate. Leah freezes halfway across the room. No one ever knocks. She waits, holding her breath. After a long moment, she opens the door a few inches.

A plastic grocery bag sits on the mat, snow dusting its handles. Inside is soap, cereal, and a small, wrapped candle. Her hands tremble as she pulls it out. A note is folded beneath it, printed neatly on the same white paper as before.

You're doing so well.

Leah crumples it in her fist. She sinks to the floor, back against the door, the candle rolling from her lap onto the carpet. Her shoulders shake. The tears come fast, unstoppable. She wants to scream, to tear the cabin apart until she finds proof that she is not losing her mind. But her body won't move. She stares at the crumpled note in her hand.

∿

Outside, Amber's car idles in the snow. She can see Leah sitting on the floor, motionless. Amber's breath fogs the glass. She smiles faintly.

"Almost there," she whispers.

The snow thickens, covering the road, the parked cars, the footprints that led to Leah's door. Amber reaches forward, turns off the headlights, and lets the darkness close around her. The hum of the engine fades into the quiet, leaving only the sound of falling snow.

24

Leah sits on the floor, knees drawn up to her chest, surrounded by unopened parcels, half-filled notebooks, and the ever-growing pile of papers about Sam. The words blur together in a list of dates, times, names, but she can't stop reading them.

Thunder cracks overhead, close enough to shake the glass. The lights flicker, casting the room into momentary darkness before stabilizing again. And another flash of lightning illuminates the room, bleaching everything white.

Then comes the knock. It's faint at first, almost lost to the storm. Then it comes again, louder and more deliberate. Leah freezes. The air feels charged and heavy, and not just from the storm. She waits, holding her breath, hoping whoever it is will go away. But it comes once more, three short raps, measured and certain.

Her body moves before her mind catches up. Barefoot, she crosses the cold floor and presses her eye to the peephole. Amber stands outside. Rain streams down her face, her hair plastered to her cheeks. She clutches a bottle of red wine against her chest like an offering.

Leah's pulse quickens. She doesn't open the door. Amber leans closer, her voice muffled through the wood.

"I just want to talk."

Leah stays silent.

"Please, Leah. You must be exhausted."

Leah closes her eyes. She should tell her to leave. She should call someone. Tanya, the police, anyone. But her phone lies somewhere under the mess of papers, and even if she found it, what would she say? A colleague from work is knocking on my door with a bottle of wine in her hands? She knows where that will get her.

A longer silence stretches between them. Then Amber speaks again, her voice softer.

"I brought dinner."

Leah exhales slowly. Against all reason, against every instinct, she unlatches the door. Amber steps inside, snow shedding from her boots. The air fills instantly with her scent of lilies and laundry, something clean and wrong all at once. Her smile trembles, a mix of relief and restraint.

"I thought you might be hungry, and I hoped you might be ready to talk."

She holds up a paper bag, its handles dark with moisture. "I brought pasta. Your favorite. And this." She lifts the bottle of wine, shaking off a few drops. "Peace offering."

Leah stares at her, saying nothing.

Amber glances around the cabin, at the stacks of notes, the unopened parcels, the scattered clothes.

"You've been busy."

Leah turns away. "You shouldn't be here."

Amber sets the bag on the table and begins unpacking it without asking.

"You probably haven't eaten properly for days," she says softly. "You'll feel better once you do."

Leah wants to shout, to throw her out, but the smell of the food with its warm tomato, garlic, something herby, twists her stomach. She hasn't eaten properly for more than days. So she sits in a daze as Amber plates the pasta, pours two glasses of wine, and takes the seat opposite her. Lightning flashes again, cutting their reflections across the window.

For a while they eat, and Amber talks about the weather. The power outages. A passing comment about work. Leah answers in short, cautious phrases. Amber's tone is calm, almost soothing, the voice she uses to settle frightened callers. The pauses between their sentences stretch longer each time. Leah swallows another mouthful of wine and sets the glass down. Amber raises hers.

"To us."

Leah blinks. "What?"

Amber's smile lingers. "We've been through hell, haven't we?"

Leah doesn't move.

"Go on," Amber says, still holding her glass up. "You can at least acknowledge that."

Leah says quietly, "I'm not drinking to us. There is no us"

Amber lowers the glass slowly. The softness in her face tightens.

"You never thanked me," she says. "For everything I did for you."

Leah frowns. "What are you talking about?"

Amber's voice hardens. "For looking after you when everyone else has already turned their backs."

Leah's pulse quickens. "You didn't do that for me. You did it for yourself."

Amber stares at her, the line of her mouth trembling.

"You don't understand," she whispers. "I just wanted to fix everything. To give you calm."

Leah pushes her chair back slightly. "What happened to Sam? What did you do?"

Amber freezes. For a moment she looks genuinely shocked. Then a soft, strange laugh escapes her that sounds almost tender.

"He wanted to take you away from me," she says. "I made him go because he didn't deserve you."

The words land like ice. Leah stands, her voice shaking. "Get out."

Amber doesn't move.

"I did it for us," she says. "I couldn't lose you. You need me."

Leah's voice rises. "You're sick. What did you do? Where is he?"

Thunder booms above them, shaking the window. The lights flicker once, twice. Amber flinches as if struck. Her voice breaks.

"You promised you'd stay calm."

Leah stares at her. "What?"

Amber's expression twists with grief, confusion, and anger all at once.

"You promised," she repeats, softer this time, almost pleading.

Leah backs toward the counter. "You need to leave. Now."

Amber steps forward. The wine bottle dangles from her fingers, her grip tightening. For a heartbeat Leah thinks she's about to swing it. Her body tenses, ready to duck. Instead, Amber sets it down hard on the table, where it overbalances and falls to the floor. It doesn't break, but the thud echoes through the small room. Tears streak down Amber's face.

"I saved you," she says, her voice cracking. "You're supposed to thank me."

Leah points to the door. "Just go."

Amber doesn't move.

"Leave," Leah says again.

Amber's breath comes shallow and uneven. The fury in her eyes flickers, replaced by something hollow. She nods once, slowly.

"You'll regret this," she whispers.

She picks up her coat from the chair, shoulders trembling, and walks to the door. When she steps out, the storm swallows her instantly. Leah slams the door and throws the bolt. The cabin is silent.

Leah slides down against the door, her back pressed to the wood, her hands shaking. Her breath comes in short bursts, her heart still hammering.

The wine bottle lies on its side, dark liquid spreading across the floor in a slow, widening pool. She stares at it, at the red stain seeping into the cracks of the wood, and thinks of blood.

Her phone buzzes once. She jumps, fumbling for it. There's a new voicemail. Tanya's voice fills the small space, soft and uncertain.

"Hey, Leah. It's me. Call me back, okay? I'm worried about you."

Leah wants to call back. To tell Tanya everything. But she's too tired. The words feel too heavy. She sinks down to lie flat on the floor, listening to the storm rage on, and whispers the only word that still feels real.

"Help."

25

The storm has grown louder. Snow being blown in flurries and drifts by huge gusts of wind that rattle the glass as if the house itself is coming undone. The heating has cut off again, and the air feels cold enough to sting. Leah sits on the living room floor, her back to the wall, still trembling from the dinner that ended in a threat. Amber's voice still echoes in her head. The calm, reasoned tone twisting into fury.

Her stomach churns. She clutches her phone in one hand, her car keys in the other, ready to run if she has to. She doesn't know where to, but she feels she needs to get away. A flash of lightning splits the night. For a heartbeat, the entire room is illuminated again, and she sees the overturned wine bottle, the dark stain spread across the floor like blood. Then the thunder comes, a violent crack that shakes the walls. The lights flicker once, twice, and then go out for good. Everything falls silent. The darkness is total except for the dim glow of her phone screen reflected in her shaking hands.

Leah's breath quickens. "No," she whispers. "Not now."

She moves toward the window, trying to peer through the snow, but the outside world is only a blur of shadows and white.

Then she hears a dull thud from the kitchen. Her body goes rigid. Another thud, closer this time. She swallows hard, forcing sound through her dry throat.

"Amber?" Her voice cracks on the name.

No answer. Something glass shatters. The sound ricochets through to the lounge like a gunshot. Leah flinches and steps back. A silhouette moves past the doorway in the kitchen. Leah's heart slams against her ribs. She backs toward the bedroom, the only route she has, whispering into the dark.

"Please... go away."

Footsteps from the kitchen come slow and careful. The scrape of metal follows, a knife against the counter. Leah's hands shake as she clutches her phone. The emergency number glows on the screen, her thumb trembling over the call button. Then she hears Amber's voice, low and broken, drifting from the kitchen.

"You made me do this."

Leah bolts.

Her socks slide on the hardwood as she races towards her bedroom, stumbling once, catching herself on the wall. The phone nearly slips from her hand. She slams her bedroom door and fumbles with the lock, twisting it until it catches. Her fingers fly over the screen. She dials 911. The ringing sounds impossibly loud.

"911, what's your emergency?" The operator's voice is calm, steady, but Leah doesn't recognize them.

"There's someone in my house," she whispers. "Please hurry. She's here. She's got a knife."

Another crash from outside the door, the sound of a chair tipping over. Leah clutches the phone tighter. A shadow moves past the bottom of the door, then she hears a hand pressed flat against the wood. Leah whispers her address for the operator.

"Stay with me," the dispatcher says. "Officers are on the way. Can you secure the room?"

Leah shakes her head even though the operator can't see her. "It's a flimsy lock. She's right outside."

Amber's voice is muffled through the door, soft at first. "I loved you."

Leah squeezes her eyes shut.

"I kept you safe," Amber continues, voice cracking. "Why would you ruin it?"

The next words come through gritted teeth, twisted by grief and rage.

"You lied to me."

Leah's whisper trembles into the phone.

"She's in the house. Please hurry."

The door shudders under a sudden blow.

"You don't understand!" Amber screams. "I had to fix it!"

The wood splinters around the lock. Leah backs away, her chest heaving. A mirror falls from the wall, smashing into shards that scatter across the floor like ice. Another hit and the hinges creak. Leah's mind races. The window is her only option.

She scrambles to it, pushing at the frame with shaking hands. It resists, swollen with cold. She forces it open, the wind whipping her hair across her face. Thunder booms overhead again. She throws one leg over the sill, gripping the edge with both hands. It's a short drop out of the cabin and onto the snow below, but still, she hesitates.

"Leah!" Amber's voice is closer now, right outside the door. "You can't leave me!"

Another smash against the door, and the wood splinters more. Leah doesn't look back. She hurls herself out into the storm. The cold hits her like a slap. The rain soaks her instantly, her clothes heavy and clinging. She keeps low, dashing along

JENNA JORDAN

the side of the cabin, away from the porch, away from the open window. Towards the trees behind, heavy with snow and ice.

From behind, the sound of wood splintering comes again, and the door finally breaks. Amber's scream rips through the night.

"Come back!"

Lightning flashes again, and for one terrible moment, Leah sees her framed in the bedroom doorway, hair plastered to her face, eyes wide and shining.

Leah sprints through the clearing towards the cover of the trees. Somewhere behind her, the front door slams open.

"Leah!"

Amber's voice carries over the wind, raw and frantic. Leah stumbles forward, half limping, half running. The snow is thick and heavy, stinging her eyes. She heads toward the first line of trees, each step sinking into snow. Her hair clings to her face, her breath is ragged. Behind her, Amber's voice rises again.

"Don't run! I'm trying to help you!"

Leah's breath tears from her throat. She can barely see. The trees stretch out ahead like dark waves under the storm.

"You can't hide from me!" Amber's words twist with desperation. "We can start over!"

A flash of blue and red light cuts through the darkness beyond. Sirens fill the air. Leah cries out, though no sound leaves her throat. She pushes harder, stumbling through the snow drifts. A spotlight sweeps across the tree line where she's hiding.

"Police! Show yourself!"

Leah collapses onto her knees, the snow swallowing her hands. Two beams of light converge on her, voices shouting orders she can't understand. She lifts her face toward them, rain running into her mouth.

"She's here," she gasps. "Amber's here."

The officers reach her, pulling her to her feet, voices calm but urgent. One wraps a blanket around her shoulders.

"Ma'am, you're safe," one of them says. "We've got you."

Leah looks over her shoulder. The wind howls through the trees, but the path behind her is empty. No sign of Amber. The officer's radio crackles faintly.

"No sign of a second party. We're searching the area."

Leah stares into the darkness, shaking uncontrollably. Her voice breaks.

"She was right behind me."

The officer's grip tightens gently on her arm. "You're in shock. We'll take you to the station, get you warm."

Leah nods, but her eyes never leave the trees. Every shadow looks like movement. Every sound could be footsteps. The officers guide her toward the waiting car. Leah's body moves, but her mind is still back in the cabin, in the dark, hearing that voice calling through the door.

You promised you'd stay calm.

The world tilts. Her ankle throbs. The flashing red and blue lights stain the snow-bound street. Someone opens the car door and helps her inside. The blanket clings cold and heavy to her shoulders. She looks once more toward the trees. The snow blurs everything into one shifting mass of white.

"Ma'am?" the officer says. "You're safe now."

Leah nods weakly, but the word feels wrong.

As the car pulls away, she catches a glimpse of her cabin. The windows are dark, the door hanging open, snow floating in. The road outside is deserted. Then, as they turn the corner, a figure steps briefly into the beam of the headlights.

Amber. Drenched, eyes shining in the glare. Her lips move, forming words Leah cannot hear. When Leah blinks, she's gone. Perhaps she was never there.

26

The first light of dawn leaks through the narrow blinds of the interview room, turning everything pale and colorless. The air smells faintly of disinfectant and wet fabric. Leah sits hunched at the table, a grey police blanket wrapped tight around her shoulders. Her clothes are still damp from the night before, and her hair clings to her face in dark strands. Her hands, raw from the cold, tremble as she signs the bottom of her statement.

Officer Daniels sits opposite her, his voice measured and quiet.

"We've got units out searching the area. She's gone, but she won't get far."

Leah doesn't look up. Her pen hovers for a moment above the paper before dropping from her fingers.

"You don't know her," she says softly. "She plans everything. She'll lay low, and then she'll be back."

Daniels hesitates. He wants to reassure her, but the conviction in her tone silences him. He simply nods, standing slowly and gathering the pages. Outside the room, fluorescent lights hum. Someone's radio crackles faintly in the corridor with static and clipped voices. The thunder has passed, but the world is covered in deep snow, and the stillness feels unnatural.

Leah stares at the dark glass of the two-way mirror. She half expects to see movement on the other side, a figure watching, waiting. Amber's voice lingers in her mind. *You promised you'd stay calm.* Her pulse quickens at the thought of it and she looks away as a detective enters, clipboard in hand.

"We'll need to photograph any injuries, Ms. Hunter. Just standard procedure."

Leah nods numbly. She follows directions without protest as they document the faint bruise circling her wrist, the cut along her forearm, the swelling at her ankle. The camera flash bursts again and again.

"She's lucky," one detective murmurs to the other. "Could've gone a lot worse."

Leah hears it but doesn't react. The phrase she's lucky feels like mockery. When they finish, she sits again, pulling the blanket tighter around her. The door opens quietly. Daniels steps back in, face drawn. He leans down to speak to the detective beside him, his voice low enough to be almost a whisper. Leah can't make out the words, but she catches the tone. For once, Daniels looks concerned, his voice tight and serious. Then he looks at her.

"Leah," he says carefully. "We found something."

Her stomach drops.

"What?"

He glances toward the detective before continuing. "At Amber's residence. We sent a unit to check it out early this morning."

Leah's fingers curl into the blanket. "Her house?"

Daniels nods. "Small place on the edge of town. She rented it six months ago. The front door was unlocked. No sign of her. All her things are gone."

He pauses, choosing his next words.

"But there was something in the garage freezer."

Leah's voice catches. "What are you saying?"

Daniels hesitates, then meets her eyes. "A man's body."

The world narrows. The hum of the lights fades until there is only the sound of her heartbeat in her ears.

"No," she whispers.

Daniels's voice remains steady. "We haven't confirmed officially, but it matches the ID of your missing person. Sam Reed."

Leah grips the edge of the table, her knuckles white. "No. That can't be right. That can't..."

He sits beside her, keeping his tone even. "We'll run the formal identification through forensics, but we're confident. His car keys, his wallet, his phone, they were all in there."

Her voice breaks. "She kept him in the freezer?"

He exhales slowly. "We think she killed him weeks ago. Maybe the night he disappeared."

Leah covers her mouth with both hands, a strangled sound escaping her throat. Tears spill before she can stop them. Daniels waits, saying nothing. There's nothing to say.

Across town, the forensic teams continue their investigation. Amber's house stands silent and unyielding. The curtains are drawn, the yard overgrown. A single police cruiser idles at the curb.

Inside, a dispatch headset sits on the kitchen table, the cable coiled neatly like a snake. On the table, photographs of Leah are arranged in precise order. There are candid shots from work, stills from a staff event, a blurred picture taken through a café window. Each one labeled in neat handwriting. Calm. Strong.

Safe. A detective moves through the hallway, camera flashing intermittently.

In the freezer in the garage, another unit document a man's body wrapped carefully in layers of plastic sheeting. His face pale, his hands folded over his chest as if he were sleeping. Sam Reed.

∿

Back at the station, Daniels finishes describing the scene. Leah stares through him as he speaks, her eyes vacant.

"She killed him to stop him coming back to me," she murmurs. "And she kept him. All this time."

Daniels nods slowly. "We found no signs of struggle on his person. She must've..." He stops, glancing toward the recorder still running on the table. "She planned it. Down to every detail."

Leah presses her palms to her eyes. "She said she fixed everything. That she could make it calm again."

Daniels places a cup of water in front of her. "You don't have to talk anymore. Not today."

She nods, but the tears keep coming, silent and uncontrollable.

By mid-morning, news spreads through the department. Amber's car has been located. A unit found it abandoned on a mountain road twenty miles north, half-buried in snow. The keys were still in the ignition, the driver's door ajar. Tracks led a few feet into the woods before disappearing. No footprints beyond that point, they'd all been swallowed by the snow.

The temperature had dropped below freezing overnight. The official theory being bandied about was that she fled on foot and probably wouldn't survive the cold.

But there is no sign of a body. No conclusive sign of death. And that means no hope of peace or resolution.

When Tanya arrives at the station, Leah is still in the same chair, her hair now dry but matted, her face pale and swollen from crying. Tanya doesn't hesitate. She crosses the room and wraps her arms around her friend. Leah stiffens for a moment before collapsing into the embrace, her body shaking.

"They'll find her," Tanya says against her hair. "They have to."

Leah's voice is barely a whisper. "I worry that she'll find me first."

Tanya pulls back enough to look at her. "Don't say that."

Leah wipes her eyes with the back of her sleeve. "She said I should thank her. She said she saved me. But she was trying to destroy me so that she could save me."

Tanya's throat tightens. She keeps one hand on Leah's shoulder as Daniels returns with another stack of forms.

"We'll need you to go through your statement once more," he says gently. "Just to clarify a few details."

Leah nods, her voice flat. "She came in through the kitchen. I heard the glass break. She had something in her hand. I thought it was a knife."

"Did she say anything before you ran?"

Leah closes her eyes. "She said I made her do it. She said she fixed everything."

Tanya squeezes her hand. The detective writes quickly, his pen scratching across the paper.

That evening, the snow begins again, softer this time. Leah stands outside her cabin, now cordoned off with yellow tape. Two officers move inside, gathering the last of the evidence. The air smells faintly of wine and damp wood. The spilled bottle from the night before glints under the forensic lights, the dark red stains on the floor dried to a deep bloom.

Through the open doorway she can see her living room with its overturned chair, scattered notes, the stain on the floor. Everything feels smaller now that it's being contained. She wraps her arms around herself. Tanya's borrowed coat is too big, the sleeves hanging past her wrists.

"She was here," she says quietly.

Daniels stands beside her, clipboard in hand. "It's secure now."

"She'll come back."

He doesn't answer. Leah keeps her eyes fixed on the doorway until the officers close it and pull the tape across. The click of the latch sounds final, like the end of a sentence.

That night, they put her in a motel on the edge of town. It's temporary, just until she decides where to go. Tanya insists on staying in the same place, checking in every few hours.

The motel room is plain, with one bed, one lamp, thin curtains that don't quite close. Leah lies fully clothed under the blanket, staring at the ceiling. The television hums quietly, the volume turned almost to nothing. On the screen, the local news runs another report.

Police continue to search for thirty-three-year-old Amber Klein, wanted for questioning in the death of Sam Reed. Klein was last seen near Highway 89 late last night. Authorities believe she may still be in the area.

A photograph flashes up showing Amber smiling, her hair pulled back, eyes bright. A face that looks ordinary and harmless. Leah sits up, reaches for the remote, and mutes the sound. She lowers her head into her hands, whispering into the silence.

"Stay calm."

The words taste like poison now. She lies back down but doesn't close her eyes. The television flickers blue light across the room. Leah pulls the blanket higher, her body rigid, her mind unable to rest. The calm is unbearable. It feels like waiting for the worst that's still to come.

27

Snow sifts down like sifted flour, fine and relentless, softening the angles of the small house the department calls a safe address. The cottage was a county rental once used by seasonal rangers. Now it belongs to a list that changes every month. The porch boards are new. The deadbolt is not. A motion camera stares from the eave above the door with an unblinking red eye that sleeps until something moves.

Leah wakes before daylight and forgets where she is for a full breath. The ceiling is low and painted the color of skim milk. The heat ticks in the vents with a dry, brittle sound. For a second she expects the shadow of the ceiling fan from her old living room, the whisper of the tall pines outside, the muffled bark of a distant dog. None of that arrives. The silence here holds itself like a taught wire.

Her phone lies on the nightstand face down, the charging cord looped around the base lamp because the outlet is loose and the plug slips unless she anchors it. She flips the phone over with two fingers and checks the time. 5:43. A blue notification bubble sits over a name that has become both lifeline and alarm. Tanya. A new message sent at 1:12 a.m.

You do not have to answer. I just wanted you to know I am awake if you need me.

Leah stares at the words until they blur. She types a single reply.

I am fine. I'm safe here..

She does not add where here is. She promised not to. The instructions were simple. Avoid social media. Do not use the same number. Share no location data. Let the officers schedule their own checks and do not anticipate their routes. Do not assume the camera is the only eye watching.

Officer Daniels checks in twice a day. Morning before eight. Evening after six. The timing is partly random so a pattern never gels, but the call always lands. His voice stays even in a way that keeps her breathing slow. He is careful now, careful with the soft questions and the pauses that give her time to answer what she wants and leave the rest behind.

Detective Harris visits every other day. He wears a parka with fur at the hood and carries a leather notebook like a token from the world where facts line up. He always takes his boots off at the door, a small courtesy that keeps her from flinching. He speaks in plain sentences. We are reviewing local traffic camera footage along the mountain road. We are canvassing the trailhead lot for any cars left overnight. We are compiling tips. We have not found a body. He does not say the other half aloud. No body can mean many things.

Leah showers in water that goes hot and fades to temperate, then slips back toward warm. Her skin stays flushed long after she turns the faucet off. When she stands in front of the mirror, she sees that her face has thinned. Her hair hangs straight and heavy. The bruise around her wrist is a sickly yellow at the edges now, a fading cuff. It looks like something that happened to someone else. She touches it with the pads of two fingers and then lets her hand fall.

Breakfast is an apple and a bowl of oatmeal the department stocked in a cabinet with a bundle of plastic spoons. The safehouse has a list on the fridge for what the quartermaster will bring on Friday. Milk. Bread. Tea. Batteries. A flashlight with a working switch. Replacement bulbs for the porch light, which stutters to life and dies back down sometimes. She prints her name on the line where it says occupant. She does not write a last name. Names feel like clothes that do not fit.

The first call of the day comes at 8:07.

"Morning, Ms. Hunter." Daniels does not wait for her reply. "Just checking in."

"I am safe here," she says, and thinks of the message she sent to Tanya.

"How did you sleep?"

"Some."

"What about last night's noise. Any other issues."

"A truck passed around two," she says. "The sound was low. It idled for a long time and then left."

"Did you see it."

"No."

"You did the right thing not to look. If it was nothing, you did not waste energy. If it was something, you did not give away your curiosity. Either way, good choice."

She does not know if she believes him, but the compliment lands like a small stone that keeps a sheet of paper from curling.

He says he will swing by after shift, asks if she needs anything besides the items on the list. She says no and almost says yes to coffee, then thinks better of it. The house has an old percolator that works when the power feels generous. She can live without the rest.

After the call, she hovers near the front window and peels the blind with two fingers. The yard is a rectangle of hard ground ringed by shrubs that look like half trimmed hedges and half patient animals crouched in snow. Beyond the shrubs, a farm road runs past the small row of rentals. Beyond the road, a line of cottonwoods marks a creek that freezes and thaws by turns. She tries to imagine Amber in this landscape and cannot. The picture will not hold still. The moment she thinks she can see the green coat under a far tree, the wind shifts and turns the empty space into a movement her mind misreads.

The quiet inside makes her think of that last night and the way a voice can fill space with rules. She steps outside instead, coat over sweater, hands deep in pockets. The air bites her throat. She walks the perimeter of the yard because Harris told her to make a route and wear it into the ground so she will notice if anything changes. Her prints from yesterday have filled with a dusting of new snow and are soft to the eye but firm underfoot. She moves slowly, counting fence posts. Twelve down the long side. Six across the short. Twelve back. Six across. A square that does not lead anywhere.

At the rear corner near the cottonwood, the snow is thinner and the ground shows seams of brown like a closed wound. When she stands there, she can hear a faint sound that at first seems like wind. The line of power poles runs past the far end of the properties. Every fourth pole has a metal crossbar. Somewhere inside the wires a small hiss builds and fades and builds again, a sound like a voice two rooms away. If she looks up at the same time she listens, the sound dies. If she looks down and lets her attention hang in the air without grabbing, the hiss returns. It reminds her of the sound in her headset when a caller breathes without speaking. A line open on both ends. The ghost of a connection. She tells herself it is nothing. The word feels like a small blanket over a large hole.

She circles twice. By the third pass her nose burns with cold and her fingers start to ache where the glove seams are thin. She goes back inside and locks the door with her shoulder against it even though she knows the door swings cleanly.

Lunch is a sandwich with too much mustard. She eats it standing, looking at the list on the fridge like it can tell the future if she learns how to read it.

Detective Harris arrives at 1:30. He knocks once and gives his name and shows his badge through the glass before she opens halfway.

"Just fifteen minutes," he says. "Then I am out of your hair."

He sits at the small table and pulls his notebook from his pocket. The leather has taken the shape of years. "We ran the full profile on a bus depot find. A coat left on a bench three towns over. Not hers. Shoeprints by the trail were fox and a heavy man in winter boots. Not useful."

"How far does a person travel without a car in that weather."

"Not far unless she had a plan," he says. He does not add we think she always had a plan. He turns a page with his thumb. "We did another inventory at her rental. Found a folder that had logistics for two counties. Transit timetables. Church shelter hours. City bus maps for Tucson and Albuquerque. Some of it was old. Hard to say what mattered and what was just collected."

Leah looks at his hand. The knuckles are raw from cold. "And the freezer."

He nods once, just enough to mean yes and no more. His mouth tightens. "The medical examiner will have the preliminary note by end of week. The rest will take longer. We can release the body after that if his family chooses. If there is no family we will talk about the next step."

The phrase next step feels like a poor replacement for the word ritual. She hears herself ask, "Will there be a service."

"If you want one, there can be one. I will make sure you do not have to decide that alone."

She turns her face toward the window because that is the

only way to keep from crying. "He does not have parents nearby. He talked about an aunt who moved to Florida. We never met."

"If she exists, I will find her," Harris says with the quiet confidence of someone who knows how to let a computer and a phone do the slow work. "You do not have to do that part."

He closes the notebook gently. "Anything unusual in the last twenty-four hours."

She thinks of the sound near the poles and hears herself say nothing. The word comes out wrong, heavy on the first syllable. "I am fine."

He looks at her the way a person looks at snow when they cannot tell if the patch is crusted or soft underneath. Then he nods and stands.

"I will check in again Thursday."

He leaves his number on a clean card on the table even though she has it, because that is part of his ritual. He puts his boots back on and ties them neatly. When he steps off the porch he glances at the camera on the eave out of habit. She notices the gesture and feels a thin ribbon of gratitude for people who look where they are supposed to.

The afternoon smears into early evening. Tanya calls at four and again at seven. The first call is short because a holdup came over the radio on Tanya's end and a second operator called in sick and she has to grab extra lines. The second call stretches the whole length of dusk.

"You are safe now," Tanya says, the sentence quickly followed by a soft wince like she knows the phrase tastes wrong. "Sorry. I am repeating training language. I mean it, but I know it is loaded."

"It is fine," Leah says. "I used to say it all the time."

"How is the place."

"Small. Clean. The sheets smell like a new pack of paper."

Tanya laughs quietly. "That is better than mildew."

"I keep hearing a sound like static," Leah says, and swallows. She has not planned to say it. "Near the fence. It stops when I turn my head."

"Power lines," Tanya says. "When it is wet and cold they sing. My cousin's farm had that sound every winter. It feels like it is coming out of your chest."

Leah breathes out a little easier. "That is exactly it."

"You should FaceTime me in the morning. We can walk the yard together. I will be a square on your phone and not a person who breaks the rules."

"You are not allowed to know where I am."

"I will not look too closely at your shrub shape," Tanya says with a smile in her voice. "We will just count footsteps together."

They talk about nothing for a while. Tanya tells a short story about a turkey that got into the dispatch lot and chased Jason around the cars in circles. Leah laughs and feels the sound shake something loose in her chest. When they hang up, she stands in the middle of the living room and feels the strange ache of almost normal. It lasts about a minute before the quiet returns.

She reads for an hour because the therapist in Flagstaff told her to put narrative into her mind that is not her life. The book is about a park ranger who tracks fires. The sentences are clean and short. When she looks up from the page, the room has shifted a degree toward night. She washes the cup, checks the back door twice, and pulls the blind until the slats close the last crack of view.

Sleep comes fast and leaves faster.

She is not sure why she wakes. The clock says 2:31. The house holds the sound of its own systems like a held breath. She reaches for the glass of water and thinks she sees a faint glow from the front porch. It is probably the camera cycling. It is probably a car turning around at the curve. It is probably nothing. She does not get out of bed.

Morning finds her raw and rinsed out. Her throat hurts as if she has been speaking in her sleep. She makes tea because the kettle is a task she can finish. When she opens the door to get the morning air in, she stops.

A small parcel sits square on the mat that says welcome in the font every discount store uses. It is wrapped in brown paper and tied with string that has frayed at one corner. There is no label. The knot is neat and small and tied by a hand that knows how to pull evenly.

Leah stares at it like it could be a live thing. The camera is angled to see the mat and the lower half of the person who stands there. She looks up at the eave without moving her feet and sees the tiny red dot blink, alive and recording. Her body remembers last winter when red dots meant recording training calls and calls that broke people into pieces. She breathes. Then she crouches and touches the package with two fingers and feels paper give under her touch like a held breath.

Inside the paper, an inner box. Inside the box, a packet of herbal tea in a pale blue envelope printed with ferns. Beneath the packet, a folded note on clean, unlined paper. She opens it.

For calm nights.

No name. The handwriting is small and rounded and familiar. Her face drains. She can feel the blood move away from her skin. She says the word no without meaning to and does not know whether it is a refusal or a description. She calls Daniels.

"The porch camera caught it," she says before he can ask who, what, where. "There is a package."

"Do not touch anything else," he says. "I am ten minutes out."

She can hear keys and a door and a voice in the background calling a unit number. She sets the packet back into its box and the box back onto the mat as if handling an animal she does not want to startle. She closes the door softly. Inside the house, the kettle ticks as it cools and the heater hums and her heart beats too hard.

Daniels arrives with a second officer and a small kit bag that contains the tools of polite intrusion. He looks at the box and the porch and the sightlines and then at Leah with a face that says he believes what he is seeing but he also has a panel of possible explanations ready to lay down like cards.

"Reporters or internet nuts," he says lightly, because the light tone is a way to test the air. "Happens more than you would think. Someone finds a thread and pulls until a knot drops into their hands and they think it means they belong to the story."

She says nothing because the words *For calm nights* are still inside her body like a swallowed seed. They take the package inside to dust for prints and swab for any trace. The tea goes into an evidence bag like it might be powder. The note goes into another. Harris arrives an hour later to collect. He stands in the doorway and reads the words and does not change expression.

"We will run the porch footage," he says. "We will ask the county store if anyone bought this brand in the last month."

"It could be nothing," Daniels adds.

Leah hears herself ask, "What if it is not."

Daniels nods in a way that says he keeps both tracks open. "Then we treat it like not nothing."

After they leave, Leah sits on the couch with a blanket around her shoulders and tries to find the seam between fear that protects and fear that feeds. She fails. By dusk the yard looks like a small stage for heavy weather. Wind pushes the shrubs into small bows. Snow drifts into the corners of the porch. Somewhere near the back fence the wires hum again.

She walks the perimeter at sunset because routine is a leash that keeps a mind from running too far. Twelve down, six across, twelve back, six across. At the back corner she stops and listens. The static sits in the air like a thought she cannot turn into words. When she turns her head, it fades. When she looks down, it returns. She stands there until her toes go numb.

Inside, she heats a can of soup and eats it. The flavor is salt and the memory of chicken. When she finishes, she realizes that the act of finishing is the only reason she started. She puts the empty can in the trash and ties the bag and sets it by the door because Daniels said do not leave attractants out to invite raccoons and the metaphor writes itself.

Sleep finds her later than the night before. The dream is not of the cabin or the trees. It is of a dispatch screen that will not stop blinking and a caller whose silence fills the line like weather. She wakes with the sentence in her mouth. Stay calm. Help is coming. The words feel like betrayal now. She rolls to her side and stares at the tiny red blink of the motion camera notification on her phone. She has not looked at the footage yet. She does not know whether she wants to be right or wrong.

At eight sharp the next morning, Daniels calls with an update.

"We pulled the video. It is mostly wind and snow. The time stamp matches the interval you reported. We froze it frame by frame."

"And?" she asks, though she can hear what he will say in the shape of his breath.

"Two frames only," he says. "Faint outline of a figure. Could be distortion from the light. Could be a person in a dark coat. It is not clear. No face."

She presses the heel of her hand to her eye until stars bloom. "She was here."

"We do not know that yet."

"I do," she says, and the conviction in her voice makes her sit up straight, like hearing herself brought her spine back into her body. "You do not know her."

He pauses, and in the pause she hears the sound of a pen clicking and a chair creak and then a voice closer to the receiver.

"I hear you," he says. "We are rotating a car past the farm road every hour on the half. A unit will be within ten minutes of you at all times today. Harris is going to sweep later with a handheld scanner to confirm we do not have an unsecured signal bleeding onto your network. That hum you mentioned near the fence can be explained by weather, but we will check it anyway."

She wants to say thank you and also wants to say none of that is enough. She says the first and holds the second between her teeth like a coin.

The day stretches. No visitor knocks. No truck idles. A hawk lands on the far pole near noon and lifts off again like a hand opening. Leah writes one page in a spiral notebook because the therapist told her to make sentences that do not describe only fear. The sentences are poor, but they sit on the page and stay where she puts them. In the afternoon she naps in a chair because lying down makes her feel too exposed. The nap lasts six minutes and feels like a whole hour.

At 6:18, her phone buzzes with a simple text from Tanya. *I am at home. I made soup. I am sleeping on the couch with my shoes on because I want to be able to run if you call.* Leah almost laughs and almost cries and ends up typing three hearts, which she has never sent to anyone, then deletes two because three feels like a statement she cannot carry and sends one because one is still a truth.

Night tightens around the house. Wind gusts and then settles. The camera's red dot blinks in the eave like a tired eye. She makes sure the blinds fit their tracks. She sets a chair under the back knob not because it would stop anyone but because it makes her body hear that she is allowed to try.

She does not hear the step on the porch. She does not hear a car. She does not hear anything at all until the motion alert pings her phone at 6:41 a.m., which is technically morning but still feels like the dark tail of night.

She sits up too fast and the room tilts. She waits for her blood to catch up. Then she walks to the door and holds the breath that wants to run and opens it. Another parcel sits on the mat. Smaller than the first. Brown paper again. String again. The knot looks tighter.

She does not touch it right away. She looks up at the camera and then at the road and then at the edge of the shrubs where snow makes small nests at the roots. The wind is still. The world holds its breath with her. Only when her hands stop shaking does she crouch and lift the thing inside with two fingers.

Under the paper lies a single page torn from a spiral notebook. The left edge shows the clean line of pulled wire curls. The paper is water stained and smells faintly like damp cardboard and hand soap. Her eyes find the ink without her choosing.

Stay calm. Help is coming.

The words are written in blue. The handwriting is precise. The loop on the y in stay leans left. The p in help sits a fraction lower than the rest of the line. She knows both of those small habits from training notes she has read and from a shelf of staff sign-up sheets at the center back when she belonged to a room where voices saved other people.

Her throat closes. She lifts the page closer and sees that the top corner carries a faint shadow of an earlier line written hard and pressed through. A phone number has been written there once and then erased. She cannot read it all. She can see the exchange digits. She can see the way the four has a closed top instead of an open triangle. She remembers that trait like a smell.

She turns the page over. The back is blank except for the shadow of the front. She feels the paper fibers with her thumb until she is sure it is real. She calls Daniels without moving from the threshold.

"I need you to come now," she says, and her voice is soft and steady in the way that once made strangers breathe.

He asks no questions. He says he is on his way. While she waits, she looks beyond the porch to the line of cottonwoods at the creek. The sky is the color of a healed bruise. Snowflakes turn slowly in the thin air. She thinks she sees a darker shape among the trunks, the suggestion of a person turned partly away. She blinks and the shape becomes a gap in the pattern where two trees do not meet.

She closes the door. She stands with her back to it and the paper in her hands and says the sentence on the page inside her own mouth. It does not feel like comfort. It does not feel like a lie either. It feels like a thread back to the person she was before a voice took those words and turned them into a key.

When Daniels arrives, he reads the line once and folds the page into an evidence sleeve without letting his face tell her what he thinks. He asks if she looked at the camera. She shakes her head. He nods. He will pull it himself.

Harris comes twenty minutes later and runs a palm over the porch rail and then checks his scanner and says the frequency noise near the fence is real, which is what wind on wet wires does when the air holds more water than the wood can stand, and also what a small transmitter can do if it is tucked somewhere under a lip of eave. He checks the eaves with a flashlight and finds no transmitter. He checks the shrubs with a stick and finds a wintering rabbit that runs three feet and freezes and then runs again. He checks the road with his eyes and finds tire marks that belong to the plow that came through at five.

They do not find who left the paper. They do not find footprints that point inward instead of outward. They do not find anything they can take with them besides the page and the video that might show a coat that might be a shape that might be wind.

After they leave, Leah sits on the floor with her back to the couch and watches the square of sunlight move across the rug as the day lifts. The light makes a bright strip where the paper rested a minute ago, a heat that will fade to the same temperature as the rest of the room.

Her phone buzzes once with a new message from Tanya. A photo of a mug with steam and a caption that says *First shift is always the hardest. Look at us. Still here.*

Leah writes back. *Still here.*

She sets the phone down and closes her eyes. The hum near the fence rises and fades and then is quiet. Somewhere in the house a pipe clicks. Somewhere beyond the yard a truck climbs a grade and drops away. She puts her palms flat on the floor on either side of her and feels the grain and the small splinters and the realness that does not ask her to believe anything at all.

The sentence on the page sits in her chest like a slow bell.

Stay calm. Help is coming.

She does not know whether it is a promise or a warning or a taunt. She knows only that the story is not over. The quiet around her sounds like a pause in breath, not an end. She opens her eyes and looks at the door and then at the eave and then at the space between the shrubs where the wind threads itself through branches and asks for nothing back.

Outside, the snow continues to fall, soft and stubborn. Inside, she stays sitting and waits for the next inevitable sound.

Printed in Dunstable, United Kingdom